TRUE GENIUS

ANITHA SHARMA

TRUE GENIUS

This is a work of fiction. All the characters, names, incidents, organizations, and dialogue in this novel are either the products of the author's imagination or are used fictitiously.

iUniverse books may be ordered through booksellers or by contacting:

iUniverse
1663 Liberty Drive
Bloomington, IN 47403
www.iuniverse.com
844-349-9409

ISBN: 978-1-6632-4745-2 (sc)
ISBN: 978-1-6632-4747-6 (hc)
ISBN: 978-1-6632-4746-9 (e)

Library of Congress Control Number: 2022920372

Print information available on the last page.

iUniverse rev. date: 12/14/2022

PROLOGUE

Ring! Ring! The alarm rang.

"Come on, Sameera! Wake up. Today is our big day," Sahil yelled.

"Just give me a minute," I said in my sleepiest voice.

"Make it quick. We'll be late!" Sahil shouted.

I slowly got up. My hair was totally messed up. I just got it curled yesterday. *Ugh!* "What is Sahil talking about? Why is it our big day?" I asked myself. I yawned and stretched my arms. I looked at the alarm clock. It read 8:00 a.m. "Oh shoot! Today is our first day of summer camp, and I'm late. Well, I better get ready quickly." I stumbled out of bed and into my bathroom. I quickly brushed my teeth and tried to fix my hair, but my hair wouldn't stay the way I wanted it. "Ugh! This is so annoying."

"Come on, Sameera!" Sahil called from downstairs.

"I'm coming!" I called back. I just left my hair the way it was and went downstairs.

Sahil said, "Finally, you're here. Did you forget about summer camp? Mom is going to drop us on her way to work."

"Oh yeah. Summer camp is going to be so much fun!" I exclaimed with joy.

Sahil raised his eyebrows. "I'm all ready to go, but you don't seem like you're ready at all. Look at your hair, and you haven't had breakfast yet. Geesh. I'm going to go get in the car with my stuff. Bye!"

I rolled my eyes. "Don't rush me." But he was already out the door.

I am Sameera Chacko, and Sahil Chacko is my younger brother. He is eleven years old, while I'm thirteen years old—almost fourteen. He is always the first one to wake up. I don't know why he's an early bird, but I'm the total opposite. I am a night owl. I go to bed late and wake up late in the morning. Sahil and I signed up for summer camp this year. I signed up for a science camp, and my brother signed up for a sports camp. I'm a bit of a nerd, and my brother is the best at sports. If you talk about any sports, he is always ready to try them out. He's not the kind of person to use his brain to do useful things. He acts very dumb, but you won't believe what happened to him. It's a good story and let me tell you all of it.

PART I

CHAPTER 1

"See you kids later. Have fun at camp!" Mom exclaimed as she dropped us off at the front gate of the YMCA building.

"Bye, Mom. love you," I said as I got out of the car. Once we got our belongings, Mom waved to us and drove away. I looked around and saw a bunch of children around Sahil's age running excitedly across the grass with their backpacks on. I said, "Sahil, do you know where we are supposed to be?"

"I don't know about you, but I think the sports camp must meet on the fields. I'm going to go follow those kids. See ya!" Sahil said and ran off.

I called out, "Wait, Sahil! Help me find my area!" He just ran off, ignoring me. I murmured to myself, "What a brother I have." I looked to my right and saw what looked like a newly painted playground. The colors of the slides, swings, and seesaw were so bold I couldn't take my eyes off them.

Just then, a man wearing a brown hat approached me. "Can I help you?"

I said, "Do you know where the science camp meets?"

"Of course, young lady. I know where they meet. In fact, I lead that camp. Come follow me," the man said.

"Oh, that's great," I said and followed him.

"You seem very excited," the man said.

I replied, "Yes, I am super excited for summer camp this year because I had so much fun last year. By the way, what's your name?"

"My name is Chris Troop. And yours, young lady?"

"My name is Sameera."

"Nice to meet you," he said and shook my hand.

He eventually led me to a side of the building that was completely covered in jade green and had patches of graffiti stuck to the sides of it. He opened the door for me, and I walked in. He led me to a classroom that was very noisy. "All right, all you campers, listen up!" Mr. Troop screamed, catching everyone's attention. Everyone became quiet and sat down at desks. "Welcome to science camp. My name is Mr. Troop." Blah, blah, blah. He explained everything about the labs and equipment. It was boring, so I kind of zoned out. Then it became more interesting. "So now we will get into groups of three and perform a popcorn experiment. Each lab table has a set of instructions to follow. I hope you guys learn something. Let me know if you have any questions. Enjoy!" All the students scattered to different lab tables.

I slowly walked around to find a group. I was surprised to see two people I thought I recognized standing in the far-left corner. I quickly ran over to them. Meg turned around and recognized me. "Omg. Sameera? I didn't know you were going to be at this science camp."

"Same! I'm so happy to see you!" I exclaimed. Meg had been my best friend ever since we were five years old. She was kind, smart, talented, and really mature for her age. We met in preschool, and at first, I didn't like her because she seemed like a showoff, but as we spent more time together during playdates and sleepovers, we grew to be best friends. Her real name was Megan, but everyone had been calling her Meg ever since she was young.

"Hey, Mackenzie! So great to see you too!" I said and hugged her.

"Great to see you."

Mackenzie was my other best friend, and I met her in kindergarten. She was friendly, generous, and funny. She loved jokes and pranks. She and my brother were alike in some ways. I became friends with Mackenzie after an incident happened in kindergarten and she cheered me up. We were on the playground for recess one day, and one of the immature boys pushed me down the slide so forcefully that I fell and hurt my knee. I sat there crying for a few minutes, while the boy stood there laughing at me. That's when Mackenzie came to me and helped me up. Then she said, "When something goes wrong in life, just yell, 'Plot twist!' and move on." That got me to laugh and forget about my pain. Mackenzie and Meg have been my best friends ever since. After summer, the three of us will be going to high school.

"So, I guess we're a group. Shall we go and make some popcorn?" Meg asked.

I smiled. "Let's do it!"

We had so much fun and such a crazy time with the popcorn lab. Meg did most of the popping, and I helped a little, but I couldn't stop goofing around with Mackenzie and eating all the popcorn. Meg said, "Come on, guys. You're supposed to be helping me make popcorn, not having a competition to see who can eat the most popcorn."

"Sorry, Meg. You know how it is with Mackenzie. She's all about fun and games, and it's hard to be serious around her," I said.

Meg and Mackenzie both laughed. Mackenzie said, "All right, fine. No more goofing off. I'll help with the lab."

After the lab, Mr. Troop passed out some candy. "Mmm, yummy. I'm going to take some Skittles," I said.

Mackenzie said, "Me too! I love Skittles!"

"Same. I'm totally getting some. Let's be Skittle buddies," Meg suggested.

"Ha-ha! Cheers!" we all said.

We got to share our experience of the lab with the class, and we also got to give Mr. Troop some suggestions for future labs. The day went by so quickly. Mr. Troop said, "Great job today, everyone! I hope you had fun. Tomorrow we will be doing a Coke and Mentos experiment to learn about chemical reactions."

"Awesome! Don't you think Mr. Troop is a nice guy?" I asked Mackenzie and Meg. They both looked at each other and laughed. "What?" I asked.

"You like him?" Meg asked.

I replied, "Yes, of course! He's nice. He helped me find this room." They both laughed again. "What's your problem? Why are you guys laughing? Do you not feel the same way?" I asked.

"No, it's not that. Nothing, it's nothi—" Meg started and then continued laughing.

"Let's just tell her why we're laughing," Mackenzie suggested.

"Yes, please tell me so that I can laugh with you guys," I begged.

"We'll tell you, but I don't know if you'll even laugh about it," Meg said.

"Just tell her!" Mackenzie demanded.

"All right. I'll tell you, Sameera. You like Mr. Troop because he's your father," Meg said.

"What the heck? Do you even hear what you are saying, Meg? My father hasn't been around for years. After he left our family and went to California, he didn't even call us," I explained.

"No, we're telling the truth. We would never lie to you. Remember our best-friend code? Never keep secrets and never lie," Meg reminded me.

"Yeah, I remember that, but you must be joking because joking is not against our code. That can't be my father. I'm sure he looks way different than that. And how do you guys know that he's my father?" I asked.

Mackenzie replied, "Well, your mom told us this morning. She wanted us to keep it a secret until tomorrow. She was going to surprise you, but we couldn't resist telling you after you expressed how happy you were to spend the summer with him. You don't have to believe us, but we're just telling you what your mom told us."

I didn't know what to say. I wanted to believe this was a dream, but I felt a lot of emotions that I didn't want them to see. "I'll be right back. I just need to use the restroom," I said. I was about to leave when they stopped me.

"Wait, Sameera ... I'm sorry if we made you feel bad. Your mom told us to keep a secret, but you know we can't do that, especially since you're our best friend," Meg said.

Mackenzie said, "Yeah. Especially in a situation like this, we would want you to know sooner so that you're not in complete shock when you find out later."

I wrapped my hands around my head. "This is just crazy. How come my mom told you guys first and not me? Besides, the last time I saw my father was probably several years ago, but I don't remember how he looks. My mom told me and my brother that he went on a business trip but didn't know when he would be back. When I was about five years old, they got divorced. Since I barely saw him around, I asked my mom if I could speak to him. My mom told me he was unreachable by phone, but I could write a letter to him, so I did. He wrote back a few days later, saying that he had been busy with his work, so he didn't get time to talk much. He also mentioned that he would try his best to come home and visit us kids soon. That's about all I remember. Now you're telling me that my father is right in front of my eyes?" I said.

Mackenzie and Meg nodded. "People change throughout the years, and your father has changed too. You might not be able to recognize him, and he might not recognize you either, but go up to him and tell him that you are his daughter. Then I'm sure he'll recognize you," Mackenzie suggested.

I rolled my eyes and said, "Whatever. You guys are breaking the friendship code. I'm just saying."

"Well, if that's what you want to think, then you can think that way, but I guess we don't have any proof, so we can't force you to believe us," Meg said and walked away.

"Just think about it for once. He cared about your family, so he came back," Mackenzie said, then walked away. I was in a state of extreme shock.

The classroom was empty except for Mr. Troop and me. I stood next to one of the lab tables, staring at my own reflection in the sink. Staring back at me was a young woman with beautiful brown eyes and dark skin the color of milk chocolate. Her facial features were smooth and rounded. She had long, black, silky hair that grew thick enough to develop natural waves and curls. I thought about what my friends had said. *He doesn't even have the same last name as me. He's Troop, and I'm Chacko. How can he be my father?* I hadn't really gotten the chance to sit down and ask my mom about my family history, but I remembered what she told me once. Our last name had a special meaning. Chacko meant a cute, playful character. My mom only got that last name after she married my father, who was from Kerala, in southern India. They both moved to New Hampshire a few months after their marriage. Mr. Troop looked nothing like a Hindu. His eyes were blue, and his complexion was that strange bright tone that occurs when pale skin is sunburned and weathered. He was tall, probably about 5'8", wearing a basic, solid-colored shirt and some blue jeans. He had neatly cut blond hair, unlike me. I started to wonder if I was even related to Mr. Troop by blood. Neither Sahil nor I looked like him. My mom, on the other hand, was quite tall and slim. She had a round face and brown eyes. Her nose was straight and small, and her hair was long and dark. She always had well-groomed hands because she always did a manicure.

Just then, Mr. Troop approached me. "Hello, young lady. What are you still doing here? Aren't you going to go home?" he asked.

I replied, "Yeah, I was just about to go home. By the way, why are you still calling me a young lady? I told you my name this morning."

"Oh yeah. I know," he said.

I smiled and asked, "Do you remember it?"

"Yes, Sameera," he said.

I said, "Hey, can I ask you something?"

"Sure. Anything."

"Do you know my mom, Jeena Chacko?" I asked. It was silent for a few seconds, and you could've heard a pin drop.

He took a deep breath in. "Yes, I know her."

"How do you know her?"

"I … uh … she's my … okay look—I don't think I should lie to you. Your mom wanted to keep this a secret until tomorrow, but I didn't think it could last that long. Sameera, we're related."

"What! My friends can't be right," I whispered to myself.

"Excuse me?" he said.

I shook my head. "There is no way that's true. The last name? The facial features and the hair? This must be a joke."

"I'm your father … father … father … father." There was a strange echo in the room, and I snapped my head up to look at him. "Look. I can explain everything. Just have a seat." He gestured toward one of the desks close to his desk. I sat down, and he sat down at his desk.

"So you want to know about the last name?" he asked. I nodded eagerly. "Well, there's nothing special about it. It's the same as yours, but my middle name is different. My name is Chris Troop Chacko."

What? He went by his middle name. Was he ashamed of being called Mr. Chacko?

The man said, "I know you're probably wondering why I go by Mr. Troop. I'll get to it later, but first I want to tell you a little bit about how I got back here to New Hampshire. After I moved to California, people were troubling me so much, and I couldn't live there anymore. So, within a week, I moved back here and rented an apartment to stay in. Then I began looking for a job. The first job I got was a job in a German company, but they were speaking German, and I couldn't understand. So I had to quit that job and began looking for another one. Then someone offered me a job as a scrap dealer, but that didn't work out either. So I just gave up. I didn't have a job for two years and was living in debt. Then I got marr … um I mean …"

"What! You got married again? Look at my mom. It's been years since you've left us, and Mom still believes that you'll come back for her. She hasn't gotten married again. In fact, she hasn't even thought about a second marriage. I can't believe you!" I couldn't be in the same room as him anymore, so I got up and took my bag.

"Sameera dear. I can explain."

Tears were starting to form in my eyes, but I pushed them back. I barely even knew him well enough to express how I felt. "Sorry, but I have to go. I need some time to process this." I rushed out of the classroom.

Once I was out of the building, I ran into Sahil. "Hey, Samee—oh, geesh you're crying. What happened?" he asked me.

I felt that it wasn't the right time to tell him what happened. It was too much for me to take in anyway, let alone trying to get Sahil to understand. "Nothing you need to know," I told him.

He frowned. "Why not? Maybe I can help you."

I had to admit that was kind of sweet of him, but I just needed to be alone right then to process everything about my father or whoever that was. "Sahil, please—not now." I continued walking toward the parking lot. He followed right behind.

"Sameera, tell me. Tell me. Tell me."

Now he was starting to annoy me. So I did what I usually do to make him shut up—yell at him. "No! I won't!" I screamed and ran off.

"*Okay* then," Sahil said and slowly followed me to mom's car.

The car ride back home was quiet. It was surprising because Sahil didn't usually stay quiet for a second. Maybe I might've been too harsh on him, or maybe my thoughts were louder than anything else happening in the world at that moment. Mom even tried asking us how our first day at camp was, but I couldn't seem to get any words out. Sahil went on about how great his sportsmanship was and how he had the potential to one day become a professional athlete. I knew that wasn't true. You couldn't just become a professional athlete by going to sports camp, but I didn't feel like correcting him.

"What about you, Sameera?" Mom asked. I was so lost in my thoughts that I wasn't really paying attention. I was too busy staring out the window, wishing I could be at home in my room, with the door shut. "Sameera? Are you okay?"

I finally looked up. "Oh yes, Mom. I'm fine, and camp was fine too." I resumed looking at the window.

Mom asked, "Just fine? Come on, Sameera! You've gotta give me more than that. I mean, I paid so much to send you guys to camp. At least give me a reasonable explanation."

I really didn't want to talk to anyone. "Sorry, Mom."

"Sweetie, what's going on? Did something happen at camp? This is about your camp leader, isn't it?"

"Don't ask her questions, Mom. She's too self-centered right now," Sahil said.

"I am not!" I screamed.

"Yes, you are!" he yelled back.

"Am not!"

"Yes, you are."

"Both of you! Just stop it!" Mom screamed. We both went quiet. "Sahil, your turn to talk is over, and Sameera was quiet for you. Now it's her turn to talk and for you to be quiet. Gosh. I am raising two-year-olds right now!" Mom was understandably frustrated, and I didn't want to make it worse by pouring in my frustrations about Mr. Troop, even though she already knew about him. I decided to lean on the positives about the day, such as how I reunited with my friends Meg and Mackenzie and how much fun we had together during the popcorn lab. I didn't mention anything about Mr. Troop, and she didn't ask anything about him either, so it was fair.

After we got home, I ran straight to my room, while Sahil moved as slowly as a turtle. I knew he was wondering what was wrong with me, but I wasn't ready to tell him yet. I wondered how shocked or surprised he would feel when I told him that our father was in the state and was my science camp teacher. I walked into the familiar flawless room, the pastel purple sheets on the bed. The curtains were flung open. Light poured in through the window. A carefully organized computer desk sat in the corner. Poems were taped all over the walls, deep and meaningful. Next to the door, a large painting easel stood. On the nightstand, a camera glistened and begged to be used. Despite having such a beautiful room, I decided to lie down on my bed, facing the ceiling, trying to process everything that happened so far today.

After a while, I heard Mom talking to someone on the phone in her room. I slowly walked toward her room and listened in, but I couldn't hear anything but gibberish. The door to her room was closed, so I leaned with one ear on the door to listen to the conversation. I heard her saying words like "miss you," "come soon," and "waiting for you." I was wondering who the heck she was talking to. Then I heard Mom say clear sentences. "The kids will be happy to see you come home. I can't believe I met you again. You will stay with us forever, okay? None of us will leave each other, and we'll be a complete family again."

"Oh my gosh. She must be speaking to Mr. Troop," I said to myself. Then it went silent. Mom opened the door, and I dropped down. "Sweetie, what are you doing here?" she asked.

"Uh ... um." Words wouldn't come out of my mouth.

"Frogs got your tongue. Why don't you get freshened up and come downstairs for some snacks? You had a long day today. And tell your brother to come down as well." Mom skipped down the stairs. She seemed so excited. Even her tone showed that. At least she didn't bust me for listening in on her conversation. It was not nice of her to hide something like this from her children for this long, especially after I already went to camp and met Mr. Troop.

I quickly freshened up and told Sahil to come down. I went down and sat down on one of the barstools in the kitchen. I decided to play it cool and pretend I didn't know a thing. "Mom, who were you talking to on the phone?" I asked.

She shrugged and said, "It's just a friend. Nothing big."

"I heard you say that the kids will be happy to see you come home. What was that for?" I asked.

She shrugged again.

"Mom, you're hiding something. Please spill it," I begged.

"You'll just have to wait for the right time, Sameera."

I couldn't seem to fight her on that, so I changed the subject. "All right, fine. Then I have another question that you should be able answer." I paused. "Where is my father?"

She sighed and looked away immediately—the same thing she did every time I asked.

"Mom, I've been waiting for years to know. You always say you'll tell me later, but you never do. I can't wait any longer. Please tell me at least a little bit about him."

Mom opened her mouth to speak, but Sahil came and interrupted. "Why do you even care? There's no point in knowing him now, especially after all these years living without a dad. He's probably dead by now!"

"Sahil, don't make false accusations! He's not dead."

"How do you know that, sweetie?" Mom asked.

I wanted to tell her that I saw him today. *At my science camp. He's my teacher. Mr. Troop. You know that. Stop pretending you don't know. You're the one who told Mackenzie and Meg to keep it a secret from me. And he cheated on you, Mom. He married someone else.* But I didn't say all that. Instead, I said, "Well, I don't know. I just like to think that he's alive somewhere in this world. Maybe even close to us."

"That's a good thought, Sameera," Mom said.

It was quiet for a few seconds, and then I asked, "Hey, where is that photo album that had memories from our childhood?"

"Well, um, I don't know exactly. I'll have to search later. If there are any pictures, it should be upstairs in a brown box in the main closet, but I think I might've misplaced a few things when I cleaned out that closet. Don't worry about all that now. I have a surprise for you tomorrow that will be even better than pictures," Mom said.

I smirked. *Why can't you just tell us now that Mr. Troop is our father? My friends already told me everything. I've already met him, and I don't like him for cheating on you. There's no point in keeping it a secret.*

CHAPTER 2

Ding-dong! Ding-dong! Ding-dong! The doorbell rang the next morning.

"Sameera, please get the door," Mom said.

Why does it have to be me every time? I got up from the couch and opened the door. I was shocked. "Mr. Troop? What are you doing here?"

"You can call me father, and I'm here to pick you up for summer camp." He grinned.

"Thank you, but my mom will take me." I was about to close the door when he held out his hand to stop it.

"It's the same thing. Whether your mom takes you or I take you. We're a family. Come on now. Get into the car."

"I'm not going with you. You cheated on my mom. Why don't you just leave? Go back to California! Nobody wants you here anyways." I slammed the door on him.

"Sweetie, what the heck did you just do?" Mom asked.

"Um … it was someone for pest control," I lied.

"What? We didn't call anyone for pest control," Mom said.

"Yeah, same. I told him that he came to the wrong house," I said.

Mom frowned and looked like she was expecting someone. Mom immediately opened the door and looked back at me. She saw Mr. Troop in his car in the driveway and ran up to him.

"Wait, Chris! Don't leave!"

Mr. Troop looked back with tears of joy. "It's you Jeena, finally."

"Yes! Why don't you come in?"

Mr. Troop looked at me over Mom's shoulder. I looked away. "Your daughter wanted me to go back to California."

"Why? I thought she would be happy to see you," Mom said. Mr. Troop nodded. Mom called me over. "Sameera, come here. Look—it's your father. He came back."

I knew it! This whole time, this was the surprise Mom was hiding from me. More of a shock I would say.

I smirked. "I don't want to talk to him. Mom, I need to talk to you later." I looked away.

"What's wrong with her?" Mom asked.

Mr. Troop shrugged.

"Mom, I'm ready for camp!" Sahil said, rushing past me out the front door.

"All right. Your dad is going to drop you today," Mom said.

"Dad? Are you crazy, Mom? He's not even here." Sahil chuckled.

"Surprise! He's back from his trip finally." Mom pointed at Mr. Troop.

Sahil walked over to him and squinted. "Seriously? You're my dad? I don't believe it. I look nothing like you."

"Yes, I am your dad," Mr. Troop said firmly.

Mom said, "Believe it, honey. He's changed a lot over the last few years."

"Oh geesh!" Sahil remarked.

"Let's go now. You'll be late for your camp. We can all talk tonight," Mr. Troop said. Sahil nodded and got into the car.

"Thank you so much for coming, Chris! You take Sahil to camp. If you wait for grumpy Sameera, you'll be late. I'll drop moody Sameera in a while. You guys go ahead." Mom's words made me angry. She called me grumpy and moody, and I wasn't any of those things.

Mom closed the front door and turned to face me. She narrowed her eyes at me. "Sameera, please explain your rude behavior."

"*You* explain *your* strange behavior. Why would you keep something like this from us? This is a huge deal! We should've at least had some sort of notice or hint. And if you were trying to surprise us, well, I'm sorry—you failed. Not only am I shocked, but I'm really frustrated. I don't even feel like going to summer camp because of Mr. Troop."

"Mr. Troop?" Mom asked.

"My science camp teacher."

"You mean your father?"

I nodded. "I don't even want to call him my father! He betrayed you, Mom."

"What are you talking about, sweetie?" Mom asked.

I said, "Yes! What I'm saying is true. Father got married again after he left us."

Mom laughed. "Is this why your behavior was so weird?"

I nodded.

"I'm sorry, but I can explain everything, sweetie. Let's go inside," Mom suggested. We went inside and sat down on the couch. "Before I say anything, tell me, did your father talk to you at all yesterday?"

I nodded. "Yeah, he told me a little bit about his side of the story."

Mom took a breath in and murmured, "Oh no. Well, I hope what he said matches what I'm about to say."

"What is that supposed to mean?" I asked.

"Huh. Oh, well, I was just trying to say you are mistaken. Your father was about to get married again, but he figured out that he still had feelings for me. So he cancelled the wedding and gave me a call to tell me what happened. I was surprised that he did that. He told me that he wanted to get back together with me. We had a few more phone calls after that, but I kept it from you and your brother. Anyway, I allowed your dad to get back with me, and now he's here. What made you think he betrayed me?" Mom asked.

I said, "I thought he got married again and was living happily with his new wife, and when I saw him, I felt frustrated."

"Wow. I thought I could surprise you, but I guess you knew Mr. Troop was your father already." Mom chuckled.

I didn't laugh at all. Seriously, I said, "Mackenzie and Meg accidently spilled the beans yesterday."

"Oh, of course they did! Well, now you know the truth. You'd better apologize to your father for your bad behavior."

I nodded.

"He's your science camp teacher, so you should be proud," Mom tried to convince me.

"I guess I'll try."

Mom hugged me, and when she released me, she whispered loud enough that I could hear, "Phew! That was a close one."

"What?"

"Huh? Nothing. Are you ready to go now?"

I nodded. I took all my stuff and got into the car. Mom came a few seconds later. I was still a little suspicious of Mr. Troop. My mom said that he was my father, but I felt like something was fishy. None of us looked like Mr. Troop. He was an American guy with blond hair, and Mom, Sahil, and I were brown-skinned with black hair. Maybe Mom married an American guy, but then wouldn't we be white? So many questions and confusion that I didn't have a chance to clear. I'd seen pictures from my childhood but never really saw my father in any of them. I knew he used to travel a lot for his business trips, so he didn't spend much time at home with us. Plus, Mom said there might be some pictures in a box, but she doubted it, which was very disappointing.

When we reached camp, I grabbed my stuff quickly and got out of the car. "Have a great day, sweetie! And remember to talk to your father. Nicely."

"Okay, I will talk to him," I said.

Mom smiled and murmured under her breath again, loud enough for me to hear, "At least now she believes it. Mission accomplished."

"What, Mom?"

"Oh, nothing, sweetie. I was just telling you to have a great day!"

"Thanks, Mom." I quickly took my stuff and ran inside. I was obviously late.

When I got into the science room, everyone stared at me like I had just murdered someone. Everyone except for Mr. Troop. I was embarrassed, and instead of saying anything to him, not even a good morning, I just went and sat down in my seat. Meg turned around in her seat and winked at me. Mackenzie, who was sitting at the desk to the left of me, waved. I winked and waved back for no reason. Mr. Troop told the whole class how to do the Mentos/Coke experiment. Everyone got into their groups. I wanted to apologize to Mr. Troop for being rude and slamming the door on him, but before I could approach him, Meg said, "Come, Sameera. You are in our group."

"Yeah, I'll be with you guys in a second. I just need to talk to Mr. Troop," I said.

Mackenzie said, "Is it about the lab? If so, I know exactly what we're supposed to do. In fact, I'll lead you guys through the lab this time."

"No, it's not about the lab. It's a family matter," I replied.

Meg seemed surprised. "Did your mom finally tell you about your father?"

I smiled. "Yeah, I guess so. I thought about this last night, and I even had a conversation with my mom this morning. She said that he is my father, but it just seems too hard to believe."

Mackenzie said, "Oh, come on! You think your mom would lie to you about your father? That's just crazy. This is exciting, Sameera! You're getting to see your dad after a long time."

"Whatever. I need to go talk to him," I said.

Meg said, "I would say go for it, but you might want to wait until the end of the day when the classroom isn't filled with students."

I looked back at Mr. Troop; his head was buried in some cool science experiments book. "Yeah, I guess you're right. Let's focus on the lab now."

While we were performing our experiment—well, while Mackenzie and Meg were performing the experiment—I couldn't stop thinking about what my mom had said to me that morning and what Mr. Troop had said to me yesterday. Their stories matched up perfectly, but I wasn't ready to believe any of it. All this happened within a blink of an eye. I had to play along until I found out what my mom and Mr. Troop were up to. Just then, Mackenzie knocked me back to my senses. "Sameera? Hello? Are you even paying attention? Did you make note of the reaction?"

I looked at where the large Coke bottle stood on the table, bubbles and soda shooting out of the bottle in a high fountain. "Yeah, sorry. I've got my notebook right here," I said, slowly taking it out of my backpack.

"Oh, come on. She missed it, Meg!" Mackenzie exclaimed.

Meg said, "No worries. I've got it all on camera. Sameera can look at it later. The key word is carbon dioxide."

I smiled weakly.

After camp was over that day, I slowly walked up to Mr. Troop. He was writing down notes on a piece of paper. I stood next to his desk but didn't have the courage to make eye contact. So I stared at the floor. Through my peripheral vision, I saw him look up at me and then back down at his notes. "Can I help you?"

I decided that I needed to initiate the conversation. "There's something I need to say."

"Go ahead, I'm listening," he said without looking up at me.

"I'm sorry for my bad behavior. I was rude to you this morning, and I shouldn't have slammed the door on you. I was just frustrated, and I know that was no excuse for how I treated you."

He looked up at me. "You don't need to be sorry."

"Mr. Troop, I don't want you to be mad. Mom told me everything. I'm sorry I thought that you married another woman and were living a happy life," I explained.

He smiled and said, "I know you just needed an explanation. That woman I was about to marry was a bit tough compared to your mother. Being tough isn't always good. She knew how to deal with criminals and all, but sometimes she was tough with me, and I didn't feel that gentleness and love that your mom had. When they were performing the wedding rituals, I thought about how kind and gentle your mom was. I announced that I wanted to cancel the wedding right there on the stage, right there in front of thousands of people. One needs courage to do that. A lot of people were very disappointed that I did that, but I knew what was best for me. I knew that being with your mom was the best for me."

I forced a smile. "Thanks for thinking about my mother."

"Oh, it's no problem. Come here." He tried to hug me.

"Oh, I'm sorry, but I'm not ready for that stage yet," I said.

Mr. Troop smiled. "Understandable, but we're good now, right?"

"We're good," I said and left the classroom.

I walked out of the building and went over to where my friends stood in the parking lot. "So how did it go, Sameera?" Meg asked.

"Yeah. How was your first real conversation with your dad after so many years?" Mackenzie asked.

I replied, "It was good … I guess. Are your parents here?"

"They'll be on their way soon, but tell us about your conversation. What did you and your dad talk about?" Meg asked.

I rolled my eyes. "It's not a big deal. It's just personal … family stuff."

"But it's your dad! I thought you would be more excited," Mackenzie said.

I raised my voice unintentionally. "Dad, dad, dad! Just please can we talk about something else?"

"Okay. Sorry. I guess we could talk about the bizarre bake show we're entering next week. It's all about trying to make the most delicious cakes, cookies, brownies, and pies. You in, Sameera?" Mackenzie asked.

I nodded. "Sounds cool! I'm not really into baking, but I'll be there to support you guys."

Just then, Mr. Troop came up to me and said, "Sameera, your mom is busy with work, so she won't be able to pick you up. That means I'll be dropping you and your brother back to your house on my way home."

"Uh, it's okay. Don't worry about it. My friends here can drop me home. Their parents are on their way right now," I said.

"If you really want to. Why don't you go and get your brother from his sports camp? I'll be in the car," he said.

I said, "I just said my friends can drop me home."

"Yeah, I heard you, but I don't think your brother will want to ride with a bunch of teenage girls."

"Ugh! Fine. We'll let him decide who he wants to ride with," I said and went to get my brother.

When I got to the fields, I saw a boy lying on the ground and two other boys surrounding him. I went up to them and asked, "Have you seen my brother, Sahil?" The two boys standing pointed at Sahil on the ground. I kneeled and examined him. "Oh my gosh. What happened to him?"

"I think when we were playing soccer, he got hit on the head with the ball," one boy said.

"Oh no! Where is your sports instructor?" I asked.

"He left before any of this happened. We were just playing around and goofing off while waiting for our ride," the other boy said.

"What! This is just insane. Now what?" I asked. The boys shrugged. "I've got an idea. Mr. Troop is waiting in the car. I'll just go and get him." I rushed to the parking lot to find him. I was confused because there wasn't a single car left in the parking lot. "Mr. Troop, where are you?" I called out, but there was no response. "Mackenzie? Meg? Are you guys here?" I had a mini heart attack and ran back to where my brother was. He was still lying on the ground, but the two boys weren't there anymore. *They probably just left. How careless. No. They must've gone to get help.* I didn't know what to do. I tried calling my mom, but she didn't pick up. "Oh no. What a difficulty!"

Just then, I saw two girls walking down the sidewalk. I ran over to them. "Mackenzie and Meg? Where were you guys?"

"We were just taking a walk around the playground. Your dad said he had to leave because he got an urgent phone call, so I guess your brother must ride with us," Meg said.

I pursed my lips tightly together.

"You seem a little tense. Is everything okay?" Mackenzie asked.

I replied, "Well, my brother got hit on the head with a soccer ball, and he is lying down on the field. He is unconscious. So can you please help me lift my brother up?"

"Yeah, we'd be happy to. Meg is coming over to my house to hang out, so my mom will be here to pick us up in a few minutes. We should have space in our car for him," Mackenzie said.

"Thank you so much! I'll go get my brother from the field," I said.

"Let me help you," Meg said and followed me. Mackenzie waited in the parking lot for her mom.

We got to the field where Sahil was. Meg and I slowly lifted him up. He was like four inches shorter than me and very light. He only weighed about sixty-five pounds. When Mackenzie's mom finally arrived, Meg and I lifted Sahil into the back seat of the car. I begged her to take us home after she insisted on taking Sahil to the hospital. After we got to my house, Mackenzie's mom asked, "Are you sure you just want to take him in like that? Do you think it's a good idea to take him to the hospital? We could do that if—"

I cut her off. "Thanks, but he'll be fine. This has happened a couple of times before. He's always so clumsy, but don't worry; he'll recover in a few minutes. Thanks for the ride!" Meg and I lifted Sahil out of the car and carried him to my house. We made him lie down on the couch. "Thanks a lot, Meg!"

"Sure, no problem! Call us if you need anything," Meg replied and left my house.

"Hello? Mom? Mr. Troop? Anyone home?" I hollered. There was no response. *Where in the world did my parents go? They can't just leave their kids at a summer camp and run away.* I called out to my parents again, but there was still no response. I felt like panicking. I couldn't just leave my brother on the couch in such a condition. I called my mom. She didn't pick up, so I phoned Mr. Troop. He didn't pick up either. I decided I had to do something myself. I got a bucket of water and went to the sink to fill it up. I went back over to Sahil on the couch and splatted water on his face. He slowly opened his eyes. I was relieved. "Are you okay, Sahil?" I asked. He slowly nodded. "You look exhausted. Want me to make you a snack?"

"Yes, please," he said. I went to the kitchen to make a PB&J sandwich.

While I was making Sahil's snack, my phone rang. I picked up the phone. It was my mom. "Hello, Mom?"

"Hi, sweetie. Are you doing okay? How about Sahil?"

"Yes, I'm fine, and so is Sahil now. He got knocked out in the head with a soccer ball at camp, but he's fine now. Where did you guys go?" I could hear Mom breathing heavily and her voice was shaky. "Is everything all right?" I asked.

She replied, "We left town because our lives were in danger."

"Oh no! How come?"

"Well, it's a long story, but are you managing all right? Please take good care of Sahil."

I just said, "Yes, I will. Will you be okay? When will you come home?" There was a great deal of concern in my voice.

"I can't tell you anything right now. I must hang up. I'll tell you everything once we come home. I love you, sweetie. Bye!" The phone dropped from my hand to the floor. I was so shocked. I just stood there with my mouth open for a while.

"Sameera? What happened to Mom?" Sahil asked.

I lied. "She just went out."

"To where?"

"Um to … uh … to get groceries. Yeah, that's it." I didn't want my brother to get worried.

"Okay, so what's the big deal about that? You seemed really concerned."

"Oh yeah, I was … um … it's just that she … um … she forgot her cash purse at home, but no worries; she said she has her credit card with her, so it's all good." I quickly picked up my phone from the floor. I finished making the sandwich and gave it to Sahil. "Here—eat your sandwich and go take some rest." He gobbled it up and left his plate on the counter. "Hey! At least put your plate in the sink!"

CHAPTER 3

After a couple of hours, the doorbell rang. "That must be Mom," Sahil called from upstairs.

"Shut up, dummy. Mom has the house keys. Why would she ring the doorbell?"

"That's a good point," he said.

I slowly approached the front door. I opened it, but it wasn't Mom or anyone I recognized. It was a woman, a little older than my mom but not as old as my grandma. She wore glasses with a purple frame crookedly. She wore a white shirt, a long rose-colored skirt, and some black sandals. Hanging from her arm was a large handbag with the initials JT.

"Who are you?" I asked.

She replied, "I am a woman."

"I know, but what's your name, and why are you here?"

"My name is Jane Turner, and I am here to parent you and your brother," she responded firmly.

"Parent us? We have a mom for that." I chuckled a little.

"Not anymore."

My smile faded away quickly. "I don't understand. What are you trying to say?"

"I'm going to be living with you guys from now on as a mother … mother … mother … mother." There was that strange echo again.

"What? No, you must be kidding! Tell me you're kidding!" I said.

She nodded and handed me a piece of paper with a phone number on it. I slowly took it and asked, "What is this?"

"They knew it wouldn't be easy to convince you. Call that number, and you will get to know everything that has happened. I'll be in the kitchen making dinner."

I stopped her immediately. "Hey, wait! You're a stranger. You can't just come into our house and start doing whatever you want."

"Okay then. I'll wait for you to call that number and understand what's going on. Then we'll proceed from there," the woman said.

I quickly took out my phone and dialed the number on the piece of paper. There was a recorded message from my parents. They said, "Sameera and Sahil, this is your mom and dad. Remember when we told you that our life was in danger earlier? Well, it was true. We don't know when we'll be back or if we'll ever be back. There's a woman who probably came to your house. Don't send her away. She's there to take care of both of you until we're back. So please take care. Don't lose hope. I know you both will succeed in life. Just stay strong. Be nice. We love you! Bye!" I was so shocked that I crashed down on my knees, hitting the floor with a loud thud.

"Oh my … Where are they? We must save them."

"No! It'll put your life in danger if you go after them. It might be too late by the time you find out where they are and then try going there. Please try to understand. It's best if you stay here and stay safe," the woman said.

Just then, Sahil came downstairs. "What kind of chaos is going on down here? Can't you see I'm trying to rest?" he asked.

I took a deep breath. "Sahil, our parents. … They're probably never coming back," I said.

"Why not? Just because they're taking forever at the grocery store doesn't mean they'll never come back," Sahil said.

Tears flooded my eyes. "No, Sahil. It's not what you think. Listen to the message." I handed him my phone.

He looked at me like I was crazy and tilted his face at me. After he listened to the message, he said, "Psst. Whatever. Here. Take your phone back."

"Sahil? Aren't you upset? You know what this means?" I asked.

He replied, "Yes, I know. We shouldn't lose hope on them. They'll come back soon. It's probably just a prank that they're getting me back for. I'm not falling for the trap. They're probably here somewhere and pretending to be gone."

"They're not pranksters like you—well, at least Mom isn't. She doesn't believe in revenge; you know that. This can't be true. Why would they send this woman here then? Didn't you—"

Sahil interrupted. "Whether you believe it or not, I will. I believe that they'll come back for us." He went back upstairs.

Sahil does not understand that they're in danger. They might be dead. Oh no! The woman stood near the doorway, staring at me. "We can manage by ourselves. We don't need you to take care of us, but thank you for the message. You can leave now," I told the woman.

She responded, "I'm not going anywhere because none of you are over the age of eighteen. You can't live alone in this house. State rules."

I took a deep breath and then said, "Okay fine. I guess you can go make dinner. I'll find a solution to this."

The woman took her stuff and went to the kitchen. I still couldn't believe anything would happen to Mom and Mr. Troop. I wished I could do something about it. I was starving, and I couldn't think of anything. I sat down on the couch in the living room and turned on the TV.

The woman yelled from the kitchen, "Hey! Turn that thing off! It's very distracting."

I quickly turned the TV off and sat on the couch with my arms folded.

"Why don't you help me set the table?" the woman asked. I rolled my eyes and walked over to the kitchen. I called out to Sahil when the food was ready.

While we were eating dinner, I was wondering where this woman was from, but I was too nervous to ask personal questions. I kept quiet, but it seemed as though Sahil could read my mind. He asked the woman, "Can we get to know about you? Like what we should call you and where you're from. Also, how long you are staying here."

"No!" the woman screamed.

I jolted.

"Why not?" Sahil asked.

"Don't ask her anything. I think she's not in a good mood," I whispered to Sahil.

"I will tell you what you both should call me but *nothing else*!" the woman shouted. Sahil and I nodded. "My name is Jane Turner, but you both should only call me Ms. Turner."

"Okay, ma'am," I said quietly.

"Now finish your dinner quickly, and then I'll give you your list of chores to do for tomorrow," Ms. Turner said.

"Chores?" Sahil and I asked in unison.

Ms. Turner nodded. "Until you two get yourselves a real job, you guys are going to be doing household chores."

My eyebrows furrowed. Mom never made us do household chores. She would always do them and tell us to worry about ourselves. Even when we offered to help her out, she always said, "You both are still kids. You shouldn't be worrying about housework. Focus on studies. And afterward, go have fun and enjoy yourselves. This is the time to enjoy because when you get older, you will constantly be busy." I didn't understand why this woman was making us do her work. She said she was there like a mother, so housework should have been her job.

"Our mom is way nicer than you!" Sahil yelled at the woman.

Ms. Turner tightened her lips and stood up. She growled and stomped over to where Sahil was sitting. "Look at me, boy! If you speak like that to me ever again, then I will squeeze you to death. You hear me?"

My eyes got wide. "Excuse me?" I was starting to think that letting this woman into the house was a bad idea. I was just hoping that this was a dream. I pinched myself so hard to wake up in my bed but found that I was just giving myself unnecessary pain. This wasn't any dream. This was reality! We were going to be stuck with this wicked old woman forever.

Ms. Turner handed me a roll of paper and said, "Unroll the paper to see all your chores, and you too, boy!"

I took the paper and unrolled it. I read through the list and frowned.

"Get up at 6:00 a.m. tomorrow and get busy," Ms. Turner said.

"Where's my paper though?" Sahil asked.

"Your list is the same as your sister's. Split up the chores however you want, but I want them all done. No excuses. Go to bed now!"

It was only 8:30 p.m.—too early to go to bed even if we had to get up at six. She gave us a list of thirty chores to do. Sahil said, "Oh geesh. This is a lot of chores. Let's split it up this way. I'll do five, and you can do twenty-five."

"Hey, that's not fair!" I exclaimed.

Sahil rolled his eyes and said, "Okay, then I'll do ten, and you do twenty. Okay?"

"No, Sahil!" I screamed.

Ms. Turner shouted, "Will you both stop fighting! Each of you will do fifteen chores. End of discussion."

"Okay, now that's fair," I told Sahil.

"Now get to bed!" she yelled.

I went up to my room but didn't go to bed. I stayed up watching my favorite show, *Fuller House.*

In the early morning, Ms. Turner barged into my room and flung the door open wide. She stood in the middle of the upstairs hallway so her voice would be heard in both of our rooms. She screamed, "Rise and shine, children! It's already 6:00 a.m. Get up and begin your chores!"

I got up slowly and without complaining opened our list of chores. I chose fifteen chores from the list, and my brother got the other fifteen. "You get all the easy ones, Sameera!" Sahil complained.

I said, "Well, I got up earlier than you today, so it's fair that I chose first." Sahil was frustrated, but I started on my chores so he couldn't argue further. I cleaned the floors, took out the trash, and loaded the dishwasher for cleaning. I wasn't happy about doing chores, but the quicker I got them done, the more time I had for myself. I felt kind of exhausted after doing the first three chores. I wondered how Mom did it. And she didn't have any help. She did the household work all on her own. *I must appreciate her.* Since I was tired, I went to my room and lay down for a minute. I closed my eyes and was just about to fall asleep when I heard my phone vibrate.

"Hi, Sameera. It's Mackenzie. Are you excited for Monday?"

"Monday? It's only Saturday, I don't want to think about Monday yet. But anyway, what's so special?" I asked.

She replied, "Didn't you hear the announcement? We get to do the best science experiment ever!"

"Wait, but who would be the teacher? And what is the experiment about?" I asked.

She laughed. "What do you mean who's the teacher? Obviously, it's your father. He said the experiment is a surprise, but he said we'll love it! I called to ask if you knew anything about it. Did he not tell you anything?"

"Nope."

"Well, maybe he wanted to surprise you too! I guess we'll find out on Monday at camp."

"What? Oh, Mr. Troop? But he's ..." I couldn't get the words out.

"Why? Is your father sick or something? Can he not make it to camp on Monday?" Mackenzie asked.

I didn't know what to say. "Uh ... I ... don't know what's going on, but my mom and Mr. Troop are in danger, according to their voice message. I have no idea when they'll be back. I must go now." I quickly hung up the phone. Tears rolled down my cheeks. I tried so hard not to cry, but I couldn't help it. The thought of losing my mom really hurt me. Besides, I just got to know Mr. Troop yesterday, and *whoosh*—he was gone already.

Ms. Turner came into my room and asked, "What are you doing here just lying down like a lazy person? Get busy!"

"But, Ms. Turner, I'm hungry. I can't do work on an empty stomach. When's breakfast?" I asked.

She shook her head. "Breakfast? Are you kidding me? I'm not going to make you a nice, warm breakfast. The only thing I will make is dinner. If you want breakfast, then go to the refrigerator and grab some fruits or yogurt. Then get back to your chores. No wasting time chatting with your friends." Ms. Turner left my room.

I felt like I was in prison. Not that I had ever experienced prison, but it was close enough I thought. I was wondering how Sahil was doing. Was he hungry? Did he eat anything? My big-sister instincts kicked in, and I felt the need to check on him. I went to his room and was surprised to find out that he wasn't doing chores; instead, he was researching something on the computer. "Hey, Sahil. Whatcha doing?" I asked.

"Oh, hi, Sameera. I'm just researching a special formula that'll transform Ms. Turner into a nicer person. We need to mix this carbon fluid and a bunch of other fluids listed here. Do you have any of these or know where I can find them?" Sahil was researching science. *Science.* He hated science and math and all the other subjects in school. The only subject he really liked and took seriously was gym, and he loved all things related to sports.

"Since when are you interested in science?" I asked.

Sahil grinned. "Ever since that ball hit me in the head. Don't you think that's a little weird? Like a fairy tale almost. But it's true. Now, since you like science too, we both can work together to create this fluid that Ms. Turner can drink. She'll start treating us with more respect in a couple of hours after drinking this. What do you say?"

I frowned. "Not the best idea. Wrong combinations could lead to a disaster."

"Well then, do you have a better idea, smarty-pants?" Sahil asked with sass. I didn't.

I looked around Sahil's room. "What happened to the football, basketball, and all the other sports posters you had? Why do you have posters about the periodic table and stuff about photosynthesis all over your walls?" I asked.

"Oh yeah, I changed them and remodeled my room to fit my interests. The sports posters looked a little boring, and I found these cool science posters in your room. It looked very interesting, so I took them and hung them in my room," Sahil explained.

"I knew it! These posters looked so familiar to me. Sahil! Those are my posters. I care about science more than you do! Give them back!" I screamed.

"Sorry, Sameera. Finders keepers. These are my posters now. They inspire me. If you don't want your room to feel empty, then you can have my sports posters. I don't want them anymore."

I said, "But, Sahil, you're the sports person, and you care about sports more than science."

"Nah, I care about science more now. Lots of people say that I'm good at sports, but I've decided I don't want a career in sports. I'd prefer to pursue a career in the field of science."

"What! Science is my thing though. I'm a nerd. You always keep changing your mind just to compete with me!" I said angrily.

"Well, are you going to help me make the new formula or what?" he asked.

"Of course not! You're on your own, buddy!" I yelled as I approached the door.

"Okay then. We'll see who's the better science person."

I rolled my eyes and left his room.

I was in a bad mood. I was hungry and angry at Ms. Turner and Sahil. I went downstairs to get some fruit for breakfast. I wasn't going to give any fruit to Sahil. He didn't deserve it. I didn't care if he starved; I was not supporting him doing science. *That's my thing; he can't just steal it from under my nose.* After breakfast, I got busy with the rest of my chores that led me to the end of the day. What a boring day! At least I was glad to be done with chores. Ms. Turner kept us so busy today that I was ready to hit the bed.

"Children, come down! You should've finished your chores by now. I'm going to make sure you've done everything on the list before I serve you dinner," Ms. Turner said. I stumbled down the stairs weakly. I saw Ms. Turner eagerly waiting in the kitchen, rubbing her palms together. "Where's your brother?" she asked. I shrugged. Sahil had been in his room trying to do science all day. I was pretty sure that he didn't get a single chore done. He was not getting dinner. I ate fruit for breakfast, and Ms. Turner didn't give us any lunch, but I made myself a sandwich. Sahil had been in his room the whole day. I was hoping that he didn't starve to death. "Go and get your brother!" Ms. Turner yelled. I agreed and quickly ran back upstairs.

I tried to open the door to Sahil's room, but the door was locked. "Sahil, come down for dinner," I said as I knocked on the door.

He opened the door a few seconds later. "Welcome to my chemical kitchen," he said.

"Chemical kitchen what? Why are you dressed like that? And where did you get all this crazy stuff from?" I asked.

Sahil was wearing a white button-up shirt and a white chef hat with an atom logo. "I made my own kitchen in my room so that I don't have to worry about going down to get my food. I can just eat here. I got all this equipment and these ingredients from my friend. His older brother used to use this station to cook up simple things and do science experiments, but he was planning to give it away, so I decided to take it. He came over a few hours ago. I'm surprised you didn't see."

"Right. That was probably when Ms. Turner was taking her afternoon nap and I was in the basement reading and listening to music on high blast."

"Well, that's on you. Anyway, this station came with an instruction book. I've been in my room studying all the different ways you can make food interesting. All the foods here are artificially colored, but I like to call it *chemical*. Here, try some chemical burgers," Sahil said, handing me a burger with pink buns and purple patties.

"Eww! Why can't you just try to cook like a normal person if you really wanted to be a chef? Why do you have to add artificial colors and make the food look weird?"

"Well, I think the food looks cooler this way. I'm Sahil Chacko, and I just took food to the next level."

"That's not good for you, Sahil. You can't consume that much artificial coloring." I looked around his room and saw tables with colorful fluids. "Where in the world did you get all these fluids? Artificially colored drinks, I'm assuming?" I asked.

"Oh no. Those are for a science experiment I was attempting. My friend's brother had a science kit as well. I'm not finished with the experiment yet. Maybe I'll test it out tomorrow. Anyway, what would you like for dinner? I have some chemical sandwiches, chemical fries, and for dessert, I have chemical ice cream and a chemical cake. Oh, and I have—"

I interrupted. "I get the point. You have artificial foods, but I don't want any. I don't want food poisoning, okay? I guess I'll just stick to Ms. Turner's dinner, and I suggest you do the same." I smirked and left his room.

I went downstairs and told Ms. Turner that Sahil didn't want to come down for dinner. "He is eating upstairs."

"What is he eating up there? He has nothing there to eat. Anyway, I don't care. Did you get your chores done?" Ms. Turner asked. I nodded and handed her the paper. "I gave you thirty chores, and only fifteen are checked. What is this?" Ms. Turner asked.

"I did my fifteen chores, but Sahil was too busy doing science things in his bedroom and didn't do any of his chores," I explained.

Ms. Turner said, "Well, this chore list was the responsibility of both of you combined. If the thirty chores weren't completed, then I wasn't going to give you dinner. You could've helped your brother when you were done with your chores. I'm sorry, but no dinner until all the chores are completed. Good luck! And I'm taking over the master bedroom. Thank you very much." Ms. Turner headed upstairs.

"What? But that's my mom's room! You get the guest room, Ms. Turner."

She glared at me. "Well, it *was* your mom's room. Now it's mine."

I felt rage build up inside me. I wanted to run up to Sahil's room and yell at him for ruining my dinner, but that would not help the situation right then. I had bigger things to worry about. My mom and Mr. Troop were in danger, and I had to find out where they were. I pulled out my phone and tried Mom's number, but it went directly to voice mail. *She might've switched it off.* I headed up to my room and sat next to my computer, hoping to get some idea of what to do.

After a while, Ms. Turner came into my room. "All right, Sameera. Get to bed now!" Ms. Turner said and switched off the lights.

"Ugh! But I'm starving, and it's all because of Sahil. If he'd never been interested in science, then he would've gotten his chores done, and I would've gotten to eat a proper dinner. I just wish I could destroy his stupid chemical kitchen so that he'd take his chores more seriously," I said to myself. I lay in my bed and stared at the ceiling for a few hours. I couldn't sleep; my stomach was growling. "You know what? I can't take this anymore. I'm going to destroy the chemical kitchen while Sahil is asleep. And I'll make sure he won't even know a thing."

I got up and headed toward Sahil's room. I prayed that the door wouldn't squeak as I opened it. Thankfully, it didn't. I slowly went in—and shockingly, someone else was there. I could hear munching. "Ms. Turner! What are you doing here?" I asked.

"Uh oh. Shh! You'll wake your brother up. I'm just here to … well, clean up. Look at this mess," Ms. Turner whispered.

I replied sarcastically, "Right. You cleaning up? Come on. Be real now. You literally had us do all the household chores today, and now suddenly you're the one to clean up? Wow, that's totally believable."

She rolled her eyes and said softly, "Okay fine. I'm not cleaning up. You both were very loud this evening, and I heard you fight about this chemical kitchen thing. I was just curious to check it out. Anyway, I don't know why you hate this so much. Have you tried some of these foods? It's so good," she whispered, licking her fingers.

I scrunched up my face. "Eww, no."

"Well, it's your loss. I'm going to savor this."

"No, this is all junk. I'm here to destroy this thing once and for all," I said strongly.

Ms. Turner was licking some of the charcoal from a bowl. "Are you kidding? This is good! You shouldn't destroy it. I could make millions with this kitchen."

I was confused. "Excuse me? Millions of what? Food?"

"No. Millions of dollars. People would pay so much to eat this kind of food, as it's very rare around here," Ms. Turner explained.

My eyes shot up at her. "Wow, really? That's nice! Too bad it's Sahil's kitchen now, and I don't think he would want to do something like this."

"Oh, come on! Think about it. Advertising your brother's kitchen to the whole world would not only make millions of dollars but would make him famous too," she suggested.

I shook my head slightly. "Eh, I don't really think so."

"You know what? Advertising is my area of expertise. I can take care of it in no time," she said.

I looked at the chemical kitchen and said, "Wow, you're saying we can be rich with this stupid thing?" Ms. Turner nodded. I heard Sahil groan. "Oh God. We've got to get out of here," I said and motioned Ms. Turner to the door.

CHAPTER 4

It was finally morning. "New day. New feeling. Oh, wait—what is up with Ms. Turner wanting to advertise the chemical kitchen to the world?" A thought occurred to me. *What if Sahil doesn't want the whole world to know? What if he wants to keep it a secret? No, he's not like me. I'm pretty sure he'll agree to it. After all, he will be gaining fame and money. What else could Sahil possibly want?* I quickly freshened up and went downstairs.

"Morning, Sameera!" Ms. Turner hollered.

"Oh, good morning. Any chores for today?" I asked.

She laughed. "Don't worry. I don't have any chores for you right this second. Maybe later in the day. Remember yesterday's plan? I am looking for ways to advertise the chemical kitchen," Ms. Turner said, looking at her laptop.

"Oh yeah. Do you need any help?" I asked as I went to the refrigerator and grabbed a bottle of apple juice and a container of strawberry yogurt.

"I don't need any help now. Once I find something, I'll call you back to work on the plan."

"All right then. I'll be in my room."

I went up to Sahil's room and knocked on the door. He opened it and said, "Hey, Sameera."

"What's up, Sahil? Where is your chemical kitchen?" I asked. I looked around his room. There was no sign of his chemical kitchen.

No kitchen. No food. Not anything. It was like it had never been there. The whole thing felt like a dream.

Sahil said, "I thought about it. I'm sorry for not doing my chores yesterday. You had to starve, and it was my fault. So I destroyed my chemical kitchen. From today onward, I'll do my chores."

I almost dropped to the floor. "No! Why? Why would you destroy it? Ms. Turner said you could've made millions out of it."

Sahil said, "Millions? All you care about is fame and money! I heard you and Ms. Turner talking in my room yesterday. Advertising my chemical kitchen to the whole world? Without my permission? I can't believe you, Sameera."

"Wait, I thought you were asleep."

"Your loud whispering woke me up, but I decided not to get up. I stayed there with my eyes closed but my ears open. I heard everything, Sameera, and it's not fair. You are teaming up with Ms. Turner. I thought you and I were a team against her."

"Sahil ... no—that's not what—" I started.

"Anyway, I didn't want to advertise my kitchen. So I destroyed it before you could get your hands on it."

"I thought the food was good. Ms. Turner tasted it last night. You really are a better science person than I thought. I was wrong about you, Sahil. You really can do science stuff." I tried to encourage him, but he didn't seem like he was buying it.

He replied, "I don't care if I'm good at science! I'm done doing all this nerdy stuff. You hated the idea of the chemical kitchen yesterday, and now you suddenly want it back? Just because Ms. Turner said so. You know what? I want to go back to loving sports. Life was so much easier that way. Take all your nerdy science posters off my walls and keep them."

"Oh! Gosh, Sahil. Look, I'm sorry that I agreed to advertise the kitchen without your permission. Please forgive me," I begged.

Sahil responded, "You are forgiven, but the chemical kitchen is never coming back." He went over to his walls and started tearing off the science posters.

"Sahil, please listen to me. I'll do anything to make it up to you, and I mean anything. Just rebuild your chemical kitchen please."

"Oh, you'll do anything. Then let's see if you're able to ... *test this out*!" He pulled out a small bottle of green liquid from one of his desk drawers and handed it to me.

"What's this? I asked.

"I finally came up with the liquid to make people nicer. If you go and somehow get this liquid into Ms. Turner's body, then I'll get my chemical kitchen back."

"Oh, that's easy ... wait—but Ms. Turner is already nice. She didn't give us any chores today," I responded.

Sahil shrugged.

"Children, the house is dirty! We need to clean it! I mean you two need to clean it before we can advertise the chemical kitchen!" Ms. Turner yelled from downstairs.

"Well, so much for no chores. See that? So make sure Ms. Turner gets some of this liquid," Sahil said.

"Okay fine." I took the liquid and headed downstairs.

Ms. Turner said, "Sameera, you're here. I want you to clean this floor of the house, and I want your brother to clean upstairs."

"Uh, I'll do that, but first can you try this chemical lime juice? Sahil made it in his kitchen." I handed her the liquid.

She took it from me and said, "Thanks. I'll drink it later. Get busy cleaning!"

"I will, I will, but first try the juice and see if you like it. Sahil wanted to know how good it is so he can improve it," I lied.

"Why is Sahil making me try it? He should make you try it. After all, you haven't tried a single thing from that kitchen. Why don't you take a sip first, and then I'll give it a go?" Ms. Turner suggested.

"Oh, ha-ha, me? Well, I already tried some and wanted your opinion before we proceed," I said helplessly.

"Drink it!" she demanded.

I looked around for Sahil. He was standing by the stairs and moving his arms around. He was trying to tell me not to drink it, but I had no choice. Ms. Turner would know I lied if I didn't drink it. I slowly took a sip. I felt kind of dizzy, and everything around me started becoming fuzzy. "So how is it?" Ms. Turner asked.

Oh no! I think Sahil messed it up. He must've combined the wrong liquids together. "Fine. Now you try it," I said.

"It's fine. I'll drink it later. I just had breakfast," she said. I was trapped, but I didn't feel dizzy anymore. "Now, Sameera, if you wouldn't mind, please clean downstairs," Ms. Turner said.

"Yes. Right away, ma'am." I went to grab a broom.

Ms. Turner smiled wickedly. Then she looked at Sahil and said, "What are you doing standing there, boy? Go clean upstairs."

"I don't want to. I don't have to listen to you, old lady."

"Don't worry, Sahil. After I'm done cleaning downstairs, I'll also clean upstairs. You don't have to take on stress. Just relax," I said without wanting to. *I don't want to be too nice to Sahil. I know he'll take advantage of me, but I have to play along for some more time.*

Sahil grinned and said, "Thanks, Sameera."

"Anytime." I did it again.

Sahil chuckled.

CHAPTER 5

I finished cleaning downstairs and upstairs. "Great job, Sameera. Now we can work on advertising the chemical kitchen," Ms. Turner said.

Sahil came downstairs. "Hey, I found a great website for advertising this," Ms. Turner said.

I went over to her computer to get a look. "Cool. Let's use that."

"Excuse me? You didn't even take my permission. I don't want to advertise my kitchen," Sahil said.

Ms. Turner replied, "Well, that's too bad. You're too late. I've already started putting information out there. We will advertise this kitchen."

"If Sahil doesn't want to advertise the kitchen, then let's not do it," I said. "It's his kitchen after all, so his choice."

"Then how will we make millions?" Ms. Turner asked.

"We won't," I replied and closed her laptop. I started toward the stairs to my room. I wanted to convince Sahil somehow to advertise his kitchen but didn't know why I was taking his side and not doing it at all. *This is not like me. Ugh!*

"Wait … where are you going?" I heard Ms. Turner say. I saw Sahil sitting on the stairs, mumbling something to himself. He gave me a thumbs-up as I went upstairs. I just rolled my eyes and continued walking. I was helping so much for the rest of the day without really wanting to. I just hoped that this day would be over soon, and I could be myself again.

I woke up the next day and felt a bit light-headed. Sahil rushed into my room and said, "Good morning, Sameera. Ms. Turner has a lot of chores for you to do downstairs. Get ready."

I slowly got up, half-asleep. "Sahil, why do I have to do chores? I did everything yesterday. It's your turn today." I lay back down on my bed.

"What? Sameera, you said you loved doing chores and helping around the house. What happened?" Sahil asked.

"Nothing. You know what? I can't do this anymore," I said.

"Do what?" he asked with a frown.

I sighed and sat on the edge of my bed. "Your stupid science potion thing didn't work."

"Why would you say that? It totally worked. Maybe not the person I wanted it on, but you should've seen yourself yesterday, being all soft and helpful," Sahil replied.

I decided to tell him the truth. "Sahil, I was faking it."

"What?"

"That weird liquid combination you created didn't work. I was pretending that it did," I said.

Sahil gasped. "Seriously? Why would you do that?"

"I had to. I mean, you had so much faith in it. That's the first time I've ever seen you take something like science seriously. I kind of liked your courage and motivation to do that. It might've not worked the way you wanted it to, but I tried. I wanted you to believe that you invented something great, so I played along. And I thought maybe that if you saw your potion working, you would agree to rebuild your chemical kitchen. I'm sorry."

Sahil didn't say anything. Maybe he was disappointed. Maybe he felt hopeless, but it was better that I told him the truth now rather than later.

Sahil replied, "I rebuilt it last night, but I don't have a good reason to advertise it."

I said, "It's an awesome kitchen! Think about it this way. If we do make millions, we can get rid of Ms. Turner. We'll bribe her or something, so she leaves this house. Then we'll be all on our own and can do whatever we want! Think of it as a battle of you and me against Ms. Turner. That's what you wanted, right?"

"That does seem like a good plan. Fine, I'll do it, but only because you were nice to me yesterday and did my chores."

"Yes! Now let's go tell Ms. Turner that you are in. Come on." I got out of bed. I grabbed Sahil's arm and dragged him down the stairs.

Ms. Turner was sitting and staring at the laptop. "Hey, Ms. Turner," I said.

"Hello again, children."

"I think Sahil needs to say something," I said and looked at Sahil.

He said, "Okay, so umm … you have my permission to advertise my chemical kitchen. I just need to make some adjustments to it first."

"Great! I'm glad. Now we can make millions!" Ms. Turner said and cackled.

"You mean Sahil can make millions. You're just helping him out, right?" I asked.

Ms. Turner slowly nodded. "Right. Of course. Just him." She didn't seem convincing at all. It was almost like she wanted to take all the money for herself. "Uh, I guess you guys can eat breakfast if you want while I get to work on my chemical kitch—I mean Sahil's chemical kitchen." She put a bowl of fruit on the table and took her computer upstairs. "Sahil, is it okay if I go to your room to get some pictures of the kitchen?"

"Uh, sure, whatever," he said, waving his hand.

A few minutes later, my phone rang. "Hey, this is Mom's number." I picked it up. "Mom?"

"Hi, Sameera."

"Mom!"

"No, I'm not your mom. I'm calling to tell you about your parents," the lady said.

I was confused. "What? I thought they were not coming back."

"Oh really. Well, there might still be a chance for them to survive. I'll give you some information, but that's all I can do to help. Your parents are kidnapped! You'd better go save them."

"Speaker!" Sahil whispered loudly.

I put the phone on speaker. "Oh no! Where are they?" I asked, my voice tense.

"If you want to see your parents again, then you'd better go to the Cave of Doom."

"The Cave of Doom! That's all the way in Ohert City! Why are they there?" I asked. Sahil looked a little confused. The person seemed to have hung up. "Hello? Hello?" I said into the phone.

I said, "Come on, Sahil. We must go to Ohert City and save Mom and Mr. Troop. They've been kidnapped."

"What city?" he asked.

I replied, "The city that has the Cave of Doom. It's about a half hour away. Well, a half hour if we take our bikes. A taxi would be quicker, but we don't have that kind of money right now."

"Why are our parents there though?"

"You heard the call. I know as much as you do. Stop asking questions. We'll figure it out when we get there. Let's move it!" I said.

"Oh no! So this isn't a prank? It's real? Wait a minute. Now are you and Mom trying to prank me together?"

"Sahil, this is no time to joke. They're really in danger. Just come on!" I demanded.

Sahil looked upset. "Geesh. Don't we have to tell Ms. Turner?"

I took in a long breath of air. "Ms. Turner! We're going out for a bit. We'll be back soon."

"Go ahead and take your time. No rush!" she shouted.

"Well, that wasn't so hard. She didn't even ask us where we were going," Sahil pointed out. I shrugged.

We left our bowls of cereal half-eaten and rushed out of the house. We didn't know what Ms. Turner was doing with the chemical kitchen, but our focus now was on saving our parents. I started running. "Running will get you nowhere! If you need to get to Ohert City, then it will take hours. Maybe days," Sahil said.

"Sorry, I'm stressed. Let's take our bikes," I suggested. We opened the garage, took out our bikes, and put on our helmets. We rode out of the driveway and out of our neighborhood.

Sahil said, "How do we even get to Ohert City? We've never been there before."

"Just follow my lead. I know what I'm doing," I said, even though I had no idea what I was doing. We continued riding our bikes for some time.

On the way, Sahil began getting tired of riding his bike. He kept stopping in the middle of the bike lane. "We didn't even eat breakfast properly. I literally have no energy to ride this bike. Can we go to Taco Land or something?" Sahil asked.

I stopped my bike. "Seriously? Do you want to save Mom or not?" I asked. He nodded. "Then forget food! Our focus is on getting to the Cave of Doom. Let's keep moving. The faster we go, the quicker we get there."

We rode our bikes for a few more minutes. Then Sahil stopped again and said, "Sameera, I can't take this anymore. I need food. You don't want me to fall unconscious again, do you?"

"Why are you doing this, Sahil?" I asked.

"Because if I don't eat, then I'll fall unconscious, and you know that it'll cause more problems, and we won't be able to save our parents in time."

"Ugh! I should not have brought you with me. I could've just gone alone to find them! It would've been much easier!"

"I wish I didn't come with you either! You're such a bossy sister. I would've stayed home and looked after my chemical kitchen if it weren't for you!" Sahil yelled at me.

"For me? Sahil she's your mom too. Don't you care about her?" I asked.

Sahil nodded. "Yes, but she cares about us too. She would've not wanted us to try to save her on an empty stomach."

"Whatever. Just let's stop this nonsense. Tell me, what do you want to eat?" I asked.

"Something like tacos," he replied.

"I don't see Taco Land. There's a Snack Bar Express right there. That'll have to do." I pointed at the sign that I saw nearby. I had a purse with some money that I brought with me in case of emergency.

At the restaurant, Sahil ordered his burger and sat at a booth. He asked me, "Don't you want something to eat too?"

"No, I'm fine. Just eat quickly. We need to go." Sahil split his burger in half and offered me one half. "I said I don't want any."

"You'll get tired on the way, and then we'll have to stop again, and that'll waste more time. We need to save our parents, right? Eat this," Sahil said. He could sometimes be considerate and caring. I sat down at the booth, grabbed the half burger from Sahil, and took a bite. After we finished our burger, we got back on the road.

Soon we came to a sign that read "Welcome to Ohert City. We hope you enjoy the joy this city brings."

"Yes! We made it!" I exclaimed.

CHAPTER 6

The city looked so wonderful. I felt like we were in some fantasy world. Almost like a dream. There were so many things that caught my attention. I saw a large tree, the fruit of which would bring independence. We were away from the traffic and sounds. When two strangers met, they greeted each other with a "Good morning." We passed by the woods in a community free of plastic. It seemed like a world where there was no corruption, violence, or political activity and everyone lived happily. There was no leader, and everybody was their own leader. An environment where animals lived fearlessly and birds flew across the skies. This city was a haven of harmony. It was situated in a setting surrounded by great nature, hills, waterfalls, and most importantly, peace. In the middle of the city was a river running through it, which the whole city could be seen and experienced. To me, this seemed like a perfect city to live in, a place where Mother Earth was safe.

Sahil turned his bike into a vibrant-looking store. I followed him with my bike. "Sahil, we don't have all day to be in this city. We're not here for an outing. We must find our parents first," I said.

There was a middle-aged man standing outside the store saying, "Come in, come in! Our shop has a lot to offer. There is a machine in here for all your dreams to come true."

Sahil glared at me. I said, "No. We don't have time to go in there."

"Please, just one shop. Then I'll be focused on finding Mom and Dad," Sahil pleaded.

"Okay, fine. I guess one shop won't hurt," I said. We parked our bikes and went inside.

The store looked so beautiful. It was colorful and vibrant in almost every corner, surrounded with neon lights. "I wish we lived in this city so we could go to this shop every day," Sahil said.

I laughed. "You can still come here often. It's not too far from our city. Although it would probably require a taxi if you wanted to get here quicker. But it's possible."

Sahil agreed. "Let's go look at the dream machine." He started toward a big, clear globe filled with pieces of paper. I followed him.

There was a hole in the machine, and above that, a sign that said, "Put your dreams in, and this machine will give you a fortune in return." Sahil had some paper and pens in his pocket, so he took it out and started writing something. "Here, Sameera. Write your dream too." He handed me a small, square sheet of paper. I began writing about finding my parents and bringing them back home. Sahil inserted his piece of paper in the hole of the machine, and the machine started to shake. Soon it stopped, and a strip of paper slid out from another hole in the bottom of the machine. Sahil eagerly grabbed the strip and read it out loud. "You will find the solution where you least expect it."

I quickly put my wish in, and the machine started shaking—longer than usual. Then it stopped, but no paper came out. "What the heck?" I asked.

Sahil laughed. "What invalid wish did you make?"

"Just forget it! This is a stupid, broken machine," I said.

"Try again," Sahil requested.

I replied, "We've spent enough time here. Let's get out."

I began walking away when Sahil called out, "Wait! There's a piece of paper."

I looked back and immediately grabbed it. It read, "Your lost item will be found next." I kept wondering about my fortune as we exited the store. I didn't have any lost items now. Lost parents? Yes. But they were people, not items. We got back on our bikes.

Sahil asked, "Where are we going to find the Cave of Doom?"

"I don't even know. I guess we'll have to ask somebody," I said. We continued riding and saw a snack shop around the corner. An old lady was standing outside, smoking a pipe. I pointed at the snack shop and said, "That way."

"You seriously want to eat now? What about Mom and Dad?" Sahil asked.

"I'm not going to eat, dummy. I am going to ask for directions," I replied. I rode my bike toward the lady, and Sahil trailed behind.

Once I approached the lady, she put down her pipe and said, "Hello, kids! Where are your parents? You need to be eighteen years or older to roam around by yourself."

Oh, so there were rules in the city. Not as much freedom as I imagined. "Uh … our parents are stuck in the Cave of Doom, and we need to go there right now. Can you please give us directions?" I asked.

"You really want to go to the Cave of Doom?" the lady asked.

"Yes! Our parents are in danger there! We need to save them. Please help us!" I demanded.

The lady just laughed. "Think about saving your parents. You won't even be able to save yourself if you go in there."

I said, "What do you mean?"

"Yup, it's true. Do you even know how dangerous the cave is?" the lady asked. Sahil and I nodded. "The tigers will eat you. If your parents were in there, then there's no hope for them to survive. In fact, they've probably been eaten alive by now."

I said, "Hey, you can't say that about my parents! They deserve to live, and we will save them for sure. Come on, Sahil. Let's go."

"But we need directions," he said.

"Let's ask someone else. Someone who won't make fun of our parents."

"I'm just telling you the facts. I wanted to keep you both safe, but if you really want to go there, then I'll tell you. Go straight, take two rights, a left, and then go straight again until you see a sign for the Cave of Doom." The lady put the pipe back in her mouth.

"Thank you!" I said, and we took off on our bikes.

We were riding our bikes for more than ten minutes. "I don't see any signs of the Cave of Doom," Sahil said.

I glanced at him and said, "We still need to take a left. If you had paid attention to the directions, then you would know."

Sahil stopped his bike and said, "I paid attention! Stop being the boss of everything. You don't know everything!"

"I'm just telling you what I remember. Let's keep moving," I said. I saw Sahil roll his eyes and start riding again.

Sahil and I finally came to a sign that read "Cave of Doom."

"I guess we're finally here. Oh gosh, I'm just nervous about what's waiting for us inside," I said.

Sahil replied, "The tigers will just be waiting for their meal!"

"I really hope not," I said in a nervous tone. We parked our bikes outside the cave and began walking toward it slowly. Inside, it looked like any ordinary cave, nothing unusual—a characteristic void in the ground, a space enormous enough for us to enter. The cavern was shaped by the enduring rock and broadened profoundly underground.

"Wow, it's so dark in here I can't even see where I'm going," Sahil said.

I pulled out my phone and turned on the flashlight to help us guide the way.

"How are we going to find our parents in this enormous cave?" Sahil asked.

I replied, "I guess we'll just have to keep walking farther until we find any clue."

"How about calling them?" Sahil asked.

"My phone has absolutely no service now," I said. I moved my phone around here and there and held it in the air until I finally got a signal. I quickly dialed Mom's number, but she didn't pick up.

"What do we do now?" Sahil asked.

"Think, think, think. We must save them if they're really in here," I replied.

"Just saying that won't save them unless you're a magician," Sahil said.

I felt rage. "Shut up, Sahil! This is not a joke. We need to focus!" Then suddenly I heard a loud roar and jolted. "What the heck was that?" I whispered.

Sahil whispered back, "What if it is the tiger that the lady from the snack shop was talking about?"

"I … don't … know," I replied, breathing heavily.

"I'll go check," Sahil said.

I tugged on his shirt. "No! Are you crazy? If it's the tigers, they might eat you. They're very dangerous creatures."

Sahil said, "I'm not crazy. I can handle animals well." He started walking away.

"Oh no you don't," I said and started following him.

Suddenly I heard a voice behind me. "Sameera, Sameera!"

"What was that?" I slowly turned around.

"It's us, Mackenzie and Meg."

"What? It's too dark. I can't see you." I turned on my phone flashlight. Then they came into sight. "Meg! Mackenzie!" I exclaimed and hugged them. "What are you doing here?"

"We came to look for you," Meg replied.

Mackenzie asked, "But why are you here?"

"Well, my mom and Mr. Troop are stuck in this cave," I replied.

"That's not true! By the way, why are you still calling him Mr. Troop? I thought he already established himself as your father," Meg said.

I replied, "Well, it just doesn't feel right yet. I think it's going to take a while to get used to."

Mackenzie continued, "That old woman at your house was lying to you! She locked your parents up somewhere."

"Ms. Turner! Where did she hide them?" I asked.

Meg started explaining, "We were our way to your house to drop off some sweet treats that we baked, but we saw something strange. We stopped and hid behind some bushes to get a better look. That Turner lady took something called a chemical kitchen out of your house and into the garage. She seemed like she was putting on a garage sale. She put the kitchen in the driveway so that everyone who goes past your house would see it. She started yelling, 'Try some food at my very special chemical kitchen! It's all made by me!' She laughed wickedly. Apparently, she was so loud your next-door neighbor came outside. 'Wow, what's cooking?'

"'Come over and try some of these delicious organic foods. You won't regret it,' Ms. Turner said. The neighbor came over and tried something. 'That'll be fifteen dollars please,' Ms. Turner said.

"'Whoa, whoa, whoa. No way am I paying that much for a sample I ate,' the neighbor said.

"'How about I provide you a whole meal made from this kitchen?' Ms. Turner offered.

"'Sure, I'd love that.'

"'One meal coming right up,' Ms. Turner announced. Your neighbor eagerly waited. After she ate the meal, she paid and left."

Then they explained the rest of the story. She and Mackenzie walked over to my house. "Hello, ladies! Would you like to try some of my specialties?" Ms. Turner asked.

"Huh? Are you Sameera's grandma?" Mackenzie asked.

"Yeah, we've never seen you around before," Meg said.

"Um, yes, but who are you and how do you know Sameera?" Ms. Turner asked.

"We are Mackenzie and Meg. We're Sameera's best friends."

"Oh, well, then that's great! Just try some of my food," Ms. Turner said and handed them something to eat.

"Sure, but where is Sameera?"

Ms. Turner laughed. "You won't find her anywhere here."

"What do you mean? This is her house," Mackenzie said.

"Well now it's mine!" Ms. Turner said and laughed.

"I don't get it. Sameera never told us that she was moving," Meg said.

Ms. Turner replied, "Too bad she didn't. Maybe you guys don't matter to her anymore."

"Stop! You can't say that! You're lying. You're not Sameera's grandma. Who are you?" Meg asked.

"You don't need to know," Ms. Turner said.

Mackenzie said, "Seriously, where is Sameera? We need to call her."

"I'll tell you where she is, but first you have to try my food," Ms. Turner said.

Meg responded, "No, we can't trust you. We don't even know who you are."

"Yeah, what are you even doing in Sameera's house?" Mackenzie asked.

Ms. Turner replied, "Well, I'm just taking care of the house while Sameera and Sahil go look for their parents in the Cave of Doom."

"What! The Cave of Doom is too dangerous. How could you leave them alone?" Meg said.

"I didn't. They really wanted to find their parents, so they just left. Plus, they are not alone. They have each other," Ms. Turner said.

Meg said, "Oh no! Call her, Mackenzie, and make sure she's okay."

Ms. Turner immediately snatched the phone from Mackenzie. "Hey, give it back!"

"Not unless you taste my food."

"Oh no! Has she already reached the Cave of Doom?" Mackenzie asked.

"I don't know, but it's all because of this old woman!" Meg yelled. Ms. Turner laughed.

Mackenzie asked, "Why would you do this? What do you want from Sameera?"

"I'll tell you the secret if you try one of these foods from my chemical kitchen," Ms. Turner replied.

"Hey, this isn't even your kitchen! Sameera told us that she made it. Why would you steal it from her?" Meg asked.

"I want to become a millionaire! I made a fake phone call to Sameera and Sahil saying that their parents are in the Cave of Doom so that they'll be busy searching for their parents while I make millions," Ms. Turner said.

"Then where are their parents?" Mackenzie asked.

"I locked them up in … hey, wait a minute. Why am I telling you this? Just try my chemical foods or leave. I'm not giving you any more information about Sameera," Ms. Turner said.

"We're leaving! Come on Mackenzie," Meg said and left with Mackenzie.

"So that's what happened. She didn't tell us where she hid your parents, but they are not here. She gave away that much at least," Meg replied.

Then again I heard the loud roar. "Oh no! I forgot. Sahil went in to look for the tiger and our parents. I don't need him in danger along with my parents. I must go," I said.

"We'll come with you," Meg suggested, and she and Mackenzie started walking by my side.

"Why did he go alone?" Mackenzie asked.

"He told me that he can handle animals. I didn't believe it. Just because he had to take care of two class pets doesn't make him an expert at handling all animals. I told him not to go, but he didn't listen to me," I said. The three of us started running, calling for Sahil, but there was no response. "Sahil!" I screamed louder.

"Sameera, please lower your voice. The tigers might come after you," Mackenzie said.

"The tigers, my foot! I don't care anymore. I need to find my brother," I said. We continued searching for Sahil. Soon I came to a stop.

"Why did you stop?" Meg asked. I pointed at the ground in front of me. I stood in shock for a few seconds and then screamed my heart out. "*No!*" I was too late.

CHAPTER 7

My friends both stood there in shock. *Not again!* I ran up to Sahil, who was lying on the floor with his eyes closed, and this time he had red stuff coming out of him. "Sahil, get up! Get up!" I said, shaking him. There was no response. More red stuff came out of him. *Blood.* "Please just get up! Sahil!" I begged him.

Mackenzie came beside me and put a hand on my shoulder. "I think he's gone for good this time."

"Don't say that!" I yelled.

"Yeah, don't say that, Mackenzie. You don't know for sure," Meg said.

"Sorry, guys, but it's just what it seems like. With all the blood from him, I don't know if he's conscious or even alive. The chance of survival after being bit by a tiger is so low," Mackenzie said.

Meg screamed, "Shut up, Mackenzie! Keep your negative thoughts to yourself. He's not dead. What are you? A doctor?"

"Doctor! That's it! We need to take Sahil to a doctor quickly!" I suggested.

"Yes, let's go. We have a taxi waiting for us outside," Meg said.

I slowly began to lift Sahil up. Then I heard laughing, and Sahil opened his eyes. "Sahil, you're conscious?" I asked.

"Yup, perfectly fine. How'd you like my prank?" he asked.

I was about to slap him out of anger. "Sahil! I can't believe you pranked us like that! I thought I'd have to take you to the hospital.

It's bad enough we had to traipse all over this cave looking for our parents, and then you faked being unconscious!"

"Well, I had to get you back after you pranked me the other day, making me believe that my science potion worked," he replied.

I squinted. "Dude! I did it for a perfectly good reason, but you nearly scared the heck out of us! Don't you dare ever fool anyone like that again," I demanded.

Sahil laughed, "Okay, I won't. I promise. Just chill. Let's find Mom and Dad."

"No, they're not in this cave. Ms. Turner lied to us," I said.

"How do you know?" Sahil asked.

"Well, Meg and Mackenzie just told me. They came all the way to this city to inform us. Am I right, friends?"

Meg and Mackenzie nodded. "Then where are our parents?" Sahil asked.

Meg responded, "We don't even know. They could be anywhere, but we know for sure that they're not in the Cave of Doom."

"Meg, what else did you hear from Ms. Turner?" I asked.

"Well, that's about it. Everything we told you. She said that she locked your parents up somewhere so that she can make millions of dollars with the chemical kitchen or something like that you made," Meg said.

"What? That's not Sameera's kitchen! It's mine," Sahil reminded me.

"But Sameera told us earlier that she made it," Mackenzie said.

Sahil glared at me. I didn't have time to deal with this right now in the way I wanted to—with lies of course. So I just told the truth. "Sorry. I was just jealous that you're into science. I wanted it to be my thing and impress my friends, but I should not have done that. I'm sorry I lied to them, Sahil," I said.

Mackenzie smiled. "It doesn't matter how good or bad you are at science. It's cool that your brother is into science too. Probably makes it easier for you guys to get along because you have something in common." What she said wasn't true at all because Sahil and I fought more frequently ever since he showed his interest in science. But I didn't argue with her because the status of the relationship with my brother wasn't important right then.

"Thanks, Mackenzie. Anyway, do you guys have any idea where Ms. Turner locked up our parents? Did she give away any hints?" I asked.

Meg fiddled with her fingers. "No, but by common sense, I'm pretty sure she would've locked them in her own bedroom or somewhere else in her own house," Meg suggested.

"Or she might've locked them up in Sameera's house itself, to keep an eye on them," Mackenzie suggested. "I'm not sure, but we'll have to go find out for ourselves."

We heard a loud roar echo through the cave. "Uh, Sahil, stop it now with the pranks. It's not funny," I said.

Sahil shook his head at me. "That wasn't me."

I snapped my head at my friends, and we all exclaimed in unison, "Tigers! Run!" We sprinted out of the cave as fast as we could.

Once we exited the cave, Meg called the taxi, and it arrived within a couple of minutes. Sahil and I threw our bikes in the trunk and got in. Sahil got into the front seat with the driver, leaving Mackenzie, Meg, and me to ride in the back seat. After about fifteen minutes, we finally reached my house. Meg paid the taxi driver, and all of us got out.

In the garage, I saw a huge disaster. We should not have let Ms. Turner by herself in the house. She was cleaning up her so-called garage sale. We all kind of spied on her for a little while from a distance before approaching her.

Then I decided to go and interrogate her. "Ms. Turner, what are you doing?"

She jerked her head up at us like she didn't expect us to come back so soon. "Oh well, I'm just doing the ordinary household chores since there is no one else here to do them," she replied as she took parts of the chemical kitchen back to the garage.

"Ms. Turner, return our parents!" Sahil exclaimed.

"How would I know where they are? It's not like I locked them up somewhere," Ms. Turner said and laughed.

"Yes, you did!" Mackenzie said.

Meg said, "You literally told us you locked them up somewhere the last time we were here."

"Tell us what you are hiding," I demanded.

Ms. Turner dropped the parts and frowned. "I'm not hiding anything. I don't know where your parents are. I'm here to take care of you because your parents are no more."

Now she had taken it too far. "Don't say that! I know they are alive, and you're just trying to kill them. Release my parents now! Or else ..." I started.

"Or else what? What will you do?" Ms. Turner asked with her arms folded.

I thought for a second because I didn't know what else I would do. Thankfully, Meg said at the right time, "Or else we will call the police."

"Hahaha, the police. Seriously? That's not going to scare me. The police know me very well. You really think they will listen to a little girl like you?" Ms. Turner said.

"I am not a little girl! I'm thirteen years old—almost fourteen!" I screamed in her face.

"Whatever, but you don't have proof that I hid your parents." Ms. Turner chuckled.

Sahil asked, "So you did hide them?"

"Um ... no ... no ... not at all," Ms. Turner said.

Mackenzie said, "Of course, we have proof to show the police."

"What proof?" A concerned look spread over Ms. Turner's face. Mackenzie nodded at Meg.

Meg took out her phone. "I have a voice recording of you telling Mackenzie and me that you locked up their parents somewhere so that you can steal the chemical kitchen and make millions." Ms. Turner was as frozen as a statue for a minute, and then she stepped forward. She rapidly snatched the phone from Meg's hand and put it into her back pocket. "Hey, give my phone back!" Meg screamed.

Mackenzie said, "Well, too bad. I still have my phone. I'm gonna call the police."

"There's no need to do that, children. I'm sure we can work something out. If you keep this secret between us, I'll give your phone back," Ms. Turner said.

Mackenzie stepped forward. "No way. You must give back the phone, and we will call the—"

I immediately put a hand on her shoulder to stop her as an idea crossed my brain. If Ms. Turner could trick us by getting us out of the house to make money from the chemical kitchen, we all could trick her as well. I said, "Wait, Mackenzie. What Ms. Turner is saying could work. We won't call the police, and she will give Meg's phone back. Nobody gets hurt that way, and we can just forget this whole thing even happened."

Meg stepped forward. "Sameera, are you crazy? This woman deserves to be punished. I can get another phone, but this lady doesn't deserve another chance."

I tried to explain it to them without Ms. Turner getting suspicious. I clenched my teeth together and said firmly, "Meg, try to understand. Let's do what Ms. Turner suggested. It'll be best for all of us."

"I can't believe you, Sameera. You want to give this lady another chance after what she's put you and your brother through?" Meg asked.

This wasn't working, so I took the next step and asked, "Ms. Turner, could you please give us a minute? I need to talk to my friends privately."

"Sure, but make it quick. I don't have all day," she said.

I huddled my friends and Sahil together as we moved a few feet away from where Ms. Turner was standing. I said, "Guys. I have a plan that will get Meg's phone back and send Ms. Turner to the police. We must play her own game on her." The three of them eagerly listened. "Mackenzie, call the police on your phone, and the rest of us will distract Ms. Turner. We will tell her that we agree with her plan to let her loose and ask for Meg's phone back. After that, we all will have to keep her distracted and not let her leave until the police arrive. Sound good?"

"Wow, I would've never thought of tricking her like that. Your brain works fast, Sameera," Mackenzie remarked.

I smiled. "All right. Let's begin our plan."

Mackenzie pulled out her phone and started dialing the police, while Sahil, Meg, and I approached Ms. Turner. "All right, Ms. Turner, we agree to your deal. Give Meg's phone back, and we won't call the police." Ms. Turner smiled and reached her hand out with the phone. Meg snatched the phone from her. I said, "Now we need you to do something else. Since you made me do all those chores yesterday, I want you to do my laundry and fold my clothes."

Sahil jumped up and pointed his finger at Ms. Turner. "Ha! In your face, old lady."

"Girls, we had a deal. I gave your phone back, so now I get to leave," Ms. Turner said.

I looked at Meg and said, "All right, I guess we are going to have to call the police."

"No—wait, girls. What the heck? Okay fine. I'll do your stupid laundry, but that's it! I'm leaving after that," Ms. Turner said.

I smiled. "Great! Follow me. I'll show you to your task." I led Ms. Turner back into the house. I gave Meg a thumbs-up, and she winked. What weirded me out was that Ms. Turner was being such a bad-tempered child and not even acting her age. If she was supposed to be like a mother figure to us, she was clearly not living up to it.

After I handed Ms. Turner my basket of clothes and showed her to the washing machine, I went back outside to check on my friends. My brother was sitting on our bench by the tree. He got up and came over to me. "Is she going to do my laundry as well?"

"Shut up, Sahil. You don't deserve such a special treatment. You didn't even do any of your chores yesterday." Sahil rolled his eyes and went back to sit on the bench. I approached my friends, "So … did you do it, Mackenzie?"

"Yes, I called the cops and told them everything. Mission accomplished."

"Well, I would wait until the cops actually arrive and arrest Ms. Turner until I would say mission accomplished," Meg said.

A few minutes later, two cops arrived with flashing lights. The cops got out of the cars quickly and approached us. The shorter cop with a beard asked, "Who filed a complaint?"

"I did, against an old, wicked lady," Mackenzie replied.

The cops looked confused. The taller cop with a mustache asked, "How old are you girls?"

"We're thirteen," Mackenzie replied.

"Okay, well where's the lady?" the cop asked.

I replied, "I'll go get her right away." I ran back into the house and screamed, "Ms. Turner! You have a visitor."

She poked her head out of the laundry room. "Me? But I don't even live here."

"Yes, you! One of the customers who tried the chemical kitchen loved it so much they came back for seconds. Don't make them wait too long."

Ms. Turner wiped her face with a cloth and rushed outside excitedly. "I can't believe it! The chemical kitchen has demand … oh, wait—what is going on?" She saw the two cops.

Sahil screamed, "She's the wicked old lady! Arrest her!"

Ms. Turner snapped her head in my direction. "What did you do? I thought we had a deal."

"Sorry, Ms. Turner. Crime time is over."

Ms. Turner scrunched her face up at me and walked toward the police. She said, "Sir, these children have committed a crime. They must go to jail."

"I'm sorry. Proof or not, these girls are too young to go to jail," the taller cop said.

"If anyone had to go to jail, it would be Ms. Turner," I said. The shorter cop raised his eyebrows. "We have proof," I said and hinted at Meg to pull out her phone. She played the recording of Ms. Turner's evil plans and her talking about the fact that she locked up my parents. After that, the cops started at Ms. Turner.

"Sir, please just hear me out. I didn't do anything illegal. I shouldn't be punished," Ms. Turner pleaded.

The taller cop said, "That's a huge offense. You are not allowed to make children suffer like that." He looked at the shorter cop and said, "Handcuff her and put her into the car." He agreed and grabbed Ms. Turner and dragged her into the car. The tall cop said, "Thank you for reporting her."

"No problem. But what about our parents?" I asked.

The cop replied, "Do not worry. Once we reach the police station, we will know the truth and will give you a call."

"Thank you so much, sir," I said.

The cop smiled. "I'm just doing my job." He got into the car and drove away.

"Thank God they arrested Ms. Turner," Sahil said.

Meg said, "All right, now we can say it."

"Mission accomplished!" all four of us said in unison.

"Meg and Mackenzie, you can go home. Sahil and I will wait for the police to call. I'll update you. Thank you so much for your help!" I said.

"Anytime!" Mackenzie said.

"We hope they find your parents soon," Meg said.

After they left, we went inside the house. "Huh. I thought Ms. Turner would've created a huge mess here," Sahil muttered.

I laughed. "She's not a toddler, Sahil. Though she does talk like one. She might've not created a mess physically, but she sure did mentally."

"What do you mean?" Sahil asked.

I replied, "She threatened us so much, especially my friends. So that's just playing with our brains."

A couple hours later, my phone rang. "That must be the police!" Sahil exclaimed.

I said, "Be quiet. Let me talk to them." I picked up the phone.

"Hello. Is this Sameera?"

"Yes, sir, that's me."

"We wanted to inform you that we found information about your parents. We got the senior woman by the name of Jane Turner to tell us everything," the cop said.

"What happened to them? Please tell us," I begged.

"The woman told us that she locked your parents up so she could steal some valuable items from the house and take advantage of you kids to reveal the information. She also mentioned that after her arrival, she discovered some treasure and started making money with it. Young lady, do you happen to know what this woman was using to make money?" he asked.

I replied, "Yes, yes, I know! It's my brother's chemical kitchen. He made artificially flavored foods using that."

"Ah, that is what it is."

"Sir, we know that Ms. Turner used my brother's kitchen to make money. We want to know about our parents," I said.

He responded, "I am afraid she hid them in the closet at her own house."

"Oh no! We don't know where she lives, so how do we find them?" I asked nervously.

The cop replied, "There is no need for you to worry. That is our job. We have the address and permission of Jane Turner. I have sent a few officers to go to her house and retrieve your parents. You and your brother need to stay put, and my officers will escort your parents back to the house."

"Okay, we will stay here. Thank you, sir. I'm so grateful," I said.

"We're doing our best to keep you and our community safe. The officers will inform me once your parents are released. Take care," he said and hung up.

Sahil asked me, "Are Mom and Dad going to be all right?"

"Yes, the cops told me that everything is under control. Ms. Turner hid our parents in her own house. Can you believe it? So now the cops are going to go and rescue them."

"Phew. Thank God. At least they're still alive. That old woman scared the heck out of me."

"The cops also told us to stay put until our parents are back," I told him. Sahil decided to go to the basement to play video games, and I went to the kitchen to grab a snack. Just then, I remembered my friends and decided to call them and tell them everything. "And thank you once again, Meg, for being proactive and recording Ms. Turner's words as proof. That really helped make things a lot easier."

"No problem, Sameera. That's what friends are for."

CHAPTER 8

A few hours later, the doorbell rang. *Ding-dong, ding-dong, ding-dong.* Sahil and I stopped what we were doing in the basement and rushed upstairs. "I'll get the door!" Sahil exclaimed.

"No, Sahil. I'll get the door. I usually do it all the time," I responded.

Sahil argued, "Yeah, so for a change, I'll open the door this time."

"Sahil, I'm older than you, and I get these privileges, so I'll open the door," I explained.

Sahil said, "What privileges? Anyone can open the door in this house. You don't have special privileges!"

"Fine. Just open the door already," I said and rolled my eyes.

"Thank you," he said and opened the door. There they were, standing in front of us. "Mom, Dad, it's you!" Sahil exclaimed.

I went up and hugged Mom. "Oh, sweetie, we missed you so much!" Mom said.

Sahil complained, "Why did you guys send an evil woman to take care of us?"

"Oh, honey, we didn't do that. That old woman kidnapped us and threatened us. She made us say all those things you heard in the message. If we didn't obey her, she would've caused harm to you both," Mom said.

Mr. Troop said, "Well, it seems like she really ruined things for you guys here."

"Yes, she did. She even made us do chores! Can you believe it?"

"Honey, I'm so sorry. Come here," Mom said and hugged Sahil.

I said, "She lied a lot to us about you both. She even cheated Sahil by stealing his chemical kitchen."

"Chemical kitchen? What in the world is that, Sameera?" Mr. Troop asked.

I replied, "We'll tell you the whole story later—our side of the story. But we want to know yours first. Tell us how the old lady kidnapped you."

"Let's sit down, and we'll explain everything."

The four of us went to the living room and sat on different sides of the couch.

"So the bank branch where your mom kept her precious belongings was closing, so she went over there to collect her valuables. She told me this later, but she noticed an old woman watching her suspiciously for a while. After she got out of the bank, the lady approached her, so she immediately called me. She was able to say a few words, and then she got knocked out. I figured she was in some sort of danger. I had to leave the YMCA immediately. I tracked her location and got there as soon as I could. I reached there at the right time because I saw the old lady, along with some other guys, pick up your unconscious mother and put her in the back of a truck. I immediately rushed over to the truck, but before I could do anything, one of the guys knocked me unconscious too. I'm pretty sure they put me in the back of the truck as well, and the old lady stole her valuables," Mr. Troop explained.

Mom continued, "A few hours or so later, we woke up in the closet of someone else's house. Then the same old lady appeared and threatened us. She made us give out our house address, which is probably how she got to you. She told us that if we didn't do what we were told to, then she would come after our kids. I didn't want anything to happen to you both. I would throw my life in danger for you kids, so I listened to her every word. Your father was so supportive and was by my side the entire time. The old woman made us record a fake audio message that you both probably heard earlier today."

She is so evil. She has a secret gang of people working for her as well. I wish I knew that when she first walked into our house.

Sahil frowned. "So you just left us at the YMCA by ourselves to find our way back home?"

"I'm sorry, but I tried calling out to you both, and you didn't hear me, so I decided to come back for you guys after I saved your mom. But I should've waited. I apologize," Mr. Troop said.

"Did you get your valuables back, Mom?" I asked.

Mom smiled. "No, we didn't, but forget that. We got you both back, and that's enough."

"No, Dad, that's not fair! You guys need to complain to the police. They need to get you your valuables back from stupid old Turner," Sahil said.

Mom laughed. "Of course! The police will send it back to us after they investigate Jane Turner's case."

"Huh. I can't believe it. People these days are always after money," I said.

Mom replied, "But I'm just so glad that she didn't cause any harm to you both physically."

I hugged Mom again and said, "You must be exhausted."

"It seems like nothing much has happened in this house physically since we were gone," Mom said.

I nodded. "Well, she didn't destroy the place, but she sure did play with our minds, so that's big damage."

Mom and Mr. Troop both yawned at the same time. Sahil decided to change the topic. "So, Dad, what's the deal? Are you planning to remarry Mom so you can live with us in this house?" he asked.

There was no response from him. He looked at Mom, who tightly pressed her lips and scratched her nose and then looked down at the floor. "What happened, Mr. Troop? Answer the question," I said.

He widened his nostrils and said, "Jeena, I think it's time we tell the kids." Mom blew air into her cheeks and tilted her head. Mr. Troop looked up at me and Sahil. "Your mom and I talked about this, and it's straightforward. We're sorry, but we don't think it's going to work out."

"What are you saying?" Sahil asked impatiently.

Mom continued, "He will not be staying with us in this house." I was a bit shocked and surprised at the same time.

Sahil laughed. "It's because you guys haven't gotten remarried. Mom wants to wait until they get married again before Dad lives with us. Am I right?"

Mom shook her head firmly.

I gasped. "What do you mean no, Mom? You are not planning to remarry?"

"Well, kids, I won't be living with you because I got a job in California, so I must move back there. We're not remarrying or anything of that sort. We have discussed this matter while you kids weren't around, and we've decided to separate and go on our own paths," Mr. Troop explained. I just stood frozen with no reaction.

Sahil stomped his feet on the ground and said, "I can't believe it, Dad! I was really looking forward to spending more time with you. I had a lot of dad-and-son activities planned out for us to do together. You really got our hopes up, and now you crushed it!"

"I'm sorry, kids, but this is the best for all of us. Your mom agrees."

I looked at Mom, and she slowly nodded with sorrow. Sahil got up from where he was sitting and stomped upstairs angrily.

"Sahil!" Mr. Troop called out, but he kept going. I stood there, unable to speak. "I'm so sorry if I disappointed you, and I'm so sorry for not discussing this with you before," Mr. Troop said.

I frowned.

"Oh, sweetie, I know you'll really miss your father, but he'll visit often. Don't you worry," Mom assured me.

I didn't mean to be rude and talk back, but I just blurted out what was on my mind. "No, Mom, I won't miss him. I hardly even know him, so it won't make a difference to me if he leaves." I smirked and left the room. I heard Mr. Troop sniffle a little, but I didn't look back. I went straight to my room and shut the door. I sat on my bed and stared at the wall, nodding back and forth. "Everything is just happening so fast," I said to myself.

PART II

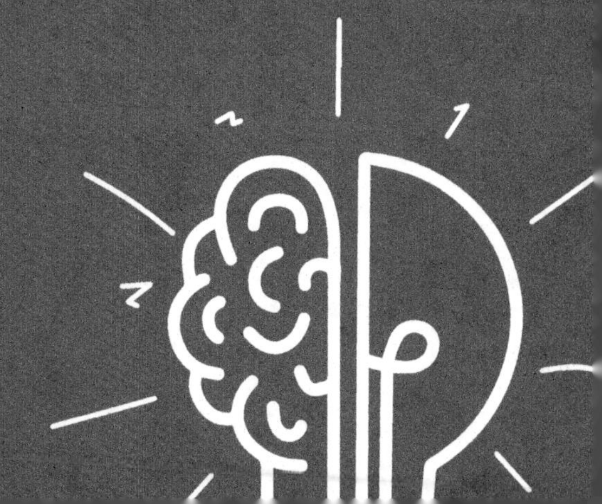

CHAPTER 9

It was a beautiful, sunny morning, and Sahil and I were sitting on the couch. Mr. Troop had bought Sahil a new video game as a going-away gift, so he was playing that. He asked me what I wanted, but I told him that no gift could make up for him leaving again. I was just sitting on the couch with my arms folded, staring at the wall. I couldn't stop thinking that Mr. Troop, who I still hadn't gotten used to as my father, would be leaving again. I had just gotten to meet him after a very long time, and since he was leaving so quickly, it was going to feel like it never even happened. Mom was in the kitchen making some breakfast.

"Mom, I'm hungry!" Sahil yelled, not looking up from his video game.

"Breakfast will be ready in a few minutes, honey," Mom responded. Then Mom saw me sitting idle and said, "Sameera, why don't you go outside for a while and get some fresh air. It's a beautiful day today."

I didn't listen to her and continued to sit there staring at the wall. "Sameera," Mom called out. I didn't listen. Mom came over and sat down next to me on the couch. "Couldn't you hear me, sweetie?" Mom asked. I nodded my head. She said, "I told you to go outside for a while until breakfast is ready. Will you go?"

I looked down and said, "No. I don't want to go outside." I thought she was going to be sympathetic like she always is and ask me what was wrong, but I think she knew.

She gazed at me for a while and then got up from the couch. She rubbed her palms on her pants and said, "Okay. Well then, that's up to you. Let me finish making breakfast for you both." I was kind of relieved she didn't ask why I was upset, because I didn't feel like talking about it.

Out of nowhere, I asked, "Where is Mr. Troop?"

"*Your father* is upstairs in the guest room, packing his stuff up. He stayed over last night since he had already checked out of his hotel before all the crazy stuff with Jane Turner happened. By the way, she's all locked up in jail now, and our valuables have been returned," she replied. I kept looking down. Mom leaned back. "Sahil, why don't you go up and help your dad pack?" Mom said.

"But, Mom, I'm not finished with this game yet," Sahil replied.

"Sahil!" Mom shouted.

"Fine. I'll finish this game later. I'll go help him," he responded.

"Thank you, honey," Mom said. Sahil got up.

I decided that I needed to figure something out, so I said, "No, it's okay. I can go help him pack." Mom narrowed her eyes on me. I said, "I have to talk to him about some things anyway, so I could help him pack while I'm at it."

Mom's gaze shifted to the wall. "All right then. You can go," Mom said and went to the kitchen.

"Thanks a lot, Sameera. Now I can finally finish my video game," Sahil said and chuckled.

I just smirked at him and said, "I didn't do it for you. I did it for me."

I went upstairs and peeked into the guest room where Mr. Troop was. He saw me and said, "Come in, Sameera. Are you all right?"

"Yeah. Mom said you needed help packing your things," I said and walked in.

"Oh really? Well, I'm almost done, so I don't need any help right now. Thanks for offering," he said. I looked down at my feet. Tears started forming in my eyes. I quickly wiped them so that Mr. Troop wouldn't see. "Sameera, are you crying?" he asked.

I fake laughed and said, "Crying? I'm not crying. There was just something in my eye, so I was trying to get it out. I think I got it out now." I turned around so that my back was facing him, but he came around to me and put his hand on my shoulder.

"Sameera, tell me the truth. I'm your father. You can talk to me about anything. You have mixed emotions now, don't you?" he asked.

I replied, "Of course I do!"

"I know it's hard, Sameera, but I can't help it either. I must go to this job. I don't think you know, but I've been waiting for this offer almost my whole life. I'll really miss you guys as well, but I'm sure we can come up with something to stay connected," he said.

I couldn't keep it together anymore, so I just poured everything out. "Mr. Troop! Stop lying! You don't really mean it. You won't miss us at all. In fact, you don't even care about your family. All you want is your stupid job in California, and you even want to leave your family to go take that job!"

It was quiet for a while, and then he said, "I'm really sorry—"

I cut him off. "You just keep coming and going. You say you are my father, but you certainly don't act like it. Fathers are supposed to be there for their kids and watch them grow. Why did you even come back if you were going to leave again? You know, when you came back after many years, Mom was happy, and I thought we could be a complete family again, but it seems that you don't like that idea. You know, you hurt Mom so much. You are so selfish. Mom and Sahil are acting like they are fine with you leaving, but I bet deep inside they are wishing that you didn't leave either. You really broke her heart! I hate you!"

I was about to storm out of the room when Mr. Troop yelled, "Enough, Sameera!" I looked back. "I got a great job opportunity. Why can't you be happy for me? Your mom is happy for me. Why do you always have to yell at me and start a fight?" he asked. I didn't say anything. More tears rolled down my cheeks, but I didn't bother to wipe them. "Answer me. You are the one who seems like you don't care about the family. You should be supporting me and telling me to follow my dreams, but you are not like that at all. Mom and Sahil are not *acting* like they are fine; they are fine. They want me to follow my dreams—unlike you," he said and walked out of the room with his luggage. I just stood there very still for a few minutes, weirded out by what he said. *Follow his dreams?*

"Breakfast is ready!" Mom yelled from downstairs. I slowly walked downstairs. I saw Sahil in the kitchen. He was gulping down some oatmeal.

"There you are, Sameera. Dad is down here, and he is done packing. What were you doing upstairs?" Sahil asked.

"Nothing, Sahil. It's none of your business," I replied and sat down.

"Yes, it is! You always tell me not to interfere, but you were talking to Dad, and he is my dad too. So it *is* my business," Sahil said.

"I don't have to tell you everything!" I got up from my chair.

"You don't even tell me anything!" Sahil screamed back.

"Stop yelling at me! You don't get to do that!" I shouted.

Mom stood up. "Enough! Would you kids just get along for once? Every time I notice, you both are always bickering about something or the other. Sit down and eat your breakfast quietly."

I wasn't in the mood anymore, so I said, "I am not hungry." I went back upstairs.

"Chill out, Sahil. Don't waste your energy getting mad at your sister. There's no point in making her understand," Mr. Troop said as he sat down for breakfast. I sat on the middle of the stairs and overheard them talking.

"Well, if Sameera doesn't want to come, it's her loss. I made her favorite breakfast—pancakes," I heard Mom say. Pancakes did sound nice, but I didn't feel like going downstairs because I didn't want to face my so-called father again.

Mom then said, "What is wrong with her today? She is acting very strangely. She didn't want to go outside for fresh air. She just sat on the couch doing nothing, and now she doesn't want breakfast. What is this all about?"

"Maybe we should leave her alone for a little while," I heard Mr. Troop say.

"Yeah, she is so bratty and shabby," Sahil added.

Mom replied, "Sahil! We don't not use those kinds of words in this house."

"Those are not even bad words, Mom," Sahil said.

"Do not talk back to me that way, mister. You'll get it from me if you talk like that ever again about anyone. Do you get it? Now go to your room!" Mom shouted. Sahil sighed and got up from his chair. I saw him pick up his video game from the couch and head toward the stairs. I quickly got up and ran to my room before Sahil saw me.

I decided to write a letter to my so-called father before he left and sneak it in with his luggage. I had so many emotions that I couldn't talk about, so I decided that writing was the best way to get everything out. I sat down at my desk with a lined piece of paper and a ballpoint pen. I tapped the pen to the paper several times, but nothing left my head. After several minutes of tapping, I finally started to get something on the paper and didn't stop until I wrote my signature at the bottom.

> Dear Father,
>
> I simply want to say thank you for never being a part of my life. Yes, you have hurt me, but you have taught me many things from hurting me. So I guess I just want to say thank you for everything

you have taught me that you didn't even know you
were capable of.

—Sameera Chacko

I folded the piece of paper into fourths and slid it into my back pocket. I decided that I would sneak it into his luggage before he left.

I decided to call Mackenzie and Meg to catch up on their lives and to get my mind off my life. Mackenzie picked up the call. "Hey, Sameera. What's up?"

"Hi. How's it going?" I asked.

"Great! Just making some desserts to practice for the bake show. How about you?" Mackenzie asked.

"Oh, desserts? That sounds delicious! What kinds of desserts?" I asked, keeping the conversation about her.

Mackenzie responded, "It's a surprise. I just joined a baking class, and I can't wait to be on TV soon, showing off my baking skills."

"Oh wow, that's awesome! Good for you!" I said.

"Yeah, I've been working on making cookies, brownies, cakes, and all sorts of sweets! You should come over and try some of them. You can be my judge," Mackenzie suggested.

"Definitely. That would be fun," I replied.

"So what's going on in your life?" she asked.

"Um ... well ... nothing much. I'm just watching some old videos," I lied.

"Oh cool! I think something is burning in the oven, so I should probably go check," she said, and I was grateful for that—grateful that we didn't have to talk about me for once.

"Sure. I'll talk to you later. Bye," I said and hung up.

Just then I got a call from Meg. I picked it up. "Hi, Sameera. I have great news!" she said.

"What could the great news possibly be? My father will be a part of my life. Sahil treats me with respect. My mom is remarrying my father?" I murmured to myself.

"Hello? Sameera, are you even listening to me, or are you in your own world?" Meg asked.

I replied, "Oh, sorry. What were you saying?"

"I was saying that I have some good news to share, but you seem so lost. What's going on, Sameera?"

I lied. "Oh, nothing at all. Go on. You said you have good news to share."

"No, you go first. You don't seem like nothing is going on. Tell me what's bothering you," Meg demanded.

"There's absolutely nothing bothering me. What makes you think that? I just wasn't paying attention to you … um … because … I was watching some old videos of myself." I told the same lie.

She replied, "We're good friends, and I can definitely sense that something is not right." Meg was that friend. The friend who knows you so well that even if you say you're okay, she will know you're not.

"All right, fine. I'll tell you, but promise me you won't tell anyone," I requested.

"Promise," she said.

"Okay, so I'm kind of upset because Mr. Troop is moving to California because of some stupid job offer that he got," I explained.

"Oh my gosh, really? That's awful! You must really miss him, right?" she asked.

"He hasn't left yet, and I tried to convince him so many times not to leave us, but he just wouldn't listen. He wants me to support him in his dumb dreams. He is so old. Now what is there to freakin' dream about? He should be supporting his children in following their dreams. He is being so selfish and doesn't even care about his family. Can you believe it? I understand now why he and Mom got divorced," I said. There was no response. "Meg, are you still there?" I asked.

"Oh yeah, I am. Sorry. What were you saying?" she questioned.

"Come on. Now you're not listening to me? The point is Mr. Troop is moving to California, leaving my mom, brother, and me alone, and I'm angry about it," I said.

"Hmmm, I see, but didn't you guys used to live like that before your dad even showed up to summer camp?" she asked.

I was quiet for a second, and then an amazing thought flooded my brain. "Yeah, we did! You know what? I'm going to act like him leaving doesn't affect me at all because I barely know him. Maybe then he'll consider not taking that job offer. Thanks for talking to me and making me understand. You're a true friend," I said.

Meg said, "No, Sameera, that's not what I meant."

"Well, whatever you meant, thanks for helping me get an idea of what I should do. I feel like I rule the world. Bye now," I said and hung up.

CHAPTER 10

I went downstairs, trying to act like a normal girl who doesn't care that her father is moving. "Sameera, there you are! Do you want some breakfast?" Mom asked in her usual concerned tone. I nodded. "All right, sweetie. I'll get you your pancakes," Mom said and got me a plate of pancakes with strawberries, blueberries, chocolate syrup, and whipped cream. She sat next to me at the kitchen table.

"Wow, it smells very nice. Thanks, Mom!" I exclaimed.

"No problem. It's your favorite after all."

I cut a slice with my fork and knife and put it in my mouth. "Mmm, so good," I said. I gulped down those pancakes quickly.

Then Mom questioned me. "Now, tell me, what's going on with you?"

I thought for a second. "There's something going on with me? I don't think so," I replied, trying to hold all my emotions in.

"I mean your emotions. I get it that you're upset that your dad is moving, but that doesn't mean that you can yell at him and fight him on it," Mom said. I looked around to make sure my father wasn't around. "He's not here, Sameera. He went to the backyard to fix something up," Mom explained.

"Oh, okay," I said.

"So? What's up? When you went upstairs to help Dad pack, you said you had something important to talk about. All I heard was screams and shouts. There was no real talking going on," Mom reminded me.

"Well, I'm sorry that I yelled at him, but I won't do it again. I promise. I really don't care that he is moving. It's up to him to decide his life. I can't decide for him," I said, looking down at my empty plate.

"Exactly. Your dad told me how you misbehaved with him. You'd better apologize to him once he gets back. Understand?" Mom asked.

I nodded. I got up to wash my plate. Just then, Mr. Troop walked in with a few wires. "Sorry I couldn't fix the pump. It's broken," he said.

"Pump?" I asked.

"Yeah, the water pump is broken, so you can't have water until you get a new pump," he replied.

"Oh, that's really unfortunate," I said. He nodded.

Then Mom said, "I have to go organize my clothes upstairs, so I'll leave you two alone for a while." She got up from her chair. Mom looked at me and gestured at my father. I knew that she was telling me to apologize to him. I gave her the weakest thumbs-up. Then Mom went upstairs.

Mr. Troop closed the backyard door and took off his shoes. I cleared my throat and then started to speak. "Uh, um. So, Mr. Troop I … um … hope you have a great life, and I'll talk to you later … that is, if we ever meet," I said.

"Oh, ho-ho!" My father laughed like Santa Claus. "Sameera, don't you worry. We'll meet up often. Either I'll come over here, or you all can come over there. Besides, technology has improved a lot, so we can video chat. I promise to call you at least once a day, and I'll send you a lot of pictures and—"

I interrupted. "Enough! I just wanted to say goodbye, but you've started rambling unnecessarily. Just … I'm sorry for yelling at you, fighting with you, and for all the other rude things I said. I'll … see you later. Goodbye." I left the kitchen. I kind of felt bad that I didn't get to properly talk to him, but I had to pretend I didn't care that he was leaving so that maybe … like maybe a 10 percent chance … he'd stay. "Come on, Sameera. Pull it together. You can keep up this act," I said to myself.

Sahil came down. He was about to say something to me and then just said, "Never mind. You won't tell me anything anyway. Let me not waste my energy on you. I'll go talk to someone more sensible, like Dad."

He started to walk away when I started to find my words. "Sahil … no … uh … I'm sorry, okay? I was just so annoyed, and I didn't want to answer you, but now I'm fine. You can ask me anything, and I'll answer properly. Just don't be mad at me, okay?"

Sahil stood there for a while and then asked, "Just sorry? You've got nothing else? Well, *I'm* sorry I can't stand around here talking to you. I have some important things to tell Dad before he leaves."

"Please listen to me," I started, and Sahil interrupted.

"Listen to you? Well, you've never listened to me, so how am I supposed to do the same to you?"

I said, "Please forgive me. I'll make it up to you somehow, but listen to me. Right now, we need each other as brother and sister for support. We're going through a rough situation with our family, so we'll need to stick together. We'll cry on each other's shoulders when our father is gone. We'll have to help Mom do chores in this house together. We'll be on our own when Mr. Troop is gone, but we can't just let our family tear apart, Sahil. We need to stick together in these tough situations. So please, if you will, can we work out our differences and join forces?" I asked.

Sahil seemed shocked. He said, "Uh sure, we can do that."

"Thanks! You can talk to me about anything you want. I'll do the same because, as siblings, I want us to trust each other with any problems or secrets or stress or anything. You get me?" I almost cried.

Sahil patted me on the back and replied, "Yes, of course, and I'm sorry too for not treating you with respect. I'll be nicer to you, and I guess we can get along."

"Great!" I said and hugged Sahil.

Mom came downstairs with a basket of laundry and said, "Whoa, what am I seeing here? Both of my children are getting along?" I nodded. "Aww, so sweet. Let me join in the group hug," she said and gestured to Mr. Troop to come join us. She put the laundry down, and we all formed a group hug.

After a while, he said, "I'll be late for my flight so I … uh … better leave now … I guess." Mom had tears in her eyes as she nodded. "I barely got to spend time with all of you, but I hope we can keep in touch," he said.

"We sure can!" Sahil said and laughed. I laughed with him. We all laughed.

Then Mr. Troop got his luggage and said, "I don't want to say goodbye. So I'll say until we meet again!"

I smiled weakly. The three of us stood near the front porch and watched him get into the car and drive away. Then I immediately realized something. *Shoot! The letter. I forgot to slide the letter I wrote in his luggage.* But it was too late by the time I remembered. He had already left.

CHAPTER 11

We all just stood there staring at the door. I guess we all were in shock that everything just happened so fast. We were quiet for a few minutes, but someone had to break the silence. "So is someone gonna close the door or what?" Sahil asked.

"Oh yeah. The door. Right. I … guess I'll do it," I said and closed the door. Mom still hadn't said anything. She was just standing there staring at the door I just closed. I looked at Sahil and gestured toward Mom. Sahil just shrugged. We were basically showing actions with our hands and mouths for a while.

Then Mom said, "You guys can stop now. I see you. I don't know why you guys are not properly speaking with your mouths. I'm fine, kids. Let's just go back to what we were doing." She sprinted into the kitchen.

"Uh, Mom? Your laundry is what you were doing, but you forgot to take the laundry basket," I mentioned.

"Oh, right. The laundry basket. I forgot. Yeah, I'll take that," Mom said and took the basket. We were talking with pauses for a while. For many hours. For many days. For many weeks. None of us could get over what had happened.

A couple of months passed by, and we slowly started to act like ourselves again.

"Sameera, come up here! I have something to show you," Sahil yelled from upstairs. I was downstairs helping Mom clean up the table and wash the dishes. Ever since Ms. Turner's incident, I felt bad that Mom had to do all the chores on her own, so I insisted on helping.

"What is it?" I asked from downstairs.

"You must come upstairs. Then I will tell you," Sahil said.

"Is it a stupid chemical kitchen again or any other dumb science projects that'll ruin our lives?" I asked.

"It's not!" Sahil yelled.

"Sorry, I can't come now. I'm helping Mom with chores, unlike you," I replied.

"It's all right, Sameera. You can go upstairs to your brother. I'll finish cleaning up the rest of the kitchen," Mom said.

"Are you sure?" I asked.

Mom nodded.

"Thank you, Mom," I said and ran upstairs to Sahil's room.

"Okay, Sahil, what is the thing you wanted to show me?" I asked.

He showed me his computer. "Come have a look," he said.

I stared at the computer screen. "It's just a website with pictures of engine tools on it. What's the big deal?" I asked.

Sahil replied, "Well it's not just any random website with engine tool pictures on it. It's my website!"

"What? Why did you randomly make a website and how?" I asked.

"I didn't randomly make it. It's for a purpose," he replied.

I asked, "What's the freakin' purpose?"

"The purpose is to solve our problems and make us happy again," he responded.

"Come on. Get to the point. How is a website full of engine tool pictures going to make us happy? It's just stupid," I remarked.

"No, it's not. I designed this website using an online software so that Dad would see it and come back to live with us," Sahil said.

"What do you mean?" I said.

He said, "So you miss Dad. I miss Dad. Mom misses Dad. We all want him to move back in with us, right?" I nodded but didn't see where he was going with this. Sahil continued, "That's the point of the website. I'm creating a fake website with a job offer that Dad will love more than the one in California. It's located close to our city, and Dad will want to come back here after seeing it."

"Are you out of your mind? Why would you fool Father like this? If he moves back here and figures out that there's no job, then you're gonna get into big trouble. He'll be jobless. Do you really want that?" I asked.

Sahil thought for a second, then said, "Um, no, but Mom works and makes good money."

"She's a single parent! You expect her to work her butt off for all of us? No, Sahil. We can't do this. If he moves back, he will neither have a job here nor in California, so it's not going to help," I explained.

Sahil replied, "But at least he'll have his family."

"Sahil!" I screamed.

He said, "Okay, fine, all right."

I hit him on the head and asked, "How could you be so dumb?"

"Ouch!" he yelled. "I'm telling Mmom that you hit me."

"Okay, okay. I'm sorry for hitting you. Please don't tell Mom because I don't want to make her furious. She's had enough of our fights," I said.

"On one condition," Sahil said.

"What now?" I asked.

"You'll help me make another plan to bring Dad back here. You're smart," Sahil said, trying to win me over.

"No, we can't do that," I said.

"Why not?" Sahil whined.

"No matter what we do, he is just not going to come back," I said.

"Why would you say that?" he asked.

"I don't know. I just feel that way. He moved so he could lead a happy life alone, with no one bothering him. I don't think he really wants to be around us or … anybody," I replied.

Sahil shut his computer and stared at me. "What are you looking at?" I asked.

"Seriously? Are you really going to be that negative?" he asked.

"I'm not being negative, Sahil. I'm just being sensible," I responded.

"Nah, don't be silly. I think Dad loves us and will come back to visit at least," Sahil told me.

I sat on his bed gathering my thoughts for a while, but chatterbox Sahil wouldn't let me think. "So are you going to help me make a plan to bring Dad back, or will you just sit there staring at the wall?" Sahil asked.

"I'll help, but I'm telling you that there's no guarantee that our plan will actually work," I replied.

"There's no harm in trying. Let's give it a shot," Sahil said.

I agreed. "So what do we do first?" I asked.

"Don't ask me. You're the one with brains. We need to think of ideas and all the possibilities that come with the ideas. We'll split up and do some thinking and write down ideas. Then we'll come together and discuss if any of our ideas can be put into action," Sahil suggested.

"Ah, well, fair enough," I replied.

"Good. So, if you have any ideas, let me know," Sahil said.

I nodded. I got up from the bed and was about to leave when I saw something glowing under Sahil's bed. *What could that be?* I thought.

"What are you waiting for? Go! Go! Go!" he exclaimed.

Now I was getting annoyed by him bossing me around. "Shut up! You can't be my boss just because I agreed to help you. I'll go when I want. Think of ideas when I want. And share them with you when I want. Don't boss me around, you dummy," I said.

"You dummy!" Sahil yelled.

"Stop!" I shouted. Then I grabbed one of the pillows from his bed and smacked him with it.

"Ouch! Don't hit me," Sahil said.

"How is a stupid pillow going to hurt you, huh?" I continued smacking him.

"Leave the room, Sameera! Go think of ideas!" Sahil said.

I stopped hitting him and said, "Okay, I'll do it. Watch me. I'll think of ideas and write them down before you can even count to ten. Waah! Waah! Sameera is so good at everything, and Sahil is not," I teased him.

"Stop it, Sameera!" Sahil said and smacked me with a pillow.

"Ouch! You can't hit me! I'm older than you," I said and hit him back.

"Well, of course I can hit you if you don't respect my privacy. Get out of my room!" Sahil shouted.

"You get out of the room!" I yelled back.

"This is my room, dummy!" Sahil just stood there for a while looking at me awkwardly.

"I mean … I'll go to my room, but you'd better not come in there," I corrected myself.

"Why would I come into your room? I wouldn't find anything interesting there. It's just gonna be stupid girly stuff. Am I right?" he asked and laughed.

"Argh!" I yelled.

Just then, Mom walked into the room. "Whoa, whoa, whoa! What's going on here? Did you guys get into a fight again?" Mom asked.

"Sameera started it," Sahil said.

I was about to hit Sahil when Mom said, "Stop! Don't hit your brother. I thought you two made up and resolved your differences. We even had a group hug. Remember? What is this, Sameera?"

"Sahil is making me upset, Mom. He is bossing me around and telling me what to do. Now look. He even hit me with a pillow," I replied.

"Sameera started it," Sahil said.

"Well, if you hadn't bossed me around, I would've just left the room on my own just fine. But no, you just had to interfere!" I yelled.

Mom said. "Stop it!" We went silent. "You guys are acting like you're two years old. Come on, Sameera. You're older. You can't be wasting your time fighting like this all the time. Find a new hobby or do something productive. Do you understand?" I nodded. "And, Sahil, may I know what you were asking Sameera to do that she thought was bossy?" Sahil opened his mouth to speak. Then I waved my hands, mouthing the word *no.* Sahil nodded. I didn't want him to tell Mom about the plan we were creating. "Tell me, Sahil. What were you telling Sameera?" Mom asked.

"Uh … nothing huge. Just fighting," Sahil replied.

"How could you just fight without a reason? There must be something. Don't hide anything from me. Tell me the truth," Mom demanded.

"Um … Sameera will tell you!" Sahil exclaimed.

Mom faced me. I said, "Me? Uh well … um … we were just fighting over this room," I lied.

"Are you crazy? This is Sahil's room, so of course he would have it. You have your own room, Sameera. Why would you want Sahil's room?" Mom asked.

I couldn't think of any reason, so I quickly scanned the room. The ripped-up science posters on the floor caught my attention. "Oh, did I say room? I meant the posters in his room. He stole them from me last year because for some reason he was interested in science. Science is my thing, so I just came here to get the posters back," I lied again. Sahil smirked at me.

"This big fuss was just for the posters? Sameera, I can buy you new posters if you just ask. Why are you making a big deal?" Mom asked.

"Well, because Sahil ripped them up, and they weren't even his. These are rare posters from last year, so you won't find the exact same ones online or in stores. I was only looking for these exact posters," I lied again.

"Really?" Mom said.

I nodded.

"Sahil, please turn on your computer and search for atomic science posters," Mom said. I got nervous. *What is Mom trying to do?* I thought.

"Uh, my computer is actually broken, so I can't search anything now," Sahil lied. I smiled because for once he was playing along well.

"Well, that's no problem. I'm pretty sure Sameera's computer will work. Right? Come, Sameera. Let's go to your room," Mom said.

My smile quickly faded. "No, it's okay. I forgive Sahil. I don't need those posters anymore. I can find new interests. I'm sorry for fighting about this petty issue, Sahil," I said.

"It's okay, Sameera. In fact, I've thought about it. You can have these posters back. I'll even help you put them back together. I don't need them anymore. The scientific liquid under my bed is good enough," Sahil responded.

"What? Scientific liquid? What is that?" I asked.

"No, not scientific liquid, silly. I meant to say … uh, my automatic light switch," Sahil replied. I didn't believe him. He was lying to me.

"Why would you have an automatic light switch under your bed?" I asked.

"Well … I invented it," Sahil said.

I squinted my eyes at him. "Why would you even need—" I started, but Mom interrupted.

"Forget that! Stop trying to change the topic. Sameera, let's go to your room and use your laptop to search for science posters,"

"Mom, I told you I don't want the posters anymore. Sahil can keep them," I insisted.

"Well then, if you don't want to buy the posters, then it's fine. But we can search for them to see if they're there, right?" Mom asked.

"No, that's not necessary." I chuckled.

"You're telling me that they're rare and we won't find them anywhere this year, right? So I just want to do a site check as well," Mom said.

"Oh, well, um … I'm not sure if any of the websites have them. It's not like I checked all of them, so maybe they might be there. I just didn't check properly," I said.

"Huh. Didn't check properly. What a great excuse, but I will not buy it. Sameera, take me to your room and show me your computer," Mom demanded.

"Fine, go ahead. I'll come behind you," I said in an annoyed voice. Mom left the room.

Then I whispered to Sahil, "This is all your fault. If I get into trouble, you'll be responsible for it. Then I won't help you with your plan. You'll be all on your own, brother."

"Sameera? Are you coming?" Mom called out.

"Yes, I am. I'll just close the door," I said. Before I left, the glowing thing under Sahil's bed caught my eye again. *What could that possibly be? Could it be the scientific liquid Sahil was talking about? How did he create that? What are its effects? Could it be part of the chemical kitchen he invented earlier?* I had all these questions running in my mind, but I didn't take the time to learn the truth.

CHAPTER 12

I took Mom to my room because she eagerly wanted to prove me wrong about the science posters. I didn't want the posters back, and I didn't check online or in any stores to see if they still had the posters. We had to make up a lie so that Mom didn't figure out what Sahil and I were up to. If she ever figured it out, we would be grounded. As much as Mom loved Mr. Troop, she wouldn't force him to live with us. Besides, she was not even going to remarry him, so what was the point of him living with us? It would just be an awkward family. I didn't care that much for Mr. Troop anymore. Sahil somehow still missed him and wanted him to come back to us. So here I was making up lies to save my brother and his foolish plans.

"Sameera, turn on your computer please," Mom requested.

"Yes, ma'am," I said as I reached for the power button.

"Now let me search what I need to," Mom said. She went to the search engine and typed in *where to find atomic science posters.* She pointed and said, "Hey, we have this exact same poster in Sahil's room." I rolled my eyes. "And this one. Oh, we have this too! Look at this. And this one also. They have these exact same posters all over the internet. All the posters you had are online. Then why were you lying to me, sweetie?" Mom asked. I shrugged. "Sameera! I can't believe you. What is going on? I just need the truth," Mom said.

I had to think of a hard-core excuse that would stop Mom from asking more questions. I thought of something, but it was a bit too extreme.

"Answer me, Sameera," Mom said.

"Puberty, I guess?" I lied.

It was silent for a few seconds. Then Mom got all soft and apologetic. I didn't like her that way, but at least it was better than getting caught in my lies. "Oh, I'm so sorry, Sameera. I didn't even think of that. You're growing up so fast. So that's what has been messing with your mood, huh?" I nodded unwillingly. "Oh, I'm sorry for whatever I did just now. I think you need to take some rest. Here, I'll put your favorite show on TV. I'll also bring you some lunch in bed after a while," Mom suggested.

"Oh, that's not necessary, Mom. I'll just come down to the kitchen when I'm hungry," I responded.

"Okay, whatever you want, my princess," Mom said.

"Mom!" I said in an annoyed voice.

"What? I can't call Sahil my princess, can I?" Mom asked and laughed. I laughed. "You are my princess after all, sweetie," Mom said and touched my face.

We were quiet for a while. Then I said, "So are you going to go down and make some lunch?"

"Oh yes! I'll go do that right away," Mom said and left the room.

Then I slowly peeked out of my door. The coast was clear. So I ran to Sahil's room and tried to open the door. "What! It's locked! Why did he lock it? Ugh! I'm going to break it open. Wait … I must be silent so that Mom doesn't know."

I whispered, "Sahil, it's me. Open the door!" There was no response, so I gently knocked. "Sahil, open the freakin' door."

He opened the door and asked, "What do you want? Did you think of ideas yet?"

"No. Just let me in. I need to talk to you," I whispered.

"Come in. Why are you whispering?" Sahil asked as he shut the door behind him.

"Mom is down there. She'll hear us, and I don't want to get into trouble," I replied.

"Oh right. Did you get into any trouble yet? Mom wanted to see the science posters online, right? How did you manage to save yourself?" Sahil asked.

"Shut up, Sahil! I had to tell a very horrible lie to make Mom leave me alone. I feel so bad for lying to her that way. She means a lot to me. You just don't understand how hard it is for me to lie to her," I cried.

"She means a lot to me too! She's not just your mother! It's not easy for me to lie to her either." Sahil got angry.

"Shh. Keep your voice down. This is all your fault! If it weren't for you and your stupid plans, then we wouldn't have to lie to Mom!" I screamed softly.

"What is a small lie going to do to you? If you just tell the truth your whole life, you'll always get into trouble. You need to lie sometimes. You're acting like you made a huge mistake," Sahil said.

"It wasn't a small lie at all! I told her that I had ..." I stopped myself right there. I didn't want to finish my sentence. I didn't want Sahil to know that I told Mom I had hit puberty. He was a young boy, and there was no point in sharing things like that with him.

"You told her you had what?" Sahil asked.

"Never mind. The point is I was able to prevent myself from getting into trouble. You know what? I feel like we should just drop this idea of trying to convince Mr. Troop to move back with us. It's hard for all of us to handle. You can do it if you want. Who am I to stop you? You won't even listen to me. So go ahead with your plans and count me out of it. Sorry. I just can't do this anymore," I said and left his room.

I didn't see the expression on Sahil's face before I left, but I'm pretty sure he was disappointed. What was I to do? I couldn't help Sahil make a stupid plan and lie to Mom about huge things. That just was nothing like me. I was always a good girl, I'm still a good girl, and I will always be a good girl no matter what. I sat at my study desk in my room, with my arms and legs crossed together. Time was ticking, but I was sitting there and literally had nothing to do. I got bored and started wondering about Sahil. Was he still trying to come up with a plan to bring Mr. Troop back? Or did he drop the plan? I decided not to care because either way I wasn't going to get into trouble. I shrugged and got up from my chair. Then I began walking around my room for no reason. I was so angry at Sahil and so ashamed to show my face to Mom. So I just stayed upstairs in my room. I decided to watch a couple of episodes of *Fuller House.*

Just then the doorbell rang. *Ding-dong. Ding-dong. Ding-dong.*

"Sameera? Sahil? Can one of you please get the door? I'm trying to cook lunch, and my hands are full," Mom called out.

"Who could that be?" I asked myself. I looked out of the window in my room, but I couldn't see anything. There wasn't a car, bike, truck, or anything.

"Kids! Could you please get the door?" Mom called out, even louder. I heard Sahil's fast footsteps on the stairs. I leaned on my door to hear what was going on downstairs. I didn't hear anything for a while.

Then Mom called out, "Who is at the door?"

There was no response. *Didn't Sahil get the door? Why isn't he responding?*

"Sahil? Sameera? Who is at the door?" Mom asked again. There was no response. *Something is fishy.* "Why isn't anyone answering me?" Mom asked me. Then after a while, I heard her footsteps. I immediately left my room and went downstairs.

"Mom, who is it?" I asked. She pointed at the door. I was confused, "You opened the door, and no one was there? Oh, our neighbor's kids might have been playing a prank on us like they do for fun. I thought you were used to it."

"No, Sameera. It can't be that. I didn't even open the door. Our neighbors can only ring our doorbell, but they can't open our door, can they?" Mom asked.

I chuckled. "No, Mom. Don't be silly. I heard Sahil go downstairs. I'm sure he opened the door, and he's careless, so he probably left the door open."

"Well then, where is he?" Mom asked.

I replied, "I don't know. Probably one of his friends came, so he took them downstairs to the basement."

"Oh yeah, that's a possibility, but it is quiet downstairs. Usually, Sahil is down with his friends making a lot of noise and mess." I agreed. Mom closed the front door and said, "I'll go check on him soon. Anyway, I made some angel hair noodles along with a strawberry smoothie for you. Why don't you go to the kitchen and have some lunch?"

I nodded. Mom went downstairs. Then I went to the kitchen and helped myself to a bowl of angel hair noodles and a glass of strawberry smoothie. I sat down to eat. I tasted the smoothie first. "Wow, this is delicious! The smoothie is so sweet I feel like I'm in heaven!" I exclaimed to myself.

Just then, Mom rushed back upstairs. I licked my lips and asked, "What's wrong, Mom? You seem tense." I took another sip of my smoothie.

Mom gasped for breath and said, "Sahil … is … not … in … the basement."

I spit out my smoothie. "What? Where did he go then? I didn't hear him come back upstairs after he opened the door," I explained.

Mom replied, "I have no idea. We must go and search for him."

"We? Right now? I'm eating, Mom."

"Sameera, how could you be like this? Do you not care for your brother?" Mom asked.

"I do! It's just … I don't … um. He must be around the house somewhere. Where else could he go?" I said.

"I don't know. I'm going to go check his room and the rest of the house," Mom said and headed upstairs.

I sighed and took a scoop of the angel hair noodles. Mom turned to look at me. "Oh, sweetie. I totally forgot you started puberty," Mom said.

I gulped down my noodles and awkwardly stared at her. *I didn't. I thought Mom would have forgotten all that by now.* "Uh … um, I don't think I really have it, Mom. I just um … thought maybe—" I started, and then Mom interrupted.

"Aww, sweetie, you don't have to take the trouble of searching for your brother. I'll search for him myself. You should probably finish lunch and go rest in your room," Mom suggested.

"It's okay. That's not needed," I said.

Mom replied, "Oh yes, it is! Rest is needed. Go upstairs once you're done, all right? I'll go look for Sahil outside the house."

"No. Please, Mom. I'll … just help you search for Sahil because I care about him," I said.

"Just a while ago, you said you didn't want to come, and now you change your mind suddenly. Oh, it must be puberty that's doing all this to you," Mom guessed.

Ugh! This is so annoying. Why does Mom think that everything I say or do is because of puberty? I shouldn't have told such a hard-core lie. "Okay, fine, Mom. I'll rest in my room," I said.

"That's my good girl," Mom said. I rolled my eyes. "All right. I must go now. I'll be back with Sahil soon. Love you," Mom said and kissed me on my forehead. She took her purse and left.

"Oh, I'm not going to stay home and rest while all this is happening. I know what I'll do. I'll gather up my team and find a solution to this ruckus," I said to myself and quickly ran upstairs. I took my phone and gave Mackenzie and Meg an urgent call. I told them to get to my house as quickly as they could and bring whoever else they could with them. The bigger the team, the better.

CHAPTER 13

Ding-dong. The doorbell rang. "Oh, that must be them!" I exclaimed and skipped down the stairs. I opened the door.

"Hey, Sameera!" Meg said.

I waved.

"Sameera, we brought whoever we could. We met them in summer camp last year," Mackenzie said and pointed at three people. "This is Lola. She has very high intelligence," she said, pointing to a girl about five feet tall with blonde hair and dark brown eyes. She was wearing a yellow flowered top, blue jeans, and pink sneakers. "Lola got a perfect score on the SAT! Can you believe it? And she's not even in high school yet!"

I raised my eyebrows. "Wow, that's a big accomplishment!"

"This is Jasper. He's very quick-witted, so he kind of has a super speed ability." Jasper seemed like he could belong to some rock band. He was wearing an oversized black vintage tour shirt from Pink Floyd, ripped jeans, and black boots. Half of his hair was dyed blue, and he even had spikes. "Did you know that Jasper has a record for running three miles in under ten minutes?" I shook my head but was really amazed.

"And last but not least, this is Apple." *Apple? What a weird name for a person.* Anyway, she had on an orange button-down top with white stripes, and her hair was up in a bun.

"Cool! What can Apple do?" I asked.

"Um … she can sit still like an apple, but she is very good at spying and not getting caught."

"Wow! It's great that all these people have a special ability," I said and closed the door.

"So, why did you call all of us here?" Meg asked.

"Yeah, why did you? We thought it was urgent, so we literally dropped everything we were doing and rushed to your house," Mackenzie said.

I replied, "Aww, that's so sweet of you, but it's not so urgent that you had to drop what you were doing."

"Hey, where is your mom by the way?" Meg asked.

I didn't even know where to start. "Well … actually … um … so … I … uh—"

"What is it? Tell us what's wrong," Meg said.

"Okay. You know what? Let's just sit down in the living room and talk," I suggested.

"All right, whatever you say," Meg said.

So I took them to the living room, and we all sat down in different areas of the room. Mackenzie and Meg sat on the large couch, Lola sat on the beanbag chair, Jasper stood in one corner of the room next to the lamp, Apple sat near the window, and I sat on the rocking chair. "Now tell us. What's been bothering you?" Mackenzie asked.

I said, "So it's a long story, but I'll try to explain everything in detail." I told them everything, from Mr. Troop leaving again, going to California, all the way up until the lie I told my mom when she caught me lying about the posters.

"Wait … what lie did you tell your mom?" Mackenzie asked.

I replied, "Uh … well … that's not important now. So anyway—"

"No, seriously tell us, Sameera. We need to know that so that we can follow along with your story," Meg said.

"Yeah, and don't worry. We won't make fun of you. We're just here to help you," Mackenzie said. Mackenzie and Meg were my best friends, so I could share it with them without being judged, but I felt kind of ashamed to share it in front of the other three. So I huddled Mackenzie and Meg together in a corner and asked the other three people to give us a minute.

"So ... I told my mom ... uh, that I-had-puberty," I whispered very quickly.

"Say what now? I did not understand a single word you just said," Meg said.

"Come on, Sameera. Just tell us what you told your mom," Mackenzie said.

I replied, "Okay, fine. I told her that I. Had. Puuuuu ..." I just couldn't say it.

"Pu what? I don't understand," Mackenzie said.

"All right, fine. I told her that I had puberty. There—I said it," I said in relief.

Mackenzie chuckled.

"See? I knew that you guys would laugh," I said, looking down.

Meg gave Mackenzie a gentle tug and whispered, "Mackenzie, come on. Be a good friend."

"Sorry, Sameera. I didn't mean to laugh," Mackenzie said.

"Yeah, Sameera. That lie is not a huge deal. We all go through it at some point in our life," Meg said.

"Well, it would seem huge if you saw how my mom was treating me. She was treating me like I was a sick child or a child with disabilities. So yes, it was a huge lie," I said. We all dispersed and went back to the rest of the group.

"Then what happened after you lied to your mom?" Mackenzie asked.

"I just stayed in my room because I was so ashamed to show my face to Mom or Sahil. After a while, the doorbell rang, and Mom was cooking, so she told one of us to get the door. I heard Sahil go downstairs to get the door, and then I don't know where he went after that," I said.

"Oh my gosh. That's *so* scary. I feel *so* bad for you, Sameera!" Mackenzie said in a very sarcastic voice.

"Mackenzie, seriously stop. Sameera, what if your brother was kidnapped? Do you know anyone who has grudges against him?" Meg asked.

I frowned and said, "I don't know—wait … oh no! I can think of only one person who might want to get rid of him. The one person who kidnapped my mom and Mr. Troop. Now she's after my brother." I gasped and shook my head.

Meg scrunched her eyebrows. "Ms. Turner? I thought she went to jail. There is no way they released her already."

"Yeah, she deserves the longest punishment possible. She's most likely going to be locked up for a long while," Mackenzie commented.

I blew air threw my cheeks. "You're right. It can't be her. Unless … she has a gang of people working for her that still haven't been arrested. They could still be out there trying to target our family. I can't think of anyone else who would've had any reason to kidnap him. Mom thought that he was upstairs with his friends, but when she checked the house, he was nowhere to be seen. So my mom went to look for him, and she wanted me to stay home and rest because of the stupid lie."

The room was silent for a second, and then Meg asked, "So do you know where exactly your mom went?"

"No. She didn't tell me. She just said that she'd be back soon with Sahil," I replied.

"Well then, why are you getting so tense? You could just wait for her to come back, or you could just ask her to keep you updated," Mackenzie said.

I responded, "I know I can, but my mom will just tell me not to worry and to rest and that she'll handle the situation alone. I'm so restless. On the other hand, I think Sahil is mad at me for dropping his fake website plan and he ran away."

"Aww, Sameera, don't say that. If that's the case, I'm sure your brother will realize his mistake and come back," Meg said with her arm around me.

I said, "How could he? He is too young to even understand that he made a mistake, so how long is it going to take him to realize it?"

"Then what do you want to do, Sameera?" Mackenzie asked.

I replied, "I want you guys to help me look for him and also find out where my mom went."

"If that's what you want, then we'll try. Lola, Jasper, and Apple could help us out with this mission easily," Meg said.

I went over and hugged Mackenzie and Meg. "Thank you guys so much!" I exclaimed.

"No problem. Anything for our best friend," Meg said.

"So how do we even get the mission started?" I asked.

"I don't know, but Lola is intelligent, so she might be able to tell us," Mackenzie suggested.

"Oh yeah. Lola, what do you think?" I asked.

Lola replied, "Well, if you want to look for your mom, we could use a tracking device to find her location ... if she has her phone with her."

I said, "I'm pretty sure she took her phone with her, but what are we going to get if we find my mom? She'll just tell me to go back home and rest because of stupid puberty. We could track my mom later, but what are we going to do about Sahil?"

Lola thought for a second and then said, "Hmmm, your brother won't recognize me, Jasper, and Apple though."

"What are you trying to say?" I asked.

"The three of us can track your brother and follow him," Lola replied.

"That's a great idea!" I exclaimed.

"Apple is pretty good at spying and not getting caught," Lola said.

"Well, yeah, I get it. Apple will be better off spying on Sahil," I replied.

"Hey, Sameera, does your brother have a phone?" Meg asked.

"No, he only has an iPad, and I'm pretty sure he didn't take it with him," I replied.

"What if he *did*?" Lola said, moving her eyebrows up and down.

"Um ... Lola, that's a little creepy," I pointed out.

"What? That your brother might have his iPad with him?" she asked.

"No, silly. Your eyebrows are," I replied.

"Oh. Sorry. I won't do that," Lola said.

"So what do we do now?" I asked.

"I'll spy and catch the thief," Apple mumbled, sitting in the corner of the room.

"Uh ... Apple? There is no thief involved in this mission," Mackenzie said.

"Yeah, we're just looking for Sameera's brother, who might have run away," Meg said.

"Yeah, I know, but I am going to catch the thief who stole my book last night," Apple said.

I hit my forehead with my hand and said, "This is going to be a long day."

"Just ignore Apple. She'll just be saying weird things like this all day. You should focus on the mission," Jasper suggested. I agreed.

Lola jumped up and said, "Jasper! Quickly, go to the brother's room and check to see if his iPad is anywhere." I stared at Lola and might've given her the impression that I didn't want strangers in Sahil's room. She corrected herself. "If it is okay with Sameera."

"Oh yeah, that's fine. I don't really care. I'll show you to his room," I said.

Lola exclaimed, "Great! Jasper, go and start our mission."

"I'm on it, boss," Jasper said and quickly left the room.

"Boss? What? What kind of a crazy team is this, Meg?" I asked.

"I don't know. It was Mackenzie's idea," Meg said.

"So is Lola also the boss of Apple?" I asked.

"I dunno. Ask her," Mackenzie said.

Apple was just sitting in the corner murmuring things to herself. I didn't know what her deal was, but she sure did seem like a great spy.

Jasper checked Sahil's room and we both headed back downstairs. "It's nowhere to be seen, and I'm telling you I literally searched all over his room," Jasper said.

"Yes! That means he took his iPad with him!" I jumped up in excitement.

"Wow. This mission just got easier," Mackenzie said.

"Yeah. Now, Sameera, everyone in your family has the *find my device* app and is sharing location, correct?" Lola asked. I nodded. Lola smiled. "Great. Now if I could have your phone opened to the app, I can connect it to your computer so we can have a bigger and better view. Let's check your mom's location first," We all left the living room, except for Apple, who was still sitting in the corner.

"What do we do about her?" I asked.

"I'll get her. You all go with Lola," Jasper said.

We all went to the study where the desktop computer was, and I gave Lola my phone with the app open. Lola connected it to the computer using AirPlay. "How's it going, Lola?" Mackenzie asked.

"Great! In fact, I've already tracked Sameera's mom based on the information from this app," Lola replied.

"That's awesome. So where is she now?" I asked.

"She seems to be near a grocery store," Lola responded.

"Um ... okay. Do you know which grocery store?" I asked.

Lola studied the computer carefully and said, "Fresh Thyme."

"Sameera, did your mom go to buy groceries or look for your brother?" Meg asked.

"I have no idea at this point," I said.

"Why would your mom look for your brother near a grocery store?" Mackenzie asked.

"She's probably just buying groceries," Lola said.

"Ugh!" I groaned.

"Hey, I have an idea! I'll send Jasper and Apple to the location that Sameera's mom is at. They can keep their phones with them and report to us on what is going on. Meanwhile, I can track Sameera's brother and see where he is at."

"You're a genius, Lola!" Mackenzie said.

"Yes indeed," Meg said.

"Are you sure about this, guys? I don't want my mom to think that you guys are spying on her," I said.

"Apple will spy, and Jasper can bring her to that location," Lola suggested. I thought for a while. Then Lola said, "If you don't trust Jasper and Apple, then maybe one of your friends, Mackenzie or Meg, can go along with them to make sure everything is going right."

"I don't think that'll be necessary. Come on, Sameera, trust them. They are experts at these things," Meg said.

"Okay, fine, Lola. You can send Jasper and Apple," I said.

"Really? Are you sure? If you don't want to, then we won't force this plan. We can come up with a different plan," Lola suggested.

"This plan is fine. Let's begin," I said.

"That's the spirit, Sameera," Meg said.

"Jasper! Apple! Come on. We need your help!" Lola yelled. They both came immediately.

Lola explained the entire plan to them and made sure their phones had enough charge. "Now go to the Fresh Thyme market and find her mom," Lola said.

"Yes, boss," Jasper said. They both left through the front door.

"I have a job for you, Mackenzie and Meg," Lola said.

"What?" they both asked at the same time.

"Keep my phone and communicate with Jasper and Apple. Tell me once they have found Sameera's mom. Let's start tracking the brother," Lola said.

"Great!" Meg said.

Mackenzie and Meg sat in a corner with Lola's phone. I stood next to Lola while she began tracking Sahil. Just then, Lola's phone started buzzing. Meg held it up. "Guys. We have found Sameera's mother," Jasper said.

"Where is she?" Meg asked.

"She's at the market buying groceries apparently. Apple is following her around now," Jasper said.

"Then what are you doing, dummy?" Mackenzie asked.

"Hey, don't call him that. He's trying to help us," Meg said.

"I'm waiting outside the market. Apple has her phone with her. She'll tell you everything that Sameera's mom does," Jasper said.

"Thanks for informing us," Meg said.

I came over to them and asked, "What is my mom doing at the grocery store? Why isn't she looking for Sahil?" Meg shrugged. "Oh, come on! There's no way that Sahil can be at the grocery store. Ask Jasper to lead my mom out of the store," I said.

"No, no Sameera. Your mother can't know that Jasper and Apple are part of our team. She'll get suspicious, remember?" Meg explained.

"Ugh! My life is over. What team do we even have!" I said in an annoyed voice.

"Just be patient and wait. We will find your brother soon," Mackenzie said.

The three of us just sat in the corner with Lola's phone, waiting for a response. Lola sat at the computer trying to track Sahil. "Anything yet?" I asked Lola in a tired voice.

"Nope. It's taking a while to load, but I'm sure if we just wait a few minutes, we'll find out," Lola replied.

"I'm so tired. Just make it quick," I blurted without thinking.

"Sameera. How rude! It's not like Lola is cutting you a slice of cake for it to be quick," Meg said. "This is not Lola's fault. It's the speed of the internet at your house. You should put yourself into her shoes. You would probably be so tense now. Poor Lola, Jasper, and Apple are all doing the work for someone they just met, while you get to sit back and relax in the corner. You should appreciate them for this."

"Yeah, Meg's right. Tracking is not a piece of cake," Mackenzie said.

I said, "I know, and I'm so sorry. It just came out of my mouth. My brother means a lot to me, so of course I'm tense that he is lost. It's not a piece of cake for me to wait for him either."

"I bet Lola could go for a piece of cake now," Mackenzie remarked.

"All right. Will you guys please stop with the cake comparisons now and focus?" Meg asked.

"Yeah, please stop talking in cake language. It's making me hungry," Lola said.

"Oh, it is? We can give you a slice of cake if Sameera has any in the kitchen," Mackenzie said.

"Shut up, Mackenzie! Lola is joking. She doesn't want cake. Let her work quietly," Meg responded.

"Well, anyway, I don't have any cakes at my house … or cookies or brownies or—" I started.

Meg interrupted. "We get it. If we are quiet, then Lola can work faster. Come on. Let's go sit in the corner," Meg suggested.

"Yeah, that'll be a piece of cake," Mackenzie said.

"Mackenzie! Seriously, shh! Now no one should talk about cake here, okay?" Meg said. Mackenzie and I chuckled. Mackenzie knew how to ease up stressful situations with her humor. I always found it easier to deal with stress when she was by my side. That was why she was one of my best friends.

We went and sat in the corner, and within a few minutes, Lola said, "So I guess Sameera's brother's location loaded after all."

Meg, Mackenzie, and I got up and ran over to Lola all at once. "Tell us. Where is he?" I asked, trying to get a better look at the computer screen.

Lola squinted at the screen. "According to the map, he seems to be in … Ohert City … City … City," Lola responded, and there was an echo.

"What? Ohert City!" I screamed.

"Why is he there?" Meg asked.

"Well, I don't know," Lola replied. I cupped my mouth with my hands and dropped to the floor.

"Sameera, are you okay?" Meg asked.

I shook my head and said, "How? How could he go there again? Who is he with? Is he alone?" I almost cried. I pulled out my phone and video called Sahil, but he didn't pick up. I tried texting him, but the message didn't deliver for some reason. I started freaking out.

"Calm down, Sameera. It's all right. He'll be fine," Meg said.

"Lola, tell Jasper and Apple to go to Ohert City. Give them the exact location," I said.

"Right away, girl. Give me my phone," Lola said.

"Oh, right. I have that, don't I?" Meg gave her phone.

Lola quickly called them. "We have a big emergency, Jasper. I tracked Sameera's brother, and he seems to be in Ohert City. You need to somehow get Apple out of the grocery store and head to that city. I'll send you the details of the exact location," Lola said.

"Thanks for the information. We will get to Ohert City as soon as we can. Copy," Jasper said.

"I told Jasper. He and Apple will go to that city and find Sahil," Lola said.

"Oh great! So now we wait even more," I said.

"Yeah, so wanna get a piece of cake?" Mackenzie asked.

Meg said, "I could actually go for a piece now."

"I told you I don't have any!" I almost shouted.

"Oh right. You're that girl," Meg said.

"What?" I asked.

Meg replied, "Never mind."

"What are you saying, Meg? I thought you were not a fan of cakes."

"I know you don't have any cakes, but Meg can go out and get a cake for us to celebrate the finding of your brother," Mackenzie suggested.

Meg frowned. "I'm not going anywhere, Mackenzie. If you want, you can go buy a cake."

"Well, I'm not going anywhere either," Mackenzie said.

"It's too soon to celebrate," Lola said.

"Why? What happened?" I asked.

CHAPTER 14

"Jasper, Apple, are you guys there yet? Did you reach Ohert City?" Lola asked.

"Almost, boss. Copy," Jasper replied.

Lola shrieked, "We need you to hurry. Sahil is in danger. Go, go, go. Copy."

"Oh no! I'm on it, boss. We'll be there as soon as possible," Jasper responded.

Lola put down her phone.

"What happened to Sahil?" I cried.

Lola took a deep breath. "Sameera, your brother is not safe in Ohert City. This tracking device app does not show it, but based on my knowledge of this location, he's near the red zone, which means he's in danger."

"What the heck is a red zone?" Mackenzie asked, pulling her hair back into a ponytail.

Lola replied, "Well, it's sort of like a dead end, except you could be dead as well."

Meg gasped. "What's that supposed to mean?"

"It's not a safe place to be because that's where all the dangerous creatures live who are always looking to make humans their meal," Lola explained.

I thought for a minute and asked, "You mean the Cave of Doom?"

"Yeah, something like that. I forget exactly what it is called."

I didn't understand why Sahil would ever go there again after what happened last time. *Is he trying to prove a point?*

My jaw dropped. Meg said, "Relax, Sameera. Everything will be fine."

"What do you mean everything will be fine? Everything was never fine, everything is not fine right now, and everything will never be fine." I got angry.

"Dang, girl, you've got attitude issues that we didn't know about," Mackenzie said.

I looked up at her like I was about to explode into anger. "Sorry. I didn't mean that. It just came out of my mouth."

"Just zip it, Mackenzie! Nobody cares. Stop making Sameera feel bad," Meg demanded.

I ran back to the corner of the room and covered myself with a thin blanket that was near the window.

"Look what you did, Mackenzie! Now she'll never come out of there," Meg said in a furious tone.

"It's not only my fault! You were talking about cakes and unnecessary stuff too!" Mackenzie yelled.

Meg shook her head back and forth and then said, "Cakes? That was all you! You're the biggest jokester around here. Instead of supporting Sameera and helping her out, you're frosting the situation with humor. That's not a great way to deal with this."

I couldn't take it anymore. I was trying to think, but Mackenzie's and Meg's bickering didn't let me concentrate, so I vented my frustration. I uncovered myself and threw the blanket on the ground. "You know what? Just get out of here! I know you guys were just trying to help, but I guess I don't need you. You guys will never realize how much I care about my brother because you are an only child. You and your stupid arguments. Please just leave me alone." They both froze, staring at me. Without saying another word, Meg exited through the front door and slammed it shut.

"No—wait, Meg. Don't leave!" Lola said.

"She's already gone; she won't hear you," Mackenzie said.

"True. Now what are we going to do without her?" Lola asked.

Mackenzie shrugged. "I don't know, but apparently Sameera doesn't want me here either, so I'm leaving. Bye."

"You too? Why? Aren't you going to help me with my mission?" Lola asked.

"Well, you have Jasper and Apple, and moreover, you have Sameera, who really cares," Mackenzie said, then grabbed her stuff and went out the door.

"Ugh, they're so childish!" Lola banged her head on the desk.

I slowly stood up. Lola looked up. "I thought they were your best friends. Why would you speak to them like that?" Lola asked.

I responded, "I'm sorry. They were being really distracting. Look, they're great friends, but right now there's not much they can do to help. You, Jasper, and Apple are my only hope now. Please help me with this mission," I said.

Lola looked up at me in disbelief and then finally said, "Fine, I'll help you, but only on one condition." I got a little nervous. *What could she possibly want from me?* I thought. "I want you to get me a piece of cake after we find your brother."

I looked at her in relief and laughed. "I'll definitely treat you once this mission is over." Lola smiled.

She sat back down and messed with her hair a little. Then she stared into the computer like a little boy staring at ice cream. "Anything interesting?" I asked.

"Nothing," Lola responded.

I sat back down. After a while, I asked, "How is it going, Lola?" There was no response. "Lola? Lola?"

"Sameera ..." Lola gasped, looking at the computer screen.

"What happened, Lola?" I asked.

Lola nodded. I immediately looked at the computer screen and was not able to understand anything. "I can't figure out what's wrong," I said.

"Sameera, can't you see? His location point is missing. That means I lost his signal. Either he switched off his device or his device lost charge," Lola responded.

"What? No way! What about Jasper and Apple?" I asked.

Lola replied, "Where am I supposed to ask them to go now? I have no leads."

"Oh no! What about my mom?" I asked, tension rising in my chest.

After a few seconds, she said, "Still at the grocery store. Wait … now it shows she's at the post office."

"You must be kidding. Is she even trying to look for my brother or just running errands? Do something, Lola. You're the expert, right?" I said anxiously.

"I can't do anything once I've lost his signal. All we can do now is wait," Lola said.

"There's no time to wait! My brother is missing, and he's more important than these stupid signals. I guess we'll have to go out there ourselves and look for him. There's no use staying at home to track him."

I was about to leave when Lola said, "No, Sameera, we can't go to Ohert City. It's too dangerous. You don't know what can happen to you."

"Nothing can happen to us, and I need to make sure nothing happens to Sahil! It's my duty as an older sister to protect Sahil. Besides, I've been to that city before, and the only thing dangerous is the Cave of Doom."

Lola looked at me with her mouth open. "What? Why are you looking at me like that?" I asked.

Lola said, "There's no way you've been there."

"Yes, I have. Last time I went there was for … You know what? Never mind. I don't want to talk about it. But right now, we must go there for Sahil—like now!" I said.

"I don't know, Sameera. I don't have a good feeling about this," Lola responded.

"Are you serious? I thought you were brave and were used to doing dangerous things," I said.

Lola nodded. "Definitely not the Cave of Doom. And besides, if I come with you, I'll be of no use. Jasper and Apple are the actual outside missions people. I am basically the backstage girl. I only come up with ideas and do all the technical stuff."

"Ugh! If you could come up with good ideas, you would've found Sahil, and he would be freakin' home by now." I lost my temper again accidentally.

Lola looked down. I said, "I'm so sorry for screaming again. This is just too much for me to handle."

"It's okay. I understand, but we need to be patient," Lola said.

I let out a sigh. "I … I can't. I've … I'm gonna go look for him myself. You can go home now. Thanks for your help!" I opened the door. Lola followed behind me.

"Wait, Samee—"

I didn't listen. I quickly took my bicycle out of the garage and rode it as fast as I could.

Halfway to Ohert City, I began to sweat and feel weak. "No, I can't stop now. I've got to keep going. I'm coming, Sahil!" I screamed, although he couldn't hear me wherever he was. I kept on going, not caring about anything else. I finally saw the sign to Ohert City and felt a wave of relief go through my body. Once I got into the city, I came stumbling upon the same fortune shop that had that foolish dream machine in it.

"Hello! Hello there! Come to our fortune shop and get your fortune from the special dream machine," an old man announced.

"It's not special. It's fake," I said to myself. I kept riding my bike. As I kept going, I recognized some of the shops from when I came last time.

"Hey, young lady!" I heard a man exclaim from a distance. I stopped in my tracks and turned around. I observed him as he walked toward me. He was by no means a young man. His life had left a profound impact on his face, making it difficult to estimate his age. His eyes, which were cast pensively into the distance, either conveyed extreme melancholy or calm serenity. His eyes seemed sky-blue from the distance and seemed to have a light winter-morning hue as he got closer. But the expression was anything but icy. His vision also appeared to be blurry, considering the spectacles that hung around his neck. The man's eyes were roving around the structures and trees on the opposite side of the street.

"Oh, hi," I said.

The man smiled and said in a southern accent, "You look familiar. I think I've seen you around before. You live nearby?"

"Uh, no … um, not here actually. I live about thirty minutes from—" I started, but the man interrupted.

"Ah, good to know. You really like this place?"

"Not really. I came looking for my brot—" I started, but he again interrupted.

"You know, most people come to this city just for the fortune shop." I rolled my eyes. He continued, "They love the dream machine because it gives them a fortune, and they look forward to it. Some of them even come back because their fortunes come true, and they want more." The man giggled. "It's where most of our business comes from. The shop is fantastic. It is the highlight of this city!" He kept praising the fortune shop, and I just couldn't bear it anymore. I was running out of time.

Dream obsessed, the guy bowed his head to his shoulder, revealing a significant scar on the left cheek, near the ear. Although the scar no longer seemed painful, it served as a constant reminder of his still young but distinctly unhappy youth. It seemed as if the guy spent his greatest years battling for survival and hope.

"Excuse me, sir … I must go now. My brother is somewhere here, and I must find—" I started.

The man said, "Have you visited the fortune shop? You seem tense, and I think the dream machine is the solution to your problem."

"Sir, please … I've been there because of my brother, and it's all superstitions. I don't believe in these things," I explained.

"Oh, ho-ho-ho-ho! Superstitious, huh? Well, we'll see about that. Why don't you make yourself comfortable at my house? You seem like you've been driving this rusty bike around for quite some time. We'll talk about the dream machine further and the miraculous things it has done for our city. You can talk to me about your stresses as well. After all, I long for people to talk to, as I live alone," he said.

"I can visit later, but I don't have time now. Maybe another time?" I asked.

The man frowned.

"Please. I promise I'll come back to the city again just to visit you. You seem like a very nice man, and I would love to talk to you and get to know you more. Maybe you can tell me your name, and I'll come looking for you next time," I said.

The man nodded and said, "That's not necessary, dear. I just wanted to help you in this situation, but if you come to me after your problem is solved, then it's useless. And I'll be useless."

"Sir, please don't say that. You're not useless at all! Don't be disheartened. I know you just want to help a lost girl, but I'm not lost. I know what I'm doing and where I'm going. It's just a matter of time. Let me go now please. I'm sure there are other kids out there who might need your help. Why don't you look for them?" The man looked up and stared at the blue sky for a while. "Sir? Are you okay?"

"Oh … yes, yes. You don't need my help. I'll just be on my way then. I'll see you around," the man said and walked away, looking at the ground.

I turned back to get on my bike when I heard someone say, "How many people are you going to upset today?"

I gasped. "Mackenzie! Meg! You guys came."

"Of course, we did! You're our best friend, Sameera. We wouldn't ever leave your side," Meg responded.

"Really? Even after I was rude and told you to get out of my house?" I reminded them.

"Well, Meg and I talked about how much you needed us. I know your brother means a lot to you, and you mean a lot to us. We can't understand sibling love because we don't have siblings of our own. So we talked through some stuff, and then we decided to come back to get you," Mackenzie stated.

Meg continued, "And when we went to your house, Lola told us that you went all by yourself to Ohert City. We were so shocked, so we came here trying to look for you."

"But how did you come so fast? And why didn't you bring Lola with you?" I asked.

Mackenzie laughed. "We don't ride bikes around like you, Sameera. We book taxis because we're cool."

I rolled my eyes.

"And Lola thought she was useless to come with us, so she stayed at home to keep an eye on the computer in case any signals came up," Meg added.

I said, "Oh, I'm so sorry for making everyone upset today. I just can't be at ease when my brother is missing. I make everyone upset to make Sahil happy. I can't live like this anymore, Mackenzie and Meg." Tears started rolling down my cheeks.

Meg came and threw her arms around me. "No, no Sameera. Don't say all that. We're here for you, okay?"

"I don't deserve great friends like you. I'm a bad girl, and I do horrible things," I said.

"Sameera! Please stop thinking negatively. You're not bad at all for us. You're one of the strongest girls we know. You might see yourself as bad, but to anyone else, you'd seem so strong to go out of your way and risk your life like this," Mackenzie said.

"Thank you so much!" I wiped off my tears.

Mackenzie hugged me and said, "Let's get you back home in the taxi. Come on!"

I released Mackenzie and asked, "Are you out of your mind? I can't just go home. I need to look for Sahil; he's somewhere here." Meg shook her head. "What is it, Meg?" I asked.

"Sameera … I don't know how to tell you this, but …" Meg began.

"Yes, Meg, just tell her the truth," Mackenzie said.

"The truth? What is the truth? Why are you guys silent? Answer me. Is Sahil okay?" I got tense.

"Sameera … I'll tell you everything on the way home. Just get into the taxi please," Meg said.

"No way! You must tell me now. I can't just leave Sahil in the middle of a random city and just go home!" I got angry.

"Cool down, Sameera. If you want us to tell you, we will. At least sit underneath this tree," Mackenzie said and pointed at a tree with colorful leaves.

I sat down on the mulch below. Mackenzie and Meg sat down next to me. "Now tell me," I demanded.

Meg began, "So, Sameera, the thing is … your brother is not here."

"What! Are you crazy? How can you say that? Lola tracked Sahil, and he was clearly in the danger zone at this city. I'm certainly sure that there's no danger zone here except for the Cave of Doom. So that's where I'm headed now," I said and got up.

Mackenzie stopped me. "Sameera, at least listen to us. We went to your house, and Lola told us more than what you know." I sat back down.

"We lied to you. Lola got a signal, but it wasn't clear, and Lola knows if a person is nearby or in a different state."

"What in the world are you trying to say?" I asked.

Meg took a deep breath and said, "Sameera, your brother has left this state."

I melted with my head on the mulch like an ice cream melting from a cone. "What! How? No! This can't happen. He ran away. What did I do wrong? I knew he was angry at me. I should not have yelled at him. Mackenzie, Meg! I made a mistake. I'm a bad sister," I said.

"Sameera. Sameera. Calm down. Here, drink some water," Meg said and handed me a bottle of water. I took a sip and sobbed more.

"Sameera, don't cry," Mackenzie said.

"Whe … whic … which state did he go to?" I asked, feeling a little dizzy.

"Cool down. Cool down. Drink more water. We'll tell you everything," Meg said.

"I can't take this much in one day," I said, shaking my head back and forth.

"Sameera, listen. Let's get you home, okay? We booked a taxi," Mackenzie said.

"Just tell me which state!" I screamed.

"We don't know the exact state, but he is going west, close to Wisconsin. At least he's headed in that direction, according to Lola," Meg replied.

I exclaimed, "That far! Why did he have to go that far to get away from me? He could've gone to New York or New Jersey. Call up Lola right now and get the exact coordinates. We must go west now."

"Sameera, please listen. Look, I haven't finished talking. Be patient. I know you're worried about your brother, but trust me. He's fine," Meg told me.

I sighed, wiping my tears. "Sorry. I'm not used to this kind of experience. This has never happened before. Maybe puberty really is hitting me."

"Oh, Sameera. Don't think about that. And we're not used to this either, so that's why we must go through this together, patiently, okay? Everything will be fine," Meg assured me. I nodded. At that point, I realized it was the second time my best friends came to Ohert City to rescue me. Last time was when Sahil and I went there to look for our parents, and my friends came all the way to inform us that Ms. Turner had kidnapped them.

"So, we sent Lola, Jasper, and Apple back to their houses. Sitting at home and tracking your brother in another state would be useless.

So that's why we thought we needed someone better than those three," Mackenzie said.

"What exactly do you mean?" I asked.

"The police," Mackenzie replied.

I gasped. "You guys called the police?"

"Yes, Sameera. We thought that's what is best for everyone now. Remember how the police helped us during the phase of wicked old Turner?" My jaw dropped. Mackenzie said, "See now, everything is going to be fine, Sameera."

"Nothing is fine! Sahil is my brother, and I should be able to find him on my own. I don't need the stupid police to look for him. I know him more than the police do!" I screamed.

Meg took a deep breath and said, "Instead of being thankful to us and making your life easier, you're angry with us?"

"Yeah, Meg is right. We did everything we could to help you find your brother faster, but you don't appreciate us at all. You should be happy at least that we're tolerating your tantrums and your anger, but now we can't take it anymore. Enough is enough. We can't follow you around and go west after we've called the police. I trust them even if you don't," Mackenzie explained.

Meg said, "You go to Wisconsin if you want, but I'm sorry we can't come with you. We trust the police. We're heading home in the taxi. Come with us if you want. Thank you. Bye!" Meg and Mackenzie walked away from me and headed toward the taxi.

I stared at them and then looked up, not knowing what to do. I was so restless and felt like throwing up. Mackenzie and Meg looked back at me and then looked away. I got up from the mulch. I looked left and right and finally said, "Wait for me. I'm coming!"

Mackenzie and Meg stopped in their tracks to look at me. I ran toward them. Mackenzie said, "Well, guess who finally decided to change their mind."

"Guys, I'm so sorry for all my tantrums and drama. I really can't explain anything that's going on in my life now. Just forgive me if you guys will, please," I said. Meg and Mackenzie thought for a second and then looked at each other. They both frowned and then opened the taxi doors. "Guys! I said I'm sorry, and I am thankful to you both. I won't throw tantrums anymore. I'll try to stay calm … and … ugh … this is so hard for me to say, but I'll … I trust the police!" I blurted out.

Meg looked at me and said, "Oh, we believe you."

I sighed in relief.

Mackenzie said, "Before this gets any more awkward, let's just get into the taxi."

I smiled, and then a thought popped into my head. "Wait, guys. Don't get into the taxi yet."

Meg had one leg in the taxi but took it out. "What is it now?" Meg asked.

"Um … if you guys could do me a favor and just wait with the taxi for some time, I'll be back in ten minutes."

Meg's eyes got wider. "I told you already! Your brother is not here. There's no point in searching every nook and corner of this city."

"Meg, I'm not going to look for my brother. I told you I trust the police."

"Then why would you make us wait for you?" Mackenzie asked.

I laughed. "Oh! I got it. You guys only see me as selfish, right?"

"Well, obviously we've only seen that side of you today. The way you said and acted toward us," Mackenzie replied.

I nodded. "Uh … okay … fair enough. But not anymore. I'm going to be nice for the first time today," I said in an epic voice.

"What do you mean?" Meg asked.

"Well, I'm off to apologize to an old man that I upset today. I know he really wanted me to come to his house and talk, and that's just what I'm going to do now," I explained.

Mackenzie's and Meg's eyes got wider at the same time, and they smiled bigger than they had ever smiled before. Their smiles were probably the best thing I had seen that day. "So what do you think of my idea?" I asked.

"It's awesome!" Meg exclaimed.

"First class!" Mackenzie said. I smiled and felt great inside. I could feel all the cells in my body were starting to smile. "We'll accompany you, Sameera," Mackenzie said.

"Yeah, we want to meet the sweet old man," Meg said.

"Then come on. What are you waiting for? Let's go find him," I said.

Mackenzie, Meg, and I were running like the wind. For the first time that day, I felt free like a breeze. No burdens to carry. The police had everything under control, and I could be at ease, without having to worry about anything.

We looked all around but couldn't find the old man. *If only I knew his name, I could ask for him.* "Sameera, where is he?" Meg asked.

I shrugged. "I'm not sure. He probably went home, and I don't know where his home is."

"There's an old man over there!" Mackenzie said, pointing straight ahead. "That must be him! Let's go!"

As we walked closer, we came upon the fortune shop again. "Are you kidding me? Why is destiny always leading me toward this shrewd shop?" I asked myself."

Any issues?" Mackenzie asked.

"Huh? Oh no, nothing. I … uh … see the man," I replied.

"Yeah, me too," Mackenzie said.

The three of us approached the man who seemed to be very depressed. He was sitting on a rusty wooden rocking chair, looking at the floor. "Excuse me, sir?" The man looked up.

"Howdy. It's you again." He got up from the chair.

"It's okay. Please have a seat," I said.

"All righty then, young lady." He sat back down. "Who are these other two beautiful young ladies you've brought with you?"

"Oh, these are my best friends, Mackenzie and Meg."

"Awesome! And what brings all of you here?" he asked.

I replied, "Well, I kind of wanted to apologize for making you upset. I was just in a big hurry to find my brother. But now my best friends have got the situation under control, so I'm a bit relaxed," I said, looking at Mackenzie and Meg.

"Oh, ho-ho-ho! No need to apologize. I wasn't upset at all," the man replied. I smiled.

Meg said, "Well, Sameera was wondering if we could all come to your house like you wanted her to."

"Of course you can! I just need to pick up something from the fortune shop, and then we can go," the man said. I rolled my eyes.

Mackenzie said, "What do you need from the shop, sir?"

"Oh, just a little something for my niece. It's her birthday tomorrow," the man replied.

I sighed. "There are so many other gift shops here. You can buy something from one of them."

The man shook his head. "No, no, no. I don't want any ordinary gifts. I'm going to get something special for her. I'm going to get her a fortune from the dream machine."

"Well, guess whose birthday is going to turn upside down tomorrow?" I murmured to myself loud enough for the others to hear.

"Excuse me?" the man said.

"Uh … well, I was just thinking … can you get your niece something else? Does it have to be from the dream machine?"

"Sameera, what is your problem? Why do you care what he gives his niece? It's *his* niece, not yours," Meg said.

"I know, I know. I'm just helping him out. I don't want his niece's heart to be broken once she figures out that these fortunes mean nothing more than pieces of paper with words on them."

The man laughed and told Mackenzie and Meg, "This girl has been opposed to the dream machine since I met her."

"Yeah, Sameera. Don't be like that. Let him give whatever he thinks will make his niece happy," Mackenzie said.

The man said, "My niece really loves fortunes. You know, she's gotten three great fortunes before. It made her so happy."

"But what if this fortune makes her upset?" I asked.

"Sameera, just let it go. It doesn't matter. You're not here to argue, are you? We want to go to the man's house. So let's not waste time. Let the man go and get his gift quickly," Meg said as her eyebrows shot up.

I nodded slowly.

"Sir, you can go and get your gift. We'll wait out here for you," Meg said.

"Are you sure you don't want to come in with me? There are some really nice things in the shop. Maybe you guys could get some fortunes too," the man suggested.

I got annoyed. "No. I told you, the fortunes are fake!"

"All right then, young lady. Don't come in then. Any of you girls want to come?" the man asked.

"I'll come!" Mackenzie replied. "I haven't seen this shop before. It looks interesting."

"Indeed, it is. Come on! I'll get my gift. You can look around or get a fortune," the man suggested.

"What are you doing, Mackenzie?" I said.

"What?"

"You're a crazy girl. Seriously? You're going into that shop?" I said.

"You know, this is the highlight of this city. A lot of people come here just for this shop," the man replied. His southern accent began to really get on my nerves.

"Let Mackenzie go if she wants to. Stop controlling everyone and everything," Meg demanded. "Sir, please, you can go with Mackenzie. You don't need Sameera's permission."

"By the way, my name is Toby Rhodes," the man said, and he and Mackenzie went into the shop.

I sat down on the rocking chair. Meg walked closer to me and sat down on the other rocking chair. "Why were you being such a fortune shop police?"

I looked up at her slowly. She held my gaze for a few seconds, and then she let go of eye contact. "The shop is fine, but the stupid dream machine isn't. It doesn't work. I've tried it before," I blurted out.

"What if it didn't work for you? That doesn't mean that it fails on everyone else. Maybe that is your fate, Sameera. Failure," Meg said.

"How dare you say that? I thought you were my best friend. Why would you call my fate a failure?" I asked.

"Well, because that's how it seems to be. Selfishness causes failure," Meg said confidently. I was so shocked by what Meg said. *I am not selfish. That's why I came all the way to this city looking for my brother in the first place. I care about him. I care about my mother too.* I tried calling my mom to see where she was or if she figured anything out, but she was unreachable.

Soon Mackenzie and Mr. Rhodes came out of the shop. "Ah, there's a nice breeze outside. Are we ready to go to my house?" he asked.

Meg and I slowly nodded, not looking at each other. Mackenzie said, "Look! I got a fortune." Neither of us said anything. "Is everything all right?" she asked. I nodded. "Oh, I see. You guys are just jealous that I got the fortune, and you didn't. Well, I guess I'll just keep it to myself and test it out to see if it comes true." Mackenzie put the piece of paper in her pocket.

"Ready? Follow me," Mr. Rhodes said and started walking. Mackenzie followed him. Apparently, Meg and I had gotten into a fight, so neither of us said anything and just walked. He led us through a path of beautiful trees and grazing grass. I looked down at the ground and saw a lot of stones shaped differently and colored as well. I saw some animals along the way, such as cows and sheep but in a barn. The wind started blowing faster, and the sun finally started to shine brighter.

CHAPTER 15

Toby Rhodes finally got us to his home, which seemed to look like an old hotel. The man seemed to love rocking chairs and had two on his front porch. "Sir, does anyone live with you?" Mackenzie asked.

The man said, "Well, my wife used to live with me, but she passed away a couple of years ago."

"Oh, that's sad," Mackenzie said.

"Indeed, it is, but I've been trying to get through my life without her. She used to take care of me so well. It's … hard, but I've been getting by." The man almost sobbed.

"Sorry. I'm sorry for making you cry."

"It's all right! It feels good to get my emotions out like this occasionally."

Mr. Rhodes climbed up the wooden stairs to his porch and unlocked the door. The three of us walked in. He took us to what looked like the living room. There were two rusty couches and a small-screen TV against the wall. "Please have a seat. Make yourself at home." Mackenzie sat on one of the big couches, and I sat down beside her. Meg sat on the small couch across from us. The man asked, "What would you like to eat or drink?"

"I would like some cold cider if you have any," Mackenzie replied.

"Of course! And anything for you girls?" Meg and I shook our heads without saying a word. "All right then. I'll go get you your cold cider. Feel free to look around," he said and went to the kitchen.

It was quiet for a few seconds, and then Mackenzie said, "So are you guys interested in touring this place?" Meg and I shrugged. Mackenzie said, "Come on! Say something. It's not like you guys are doing a silence course, is it?" We both nodded. Mackenzie hit her forehead and said, "Seriously? You guys can't do this to me."

"Why not?" Meg asked.

"Because I can't live peacefully if you guys don't ever speak to me," Mackenzie replied.

I finally said, "Well, I can talk to you, but we're not on a talking basis right now."

"Who? You and Meg?" Mackenzie said.

We nodded.

"Oh, come on! It's about the fortune shop, isn't it? We're best friends, and I get it that sometimes we have grudges, but you guys have literally been fighting and upsetting each other all day. Just grow up and get it together already. Apologize to each other and reunite. As simple as that." Meg and I just looked at each other and smirked.

Mr. Rhodes came back into the room with a glass of cider and a plate of cookies. He set it on the table and said, "Help yourself to some homemade cookies. I made them myself." He seemed very proud of his homemade cookies.

"Sure, I'll try them!" Mackenzie exclaimed.

"And here's your cold cider. Enjoy!"

"Thank you so much, Mr. Rhodes."

"No problem. You can call me Toby if you'd like."

"So what's going on in your lives?" he asked.

"Nothing much. You?" Mackenzie asked, being the lead speaker for the three of us.

"Oh me? You really want to ask about me? I can tell you all kinds of stories from my childhood to the present," the man said.

"I don't think we have time for that. I really need to get home. My mom might be home now. She must be worried about me," I said.

Meg smirked at me and said, "Well, I need to get home too. I've been roaming around with a fool all day."

"Hey! I get it. I can be dumb and stupid sometimes, but that does not make me a fool," Mackenzie replied.

Meg rolled her eyes. "I'm not talking about you, Mackenzie. There's another girl in this room who has completely ruined my day," Meg said, hinting at me.

"Whoa, whoa, whoa. Did you ladies get into a fight?" Toby asked.

Mackenzie giggled. "No … no. It's just a small misunderstanding between Meg and Sameera. It can be resolved very easily. We just need a few seconds to clear up the misunderstanding."

"Oh, misunderstandings, huh? Those happen sometimes. Do you guys want me to show you around the house?" he asked.

Mackenzie replied, "Well, that would be nice, but I'm waiting until my friends make up so we can explore together."

"Ugh! I don't even care. I'm gonna go and wait in the taxi," Meg said and got up.

"She seems so annoyed, doesn't she?" Toby said. I nodded.

"Wait … Meg! I'm coming with you. Sameera, take your time. We'll be waiting in the taxi for you." Mackenzie got up and left. It would've been nice to leave with my friends, but I had promised the man I would spend some time there, so I decided to stay a little while longer so I didn't seem rude.

I just sat there looking side to side, and some unique paintings caught my attention. One painting depicted a river flowing from a lake while being encircled by extremely thick grass. People were gathered on each side of the river. They were painted entirely in black, which was unusual. They resembled figures in a shadow. Even though they all had somewhat different shapes, it was clear they were all guys. There were five males standing on the river's upper left bank. There were four males on the river's bottom right side. The males appeared to be attempting to cross to the other side on each side. They appeared worn out and afraid. The only way to reach that safe location, where it appeared they were sheltering, was to cross the river.

Toby said, "So tell me a little about yourself."

I responded, "Me? There's really nothing special about me. I'm Sameera Chacko, and I guess I like adventures, but not to the point that someone I love goes missing."

"Wait … back up. What was that you said again?"

I repeated, "That I like adventures?"

"No, before that."

"My name is Sameera Chacko."

"Yes! That's it!"

"Yeah, what's so special about my name?" I asked.

He replied, "Chacko. I'm sure I've heard that last name somewhere. Hmm …" The man rubbed his head and thought for a while.

"I'm sure there are people out there with the same last name as me," I said, but he shushed me.

"No, no. There's someone else I had a connection with. Ahh! got it! Before I retired, I used to work with a businessman named Sabal Chacko."

"Oh cool," I said.

"But he left the company before me."

"Wow!" I remarked.

"So do you have a relationship with him in any way?" Toby asked.

"Not that I know of," I replied.

"Oh really? You look just like him. Let me tell you something about him. He is a man made of gold. If you ever meet him, oh my gosh. He's just a great man to work with. He's the reason why I am here in this condition today. He's the reason I went from poor to how I'm living right now. You know, I was homeless before I met him. He found me near the dumps one day when he was doing an environment project, and he felt bad for my condition. At that point, my life changed. He offered for me to do business with him at his company, Consider Chacker. I slowly started gaining enough money to pay off my loans and pay everyone I borrowed from. Well, I left the company after a couple of years, but I was finally able to build this house I have now. Oh, you'll be so lucky if you ever meet him," the man explained.

"Wow! He does seem like a nice guy. Do you know if his company still exists?" I asked.

"Ah, I don't think so. He left after offering for me to take over his company, and I was there for a while but I left after getting another smaller job offer. There is no way I could take care of such a huge business. This was many years ago. I'm sure Sabal would've found another place for his business to grow, and it might be prospering like crazy right now." Toby laughed.

"Yeah, he must be like a billionaire now," I said.

The man nodded. "Yes indeed."

"It's pretty interesting how these people become billionaires," I said and pulled out my phone. I searched *Consider Chacko*. No results.

"Sir, are you lying to me? There's no business called Consider Chacko," I said.

He replied, "Well, that's strange. Maybe he changed his business name as well as his location. But I'm certainly not lying. I'm living proof of that."

"Huh. That's true. What did you say his name was?" I said.

"Sabal Chacko."

I quickly searched that name up. "Wait. He lives in Wisconsin now. And … and …" I clicked on one of the website articles and skimmed through it. "He's in jail?"

"Whoa—what? That's probably fake news," Toby said.

"No! This is a legit website. How can a rich man like that go to jail so soon?" I asked, pointing my phone screen toward him. The man shrugged. I said, "Maybe some fraud happened. His kindness and wealth seemed too good to be true."

"Maybe," Toby said and looked down.

"Anyway, can I use your bathroom really quick?" I asked, changing the topic.

"Of course! The flush is broken for my bathroom downstairs, but no worries. You can use the one upstairs. Come on. I'll show you," he said and got up. I followed him upstairs.

This seemed to be a century-old house. There were simple rooms and two patios, plus a library with a fireplace. He took me upstairs and led me to a small door on the right. "Here's a much better bathroom."

I laughed. "Thank you, Mr. Rhodes."

"I'll be downstairs," he said.

After I used the bathroom, I started moving toward the stairs when an old room on the left side of the hall caught my attention. The door was slightly cracked, and on the door was a wooden sign I couldn't read clearly. The letters on the sign were losing color and seemed tarnished. Something in my body urged me to go toward the room. *Even if it's just a small peek, I'll be satisfied.* I slowly approached the room and pushed the door open slightly. It seemed dusty, and I couldn't see anything clearly. I went farther into the room. It seemed so different compared to some of the other rooms in the house. It almost seemed like I was immersing myself into a world full of memories. I didn't know why this man had a room dedicated to his past, but it sure seemed like this room hadn't been visited in a long time. There was so much dust on all the furniture, and the smell of smoke was so strong. The wallpaper had started peeling off the walls, and I noticed cardboard boxes in almost every corner of the room. I coughed up some dust. I looked around the room, and something caught my eye. A picture inside a heavy golden frame with beautiful embroidery designs. It was a photo of Toby Rhodes and another man wearing a stylish suit at a coffee shop. This picture was from years ago because Toby looked very young. I wondered who the other man was. *Maybe one of Toby's friends.* My hands went through the photo, clearing a lot of the dust. On the bottom of the picture, it read, "Cheers to the man who brought meaning into my life." *What? Who is this man? And why is Toby so fond of him?*

Sabal Chacko.

No, it can't be. How come he is so much like ...

"Sameera?" I heard Toby call from downstairs.

"Uh, yeah ... um, just give me a minute. I'll be out," I shouted back.

"Take your time. No rush. Just wanted to make sure you were okay."

I flipped the photo frame over. There was a letter sticking out from the back of the frame. I pulled out the letter and read it:

> Dear Toby Rhodes,
>
> I'm writing this letter to you because I want to thank you for all your efforts. Ever since you joined my company, the business has only gone up. You've contributed a lot, and I really appreciate it. I did the right thing by choosing a loyal employee like you. To the world, you may seem like a poor man, but to me, you are a rare gem. I'm so glad that I found you and got to know you over the years. Everyone has rough patches in their road, and I've also had mine. But after I met you, everything completely changed. I wanted to let you know that some trouble came up, and I won't be able to stay at this company any longer, so I want you to take over. I'm sorry that I couldn't convey this message to you in person, but I don't have much time right now. This letter is proof that I'm giving you ownership of the company. We may not see each other again, but I'll never forget you, and I hope you never forget me. Best of luck!
>
> —Sabal Chacko

"Oh, hello, girls! Yes, she just went to use the bathroom. She'll be out soon," I heard Toby say. *Mackenzie and Meg must've come back to get me, wondering what's taking me so long.* I quickly hid the letter and the photo. I wanted to take these items with me so I could spend some time learning about these two men, but I realized Toby would notice if his precious things were missing. I quickly took out my phone and snapped a picture of the letter and the photo of the men in the coffee shop.

I went downstairs and heard Mackenzie telling Toby that we were leaving. He said, "Are you sure? You can stay for as long as you want."

"I'm back! My mom is probably waiting at home for me. So I really must go. Thanks for all your kind gestures," I said to him.

"No problem," he said and opened the door.

I quickly ran to the taxi, and Mackenzie and Meg followed me. "Have a great day and stay safe!" Toby shouted from the door. I waved goodbye and got into the front seat of the taxi. Mackenzie and Meg got in the back.

"Come on, driver! Take me home quickly," I said. The driver nodded and started his engine.

After I got home, I paid the driver and ran inside, with Mackenzie and Meg following behind me. When I unlocked the front door, I saw Mom standing by the stairs. "Mom!" I ran up to her and embraced her.

"Sameera, sweetie! Where were you?"

"It's a long story, but I'll shorten it. After you left to search for Sahil, I couldn't just rest at home. I had to do something to help find Sahil. So I called Mackenzie and Meg to come help me. We tried to track Sahil's iPad, but we lost the signal after it showed that he was in Ohert City. I didn't know what to do, so I drove my bike to Ohert City to find him. I looked everywhere and couldn't find him, but I met an old man who was nice enough to let us into his house, so we were there for a while."

"Wait … so you went into another man's house who you don't even know?" Mom asked.

I slowly nodded. "But, Mom, he was really nice, and he told me his story of how he went from poor to middle class."

"Sameera! You can't just go into someone's house who you don't even know. He could've been a dangerous person who was just trying to lure you into his trap."

"I know. I'm sorry, Mom."

"Oh, Sameera. You went through so much despite starting puberty. I told you I could've handled the situation alone." I rolled my eyes.

Meg tapped me and whispered, "It's now or never. Tell her it was a lie before it's too late."

I took a deep breath and said, "I don't have puberty."

"Sweetie. I know you just don't like a lot of attention so you're saying that. It's okay. I understand, and I won't be so touchy anymore. You take it slow."

"Mom! I am serious!"

Mom looked at me, her eyes twitching. She said, "I get it if you don't want to talk about it in front of your friends. But we can talk later."

"I'm not joking. Even they know it. I don't have puberty."

"Okay, sweetie. Whatever you say."

"Anyway, Mom, any news about Sahil?" I asked, changing the topic.

Mom opened her mouth to speak, but Meg said, "Sameera, I must go now. I just realized I have a baking class in an hour."

"I must go too. I was supposed to babysit my cousins today," Mackenzie said.

I replied, "You guys can go now. We'll handle it from here. Thank you so much for your help."

"No problem. Anytime!" Mackenzie said, and they both left.

"So, Mom, about Sahil?"

She responded, "Yes, I know Sahil's whereabouts."

"Tell me everything," I demanded.

"Sweetie, it's not that simple," she said.

"I don't care. I want to know! He's my brother, so I have every right to know," I shouted.

She pointed to the couch. "Let's sit down. I'll try to explain."

We both sat down on the couch to talk. Mom took a deep breath.

"Where is Sahil? Is he mad at me? Is that why he ran away? I'm so sorry for yelling at him. I'll apologize, I promise. Please bring him back!"

"Cool down, Sameera. I said I'll explain. Why are you so impatient?"

"Sorry. I'm just worried. Go on," I said.

She said, "I understand how you feel. All I can say is he is in safe hands. He's with your dad."

I was so shocked. "Who?"

"Your father," she said. I just stared. "Mr. Troop."

"I know who you're talking about, but why is he there?" I asked.

She put one of her hands on my shoulder. "Sometimes one needs their father's love to live."

"Oh my gosh, Mom. Stop beating around the bush. Just tell me clearly already!" I said.

"I don't know much either. Sahil called earlier and told me that he went to meet his father," she replied.

"By himself?"

"Well, no. He said he was with his friend Carson earlier, and he went with him. Don't worry. A parent guardian was with him."

"He went all the way to another state. Without telling you?" I questioned.

"I was very disappointed at first, but Carson's family was traveling to the state that Chris lives in, and he wanted to go. I talked to Carson's parents as well, and they were okay with him tagging along. He missed Dad very much, so I let him go."

"And you just believed him?"

"Of course. He's always honest. Unlike you, who lied about the science posters recently."

"But … but," I started.

"No, Sameera. I trust him. End of discussion." Mom got up from the couch, and then I remembered something.

"Mom, I have another question," I said, and Mom turned around to face me.

"Who is Sabal Chacko?" I asked. Mom froze. I could see her body tensing and her smile fading away. "Mom, I asked you a question."

"Samee … what kind of a ques …? Where did you get that name from?"

"You answer me first," I demanded.

Mom replied, "I don't know. Okay? You find a random name and ask me who that is. How would I know?"

I got up from the couch and stood facing her, staring directly into her eyes. "Businessman Sabal Chacko. He had a business called Consider Chacko. Does that ring a bell?"

Mom looked up. "I don't know who you are talking about. Where did you get all this … this fake information from?" She looked at me again.

"Remember that old man I was talking about earlier. Uh … what was his name? Oh yes, Toby Rhodes. When I went to his house, I learned about Sabal Chacko. Mr. Rhodes went from poor to middle class after joining that business. Here. I'll show you a photo. Then maybe you'll remember." I pulled out my phone to show Mom the picture I took from the house of the two men at the coffee shop.

"What is this, Sameera? First you go into a random man's house, and then you learn about another … random man, and you ask me who that is? I can't waste time right now. I … I have a lot of work to do in the kitchen. Go upstairs and do your work," Mom said and went to the kitchen.

I stood there looking at the photo on my phone. "Sabal Chacko. Sabal Chacko. Sabal Chacko," I kept repeating to myself.

"Sameera, what nonsense is this? I thought I told you to go to your room," Mom said from the kitchen. I glanced at her and then walked upstairs staring at my phone. I went to my room and closed the door.

CHAPTER 16

I sat on my bed thinking for a while, and then I got a text message from an unknown number:

"Hello there, Sameera! How have you been?"

"What the heck?" I said.

I texted, "Who is this?"

Unknown: *typing …*

They were typing for a while, so I put my phone down and said, "Someone is trying to waste my time. I'm not falling for it. I'm gonna go work on something." I got up, sat at my desk, and opened my laptop. Just then, my phone buzzed.

Unknown: "I'm not trying to waste your time, but I know something."

Wait … did they just hear what I said about wasting my time? Uh … a little creepy.

Me: "About what?"

Unknown: "Sameera, I'm sorry."

Me: "What? Who even is this? How do you know my name?"

Unknown: "I shouldn't have done what I did, but I did learn some very crucial information."

Me: "Oh my gosh. What did you do, and why don't you tell me who you are?"

Unknown: "I can't. At least not now …"

Me: "Why not?"

Unknown: "You'll be angry with me."

Me: "Huh? I don't even know who you are, so how could I be angry?"

Unknown: "I'll tell you all that later, but please listen to me. Don't go anywhere or do anything. Whatever you're worried about right now will ease up. I'm telling you, just hang in there. The solution to your problem will arrive soon."

Me: "How do you know I'm worried?"

Unknown: "I know because I'm ..."

Unknown: "Never mind."

Me: "Tell me."

No reply.

Me: "Hello? Are you still there?"

Me: "Please! Don't leave me hanging like that. I need to know more."

Unknown: "I've said too much already."

Me: "No, you haven't said anything!"

Unknown: "Sorry, but if I say any more, it'll reveal my identity."

Me: "That's okay. Is this some sort of prank?"

Unknown: "Definitely not. Just listen to my advice and don't go anywhere or do anything."

Me: "Why should I listen to some stranger? I'll do what I want when I want and where I want!"

Unknown: "Please don't. You'll face big trouble if you do."

Ugh! What is this person even talking about? I'm so confused. Let me call Meg. I was about to call Meg when I received another text.

Unknown: "One more thing. Don't tell anyone about our conversation. It must be kept private."

Me: "I don't have to listen to you. I will tell my friends about you."

Unknown: "Fine then. Your loss."

Me: "Are you trying to blackmail me?"

Unknown: "I'm being serious. Don't tell anyone."

I didn't know what to do. Should I inform my friends about this stranger? Should I inform my mom? What would happen to me if

I didn't? What loss was this person talking about? How would my worries ease up? I had so many questions running through my mind. Nothing made sense.

"Sameera!" I heard Mom call from downstairs.

"Ah, forget it! I can't tell anyone right now," I said to myself and rushed downstairs. "Uh, yes, Mom? Is everything all right?"

"No! How could everything be all right? You called the cops!"

"Oh shoot. I forgot! I'm sorry, but my friends called them before you told me everything. I thought they would've told you." I felt bad.

She replied, "They didn't. You could've told me. We would've called them and told them you wanted to take back the case. Now they're calling me to ask for more information about Sahil," she said.

"You can tell them to discontinue the mission. You know where Sahil is. We don't need their help anymore," I suggested.

Mom nodded in frustration. "Sameera, Sameera. It's not that easy. You and your friends have created havoc in the police station. You really should've told me about this earlier."

"I'm sorry. I was too tense to think about anything," I told her.

Mom responded, "Let me go deal with this now." She went to the study with the phone and shut the door. I felt bad. *How could I forget that my friends called the police for Sahil? We solved the case of missing Sahil and didn't inform the cops. I just hope they don't send Mom to jail for our mistake.*

After a while, Mom came out of the room. I went up to her and asked, "What happened? You're not going to jail, right?"

"Sweetie. Why would I go to jail?"

"For what we did. I'm so sorry, but you know I would've told you if I remembered," I said.

"Yes, I know, and it's fine. They are willing to let us take back the case."

"Phew! That's good." I sighed in relief.

"Just make sure to tell me next time you do something like that," she said.

"Yes, for sure."

"Anyway, are you busy right now?" she asked. I shook my head. "Great! Can you help me in the kitchen?"

"With what?" I asked.

She replied, "To make dinner."

"Really, Mom? Now?"

"Well, of course. It's getting late. And it's been a long day for us, so it'll be good if we can get to bed soon."

"Fine, I'll help you. What are we making?" I asked.

"Awesome. I'm making some stuffed ravioli with spinach and feta. Help me boil these on the stovetop," she said, handing me a tray of frozen ravioli.

As I was helping Mom with the ravioli, my mind was whirling with so many thoughts. I kept thinking about the unknown person who messaged me. I also thought about how Sahil would be having dinner with Mr. Troop right now. That didn't feel right to me. I felt a little dizzy just trying to imagine that, so I grabbed a glass of water.

"Sameera, are you all right?" Mom asked, always concerned about my well-being. The thing about mothers is that they always work around the clock without any complaints to keep their children happy. They are there to care for you when you need it the most. When it comes down to it, a mother will always be one of the most important people in your life. I really wanted to tell her about the unknown number that messaged me, but I wasn't supposed to tell anyone, and Mom had already had enough tension for the day. "Sameera? I'm talking to you," Mom repeated.

I looked up. "Oh, sorry, and yeah, I'm fine. I was just a little thirsty," I said and continued cooking the ravioli.

"If there's anything you want to talk about, sweetie, we can," she said.

"No, Mom. I'm fine, really," I lied.

"If it's about the police situation, I said it's okay. No need to stress about it anymore. I took care of it." She tried to make me feel better.

"I know, Mom. I'm not worried about that anymore," I said.

"If there's anything else bothering you, sweetie, please let me know."

I nodded and said, "I really miss Sahil."

"I do too, but we must wait. Time is all he needs, and we must give him that. He just wants to spend some time with a father figure, so let it be. Don't worry. He'll be back soon," she assured me.

I said, "Okay. Can we eat now?"

"Go ahead and set the table. I will bring the food," she said.

After dinner, I went straight up to my room. I thought, *If this unknown person knows me, does he know Sahil as well? Will he do any harm to Sahil? Oh no! I must protect him. Wait, but this stranger told me not to go anywhere or not to do anything. Darn it! I'm helpless.*

Just then, I got a call from Mackenzie. *Should I pick it up or not? What if something about the unknown person comes out of my mouth? That's the only thing on my mind right now. No, I can't take the risk.* I declined the call. She called again. I declined again. Then she texted me.

Mackenzie: "Why aren't you picking up my calls?"

I didn't respond.

Mackenzie: "Sameera, is everything okay?"

I still didn't respond.

Mackenzie: "If you don't respond, I'll come to your house."

I couldn't allow that. Talking to her on the phone was going to be hard for me. How would I be able to talk to her in person? I texted back.

Me: "I'm fine, just a little busy."

Mackenzie: "With what? School hasn't even started yet!"

Me: "Why do you care? What do you even want?"

Mackenzie: "Call me."

Oh, I was not going to do that.

Me: "I don't feel like talking right now. Can you just tell me in text?"

Mackenzie: "I wanted to ask about your brother. Did your mom figure out anything about him?"

Me: "Yeah, apparently, he's with Mr. Troop. His friend was traveling, and he wanted to go see his so-called father, so he tagged along."

Mackenzie: "Without telling you and your mom?"

Me: "Yeah, well, we can't do anything about it now. My mom was a little disappointed at first, but then she supported him seeing his dad or whatever, you know?"

Mackenzie: "I can understand, but that's a drastic step, and it would've required a lot of confidence."

Me: "Probably."

Mackenzie: "So what about the cops we called? We must call them at some point and tell them that we know where your brother is."

Me: "Yeah, about that. My mom got a call an hour ago from the police station, so she explained everything and took the case back."

Mackenzie: "Oh, well, that's good."

Me: "Anyway, I feel kinda tired right now because it's been a long day, so I'm gonna go to bed. Good night, Mackenzie."

Mackenzie: "Okay. Good night, Sameera."

I turned off the lights and lay in bed, but the thought of the unknown person wouldn't go away. I needed to know what that person was up to. So I grabbed my phone and sent a message.

Me: "Hey, if you know me, do you know my brother too?"

Unknown: No response.

I put the phone down and closed my eyes. Soon, I drifted into a deep sleep. The next morning when I woke up, I was quite surprised that I slept well despite all my worries. I checked my phone for any new messages from the unknown number, but there was nothing. I was getting worried. I couldn't be kept on a cliff-hanger, so I texted again.

Me: "Hello? Are you there?"

No response.

"Ugh! This person is not letting me do anything or go anywhere. At least respond. Come on, man, I'm gonna start doing something sooner or later. The person can't keep me in control for long," I said to myself. Just then, Mom came in. I quickly swiped out of my messages.

"Good morning, sweetie! You're up early. Didn't get much sleep last night?" she said.

I responded, "I actually slept pretty well."

"Wow, that's amazing. I did too. Since we're up so early, do you want to go out somewhere for breakfast?"

"Yeah, I would love to ..." I began but then remembered that I was not allowed to go anywhere, according to the stranger.

Mom said, "Great. Then where do you want to go?"

"As I was saying, I would love to, but I can't. I ... uh ... I have some work to finish."

"Work? During summer break? Sameera, are you okay?"

"You have a good point, Mom. It is summer break, which means time for me to prepare for high school," I said.

"Why do you want to prepare for high school now? We still have a lot of time left. You'll be fine. Come on. Let's go get breakfast," Mom said.

"No. I want to be prepared and research before selecting my classes," I lied.

Mom stared at me for a moment and then said, "Sweetie, I know you're stressed about Sahil and your father, and so am I. It's a good idea to be outside the house for some time. At least, if you don't want to go anywhere and eat, we can pick up some breakfast from your favorite restaurant and bring it home."

"No, I can't," I began to say and then got a text message. I looked down at my phone, and it was from the unknown person.

"Who is that?" Mom asked.

"Uh ... the text message? Oh, well ... that's from ... Mackenzie. Yup, she just ... said good morning," I lied.

"Hmmm, okay. I'll be in the car waiting for you. I know a good restaurant we can go to." She left the room. I quickly opened my text messages.

Unknown: "Hello. Yes, I am still here."

Me: "Oh my gosh, I was worried."

Unknown: "There's nothing to worry about. I told you, I got you. You don't have to do anything."

Me: "Answer my previous message about my brother. Do you know him?"

Unknown: *typing …*

Me: "What?"

Unknown: "Yes, I know him."

Me: "How? You'd better not mess with him the way you're messing with me."

Unknown: "No worries, I won't. I know how much he means to you."

I went downstairs, put on my shoes, and joined Mom in the car. I wasn't going to let the unknown person mess with me or give me fear. "Are you finally ready?" she asked.

"Yup! Where are we going?" I asked.

"You'll see," Mom said and started the engine.

"Mom! I don't want any surprises; I've had way too much of that already."

"What do you mean?" she asked.

"I mean, I've had enough shocks and surprises about Sahil. I don't want any more of it. Just tell me where we are going," I said.

"Okay. We're going to Big Waffles. You can get anything you want from there."

"That's a pretty good place," I said, and my phone buzzed. I looked down to see a message from the unknown person.

Unknown: "You must do something for me."

Oof! I knew this moment was coming. Strangers that say they've got your back don't do things for you without you doing something for them.

Me: "What?"

Unknown: *typing …*

"Who's texting you?" Mom asked.

I hid my messages. "It's Ma … Mackenzie," I lied.

"What does she want?"

I made up something on the spot. "Um, she is, like, concerned about me—you know? After what happened yesterday. She and Meg want updates on Sahil and how I am doing."

"Okay, but this was meant for us to get our minds off all that. If you're still talking about that, then that defeats the whole purpose of going out for breakfast," she said.

"That's true. I'll put my phone away now," I said, and then my phone buzzed again. I looked at it.

Unknown: "Don't tell your mom this, but I know about your real father and where he is."

I was shocked and froze. I told this person not to mess with my brother, so was he going to mess with my father, whoever he was?

"Sameera, what happened to putting your phone away?" Mom asked.

I replied, "I know. Let me just tell Mackenzie that I'm outside now and can't talk." I texted the unknown person.

Me: "Stop texting me. My mom is right next to me, and she will get suspicious. Tell me more later."

As I put my phone away, my mom pulled into the parking lot of Big Waffles. The place looked a lot different than I remembered it. When we went in, I saw a lot of the renovations. Big Waffles had large, mullioned windows, long embroidered curtains, dark walnut tables with flowers on each table, delicate live piano music, a flagstone tile floor, and a lounge area with embroidered couches and tea served from silver trays in white teapots. One waiter approached us. "How many?"

"Just the two of us," Mom replied.

"Follow me," the waiter said and led us to a table.

"Wow, this place looks so fancy!" I said.

"Yes, we've remodeled this place. What can I get started for you?" he asked, handing us menus.

"I'll take a cup of black coffee," Mom said.

I added, "I'll take some orange juice."

The waiter took out a notepad and wrote down our orders. "Be right back with those," he said and left.

My phone buzzed again, but I didn't look at it. Even though I knew it was from the unknown person and it was tempting, I couldn't make Mom suspicious of me. I kept staring at my menu even though I'd been there before and knew exactly what I wanted to eat. Mom said, "So, Sameera, what do you want to do today?"

"Um, nothing much. I'll probably just read some books and research high school," I said, not meaning it.

She replied, "Well, that's not like you at all. Since your brother is spending time with Dad, I thought we could have a mother-daughter day. We could go and get a mani-pedi done and then spend the day at the mall, shopping, watching movies, and getting some ice cream. It'll be fun. What do you say?"

"No, I don't want to do all that," I replied.

Mom frowned. "Something has changed about you. What's with this new behavior?"

I looked around for ideas but couldn't think of anything.

Then the waiter arrived with our drinks. "Here you are, ladies. One black coffee and one orange juice. What else can I get for you?"

"I'll take a Nutella crepe with whipped cream and strawberries," I said.

Mom looked at the menu and said, "Hmmm, I want to try something new, so I'll take the cinnamon roll French toast."

The waiter scribbled on his notepad and said, "It'll be fifteen minutes."

"That's fine. We can wait," Mom said, and the waiter left. It was quiet for some time, and all I could hear was the melodious piano music and some voices from other tables. I don't think Mom wanted to talk after I said I didn't want to do mother-daughter day. "I'll just go wash my hands and use the restroom," Mom said and got up. When she was gone, I knew it was my chance to use my phone. I pulled up my messages.

Unknown: "Your father is not who you think he is. The man pretends to be your father."

Me: "What are you saying? Mr. Troop is not my father?"

Unknown: "No, he's not. That's what I wanted to talk about."

Me: "Wait … how do you know this? Stop spying on my life."

Unknown: "I'm not spying on your life. It's my life too."

Me: "I don't understand."

Unknown: *typing …*

Me: "Why aren't you saying anything? How can my father be a part of your life?"

Unknown: "Chris Troop is not your father. That's all I can say now."

Me: "Why should I believe you?"

Unknown: "Trust me. I know."

Me: "Fine. Then who is my father?"

Unknown: *typing …*

Unknown: *typing …*

Unknown: *typing …*

Then Mom came back. I quickly hid my phone from her. She sat down across from me at the table without saying anything. She didn't look at me. I knew she wanted me to apologize to her and say that mother-daughter day was on, but I wasn't going to do that. Instead, I said, "Mom, can you tell me something?"

She looked up.

"Who's my real father?" I asked.

Mom's eyes got wide. "What? You already know. Chris Troop."

"He isn't my real father," I said confidently.

"Sameera, just because he's not here doesn't mean he's not your father. You're jealous of Sahil, aren't you? Well, if you really want, we can go all the way to California to meet h—"

I interrupted. "He isn't Sahil's father either. I don't know where Sahil is now, but I doubt he's with Mr. Troop."

"Sameera, stop! Just stop it! Enough with this behavior," Mom screamed, and everyone around us stopped what they were doing to look at us.

"Mom, lower your voice," I whispered.

Mom got irritated. "Why should I? Huh? You're falsely accusing your brother of being somewhere else and asking me to lower my voice. Don't try to change the truth. Chris Troop is your father, and Sahil is with him now! End of discussion." I didn't say anything. "You know what? Forget mother-daughter day! You're grounded!"

CHAPTER 17

The ride home from Big Waffles was quiet. After the chaos at the restaurant, neither of us wanted to speak. When I got home, I knew what to do. I went straight to my room and closed the door. Thankfully, Mom didn't take my phone away. I could still get updates from the unknown number. Then Meg texted.

Meg: "Sameera, how's it going?"

Me: "My mom grounded me for some stupid reason. I asked her a simple question, 'Who is my real father?' She's the one who raised her voice and created chaos, and then she grounds me?"

Meg: "OMG! That's horrible! But don't you know your real father already?"

Me: "No. Mr. Troop is not my real father. He can't be."

Meg: "How do you know?"

Me: "Because someone told me."

I stopped right there. I couldn't say anymore without revealing the unknown person.

Meg: "Who is someone?"

Meg: "Just because some random person tells you that he's not your father, you believe them?"

Me: "No, it's not a random person. I have a connection with them."

Meg: "Like how?"

Me: "You know what? Just leave it. It's my problem. I'm grounded, so I can't do anything anyway."

Meg: "Sameera, if you need anything, please call me."

Me: "Sure. Thank you, Meg."

I texted the unknown person again.

Me: "Tell me who my freakin' father is! I got grounded for asking my mom that question."

Unknown: "Oh, I didn't mean to get you grounded."

Unknown: "You shouldn't have told your mom. I told you to keep our conversation private."

Me: "I didn't tell my mom about you or what we talked about. I just asked her that simple question."

Unknown: "Still ... you shouldn't have said anything. I'm trying to keep you out of trouble."

Me: "No, you aren't! You're getting me into more trouble!"

Unknown: "It may seem like that right now. You'll thank me later."

Me: "I don't think so."

Me: "Just tell me who you are already!"

Unknown: "I can't do that so soon."

Me: "Fine. At least get me out of this mess. Tell me how I can be ungrounded."

Unknown: "I'm sorry, but I don't know. That's up to you."

"Ugh! This person is driving me insane," I said to myself. Mom knocked on the door. I quickly swiped out of my messages and put my phone under my blankets. "Come in."

Mom came in and said, "One more thing. While you're grounded, you're not allowed to have your phone with you. Hand me your phone."

"No, Mom. I can't. I need my phone," I said.

"Sweetie, you're just like any other teenage girl. It's not like you're going to call someone to come save you. Hand it to me now!" Mom demanded.

Oh no! What if Mom sees my conversation with the unknown number? She might ground me for longer. "Mom, I won't even use my phone. Please, just let it stay in my room."

"Sameera! The phone, *now*!" Mom yelled, reaching her hand out.

I'll have to see where she's hiding it and steal it back. I grabbed my phone from underneath the blankets and handed it to mom. "Aha. I see. You were trying to hide the phone from my sight. Oh, Sameera, I'm your mother. You can't fool me," Mom said, and she left my room with my phone. I slowly went near the door and peeked to see where Mom was taking my phone. She was going toward Sahil's room. "Sameera, I know you're there. Go back inside," Mom said without looking back. I quickly went inside.

"Now what? She has my phone. I can't contact anyone. I guess I'll just have to wait until Mom goes downstairs, and then I'll sneak into Sahil's room," I said to myself.

After a few minutes of sitting on my bed staring at the wall, I peeked out of my room. The coast was clear, so I tiptoed to Sahil's room. After I got inside, I shut the door and began searching for my phone. I looked everywhere but couldn't find it. "I'm pretty sure I saw Mom going toward Sahil's room. She must've hidden it somewhere here." I forgot one place, and that was underneath Sahil's bed. I bent down to look under his bed, and there it was—not my phone but the glowing liquid I had seen under there earlier. I grabbed the bottle of glowing liquid and held it up to my eyes. "What is this?" Before I could proceed any further, I heard a phone ringing. The ringtone sounded familiar. "That's my phone! It's somewhere here." I placed the liquid on the floor and began following the noise outside Sahil's room. I followed the noise all the way to Mom's room. I opened the drawer on the nightstand, and there my phone was. I tapped on the screen. There were no new messages, but there was a phone call from the unknown number. *Why did they call me? Maybe it is time to find out this person's identity. I must call back, but not in Mom's room.* I quickly took the phone and went to my room.

I went to the unknown person's contact information and was about to click the call button when I heard a bunch of pots clash and fall downstairs. I put the phone down and rushed downstairs. I saw Mom standing in the kitchen, staring at her phone on the table, in shock. "Mom, are you okay?" Mom shook her head. "What happened? Why are you staring at your phone like that?"

Mom came up to me and put her hands on my shoulder. "Sameera, I don't know how to tell you this, but Sahil—" she started.

I interrupted. "What? What happened to Sahil?"

"He's not with Chris," Mom said.

My mouth opened. *I knew something was fishy from the moment Mom told me Sahil was with Mr. Troop. I mean, it seemed too good to be true.* I asked, "How did you find out?"

"Sweetie, Chris just called to check how we were all doing, and I asked to speak to Sahil. He told me that Sahil didn't even go over there."

"He lied to us! Where did he go then?" I asked.

Mom shook her head with tears rolling down her cheeks. "I don't know anymore. I tried to call Carson's parents, but they are unreachable. This whole time, I was in the belief that Sahil was safe with Chris, but I was wrong. It was my mistake. I should've at least called Chris when Sahil mentioned he was there. It's all my fault." Mom sat on the table and hit her forehead.

"Mom, stop! Don't do that to yourself. We'll find Sahil," I assured her.

"I'm so tired of hearing that! We're not able to find him. Oh God, where's my son?" My mom put her hands up to her face.

I had an idea. *The unknown number. The person said they knew Sahil. He must've done something. No! I warned him not to go near my brother.* "I'll be right back, Mom," I said and headed upstairs.

"Where are you going, sweetie?" she asked, but I ignored her.

I took my phone and immediately called the unknown number. They didn't pick up. *This is so annoying.* I texted them.

Me: "Where is my brother?"

Unknown: *typing* ...

Me: "Answer me!"

Unknown: "Why are you asking me? How would I know?"

Me: "I know you have him. Let go of him. I'm willing to do anything."

Unknown: "Anything?"

Me: "Well ... yes. It's my brother we're talking about."

Unknown: "I'm telling you, I don't have him."

Me: "Stop lying! I'm gonna call the cops and tell them about you."

Unknown: "Do whatever, but you'll just be getting yourself into more trouble."

Me: "I don't even care anymore. I'm gonna ask my mom to call the cops."

Unknown: "Okay, fine. Your loss."

Unknown: "Also, do you want to meet your dad or not?"

Me: "Seriously? My brother is in trouble, and you're making up some stories about my father so that I get distracted. I can't believe you!"

Unknown: "Come on, Sameera! Your brother is completely fine. Just listen to me. Meet me at Madison County Prison. You can meet your biological father there."

Me: "Are you kidding me?"

Unknown: "I'm not. Geesh! What is it going to take to convince you?"

Me: "Revealing your identity."

Unknown: "Um ... not just yet. Also, bring your mom with you. She needs to be taught a lesson."

Me: "I'm sorry, but I can't let you harm my mom."

Unknown: "I won't! I'm just trying to help you."

Me: "How?"

Unknown: *typing* ...

Unknown: *typing* ...

I put my phone down and lay in my bed for some time, staring at the ceiling. I didn't know what Mom was up to. Neither did I know what I was going to do now. I closed my eyes, trying to escape from reality, hoping this unknown person would just disappear and my brother could come back. I think I fell asleep because the next thing I heard was, "Sameera, sweetie. Wake up. You've been asleep for a couple of hours."

I slowly rubbed my eyes and allowed them to focus. I sat up on my bed and looked around. Mom said, "What have you been doing? You said you'd be right back, and it's been a couple of hours. Are you okay? You said you slept well last night. How come you're falling asleep again?"

"Sorry. I think it's just the stress," I replied.

Mom sat down next to me on the bed. "Aw, I know how you feel about Sahil. I feel the same way. We … we'll figure something … oh, who am I kidding? I don't know what to do. I've been thinking and thinking, and I'm ashamed to say that I have no idea how to find Sahil."

"It's okay, Mom. I'll find a way. We'll find Sahil soon," I assured her.

"You're so optimistic, sweetie, but I don't think it's that easy," Mom replied.

"I know it isn't, but we can't give up. Sahil is a part of our family, and we can't rest without finding him."

"Then what do you say we do?" Mom asked.

I smirked. "Well, there's no point of doing anything because I'm grounded anyway." Mom took a deep breath. "Oh, forget all that! I'm ungrounding you. Anything to find Sahil."

"Really?" I asked.

"Yes, and you can have your phone too. I'll go get it for you," Mom said and got up.

"Actually, I got it already." I held up my phone.

"Samee … where did you find that?" Mom asked.

"Sorry, but I just had to. After you left, I sneaked into your room and got it." I looked down, feeling a little ashamed.

"You went behind my back! I … I'm tired of controlling you. You won't even listen to me. I take my words back. You're still grounded! I'll figure out a way to find your brother, and once I find him, I'll tell him how disobedient you are." Mom left the room. I'd never seen her so angry, but I understood her emotions. I wasn't cooperating with her, and Sahil wasn't either. It is not easy being a parent, especially being a single one. But I couldn't give up. Even if I was grounded, I'd stay in my room and find a solution.

I thought about what the unknown person had said. Madison County Prison. I scurried over to my desk, opened my laptop, and searched Madison County Prison on the internet. There was a map that showed exactly where that was located and how to get there from my location. *Why, though? Why does this person want me to go to some jail? To meet my biological father. The person said it's not Mr. Troop, and I don't even feel like Mr. Troop is my biological father. Who is my real father?* I looked around in desperation for ideas in my room, but there was nothing. *Why doesn't Mom just tell me the truth?* Then I heard a ding. It was from my phone. It was the unknown person again.

Unknown: "I'm sorry for running away."

"No way!" I exclaimed. I knew who this was, and I was not happy about it, but I decided to play along until the person revealed themself.

Me: "What are you talking about?"

Unknown: "You know what I'm talking about."

Me: "Maybe I do, maybe I don't, but if you don't tell me, I'm blocking this number. You're wasting my time."

Unknown: "Geesh, Sameera. You know who I am."

Me: "Where did you say you are right now?"

Unknown: "Well, I'm in Wisconsin. About to head to Madison County Jail to meet my biological father. Are you coming?"

Me: "I knew it! This whole time, it was you! Whose phone is this anyway?"

Unknown: "My friend Carson's. My iPad ran out of charge, and I forgot the charger at home."

Me: "Why did you do this to me and Mom? You know how much we were worried about you. Why didn't you tell me in the first place that it was you?"

Unknown: "I know you have a lot of questions, and I have a lot of explanations. But right now, I don't have time to answer all that. If you want to come here, then come, and we can talk."

Me: "I can't right now. I'm grounded. Plus, even if Mom and I leave now, we won't be able to reach there before dark."

Unknown: "That's okay. Carson and I can wait for you."

Me: "I don't understand. Mr. Troop is not my biological father. Then who is?"

Unknown: "Only one way to find out."

Me: "Call me."

Unknown: "Why?"

Me: "Just do it. My hands are getting tired of typing."

Unknown: "Then don't text anymore. You know what to do. Call me after you reach Madison."

Me: "Wait, but how do I convince Mom without revealing that we're going to meet our biological father?"

No response.

Me: "Hello? Sahil? Are you still there?"

Unknown: "That's up to you. Also, one more thing. There's a small vial of glowing liquid under my bed. Bring that with you. Do not open it or mess with it in any way. Just put it in your bag and don't take it out till you see me. See you soon!"

Me: "Wait, what? What the heck is that?"

No response.

"Ugh! My life is over! Sahil, Sahil, I can't believe this mess you've created. Mom won't buy anything I say anymore. I guess there's nothing else to do but give it a try." I went downstairs to talk to Mom. She was sitting on the living room couch with her back facing me. I sat down next to her on the couch. I knew this was going to be a tough conversation, but I came straight to the point. "Mom, we have to go to Wisconsin." Mom didn't say anything. Instead, she was shaking her head back and forth. "Mom?" I said again.

"No, Sameera, we're not going anywhere," she replied without looking at me.

"Please! We must go. It's very important."

"You're grounded, so you can't go anywhere," she said.

I kept quiet. *There's no way she'll agree to come unless I tell her the truth.* I wasn't going to tell her about meeting my biological father, but I would tell her about Sahil.

"Here's why I want to go to Wisconsin. Because Sahil is there!"

Mom finally turned around to look at me, her eyes wide.

"Yes, you heard me right. Sahil texted me, and he said he's somewhere near Madison County Prison."

"What! Prison! No!" Mom screamed.

"No, Mom, he's not in prison. He's near it. He's too young to go to prison anyway."

"When did he text you? I want to speak to him," Mom said.

"He won't speak now. He didn't even speak to me when I asked him to call. He wants us to meet him there. We have to go now."

"How can we go now, Sameera?" Mom asked.

"Just book a flight or something," I suggested.

"We can't book a flight today and leave today. That's just not how it works," Mom explained.

"Ugh! Then let's just … um, drive. Okay?"

"Drive? You know how long it takes to get from here to Wisconsin in a car?"

I nodded. "Yes. I searched. It's long, but we can drive nonstop."

"Sameera, just listen to yourself. We can't drive nonstop for seventeen hours with me being the only driver."

"That's true. How about we ask Mackenzie's and Meg's moms to help us get there?" I said.

Mom thought for a second. "That does seem like a good idea. Three moms to tackle a seventeen-hour drive. But I really don't think they should get involved in our family matter. I mean, we don't even know what happened to Sahil."

"Then what do we do? Do you care about your son or not?"

Mom replied, "Of course I do, but this is just so sudden, and without planning, it's going to be tough."

"Please, Mom, I want to see Sahil and also my bio—" I began to say but then stopped myself.

"And your what?" Mom asked.

"Nothing. Just see Sahil."

Mom sighed. "First of all, how did he text you? And second, why is he in Wisconsin and not in California with Chris like he told me?"

"He texted me through his friend's phone. Carson is with him too. And why he is in Wisconsin, I don't know. But the only way to find out is to go there," I said.

"We will go there, Sameera—we have to—but I just don't know how," Mom said.

"Mackenzie and Meg are my best friends, and best friends are supposed to help each other. They are willing to help me anytime. We'll return the favor, maybe buy them food, and I'm sure we'll think of other things on the way. I promise."

"Fine. I guess they are our last hope. Right now, it's 11:00 a.m., so if we drive for seventeen hours with breaks in between, we'll probably reach there by tomorrow morning, maybe around five or six. Sounds fine. I'll contact them," Mom said. I smiled.

After Mom contacted them, she said, "All right, let's pack our stuff and pick them up. They're in."

"What do we pack?" I asked.

"Just pack everything you need. We don't know how long we're going to be there," Mom said.

I went upstairs and put half of my wardrobe into my duffel bag. I also packed some necessities, such as toothbrush, toothpaste, hairbrush, shampoo, and towel. I sneaked into Sahil's room, took the glowing liquid vial, and put it in my bag like he wanted. *I wish I knew what this was. Probably something he saved from his stupid chemical kitchen.* I zipped up my duffel bag and rushed downstairs. "Mom, I'm ready to go," I said.

"Great. So am I. I pulled the minivan out into the driveway. Get in there, and I'll be there in a minute."

I took my stuff, put on my most comfortable shoes, threw my stuff in the trunk of the minivan, and got into the front seat. Mom followed right behind. We drove to Meg's house first and picked up Meg and her mom. "Sameera, is everything all right?" Meg asked as she got in.

I replied, "I'll tell you guys everything on the way. Let's pick up Mackenzie now."

Meg and her mom got into the second row of the minivan. Then we picked up Mackenzie and her mom. They got into the third row of the minivan. "Are we all ready to go?" My mom asked.

"Yes!" we all shouted. "Off to Madison we go."

"What exactly happened?" Mackenzie asked. I told them everything—about Sahil. Not about my biological father, because Mom was right there. I had to keep that part to myself until we got there.

CHAPTER 18

After driving for about four hours straight, my mom pulled over at the Amoco gas station. While she was filling up the gas on the minivan, Mackenzie, Meg, and I went into the store to grab some snacks for the duration of the road trip. We grabbed some chips, cookies, sodas, candies, and fruit snacks. By the time we got back, Mom was done filling the gas. Meg's mom was sitting in the driver's seat. and my mom was sitting in the passenger seat, so Meg and I got into the second row. As Meg's mom started the car, we passed out the snacks to everyone. "Wow, are you guys trying to load up on calories here?" Mackenzie's mom asked.

"No, Mom. The store only had these kinds of snacks," Mackenzie said.

My mom said, "There's no need for junk food right now. This is not some fun trip. Okay, girls?"

"We know, Mom. We just got something to satisfy our hunger. Didn't know it had to be healthy," I said.

"Well then, it's better to eat nothing than these junk snacks," Mom said.

Mackenzie and Meg got frightened and slowly placed their snacks back down. "Mom, please. Just take it easy," I said.

Mackenzie's mom said, "Yes, please take it easy. If you don't want them to eat those snacks, then no problem. They can save the snacks for later. Right, girls?"

We slowly nodded. "But then what can we eat?" Mackenzie asked.

"Well, there's a salad bar in a couple of miles. I'm sure we can all get something healthy from there," Meg's mom replied.

Meg rolled her eyes. "Seriously? Salad? Eww, gross! I would rather eat nothing than that."

"Megan! Watch the way you speak. And all of you need to stop acting like toddlers. We're getting salad, and everyone will eat it. End of discussion." Everyone went silent. I'd never seen Meg's mom so upset. And my mom too, but I could understand why my mom was upset. Sahil ran away from home. Which mother wouldn't be upset in a situation like this?

A few minutes later, we arrived at the salad bar. We all got out of the minivan and went into the restaurant in silence. We ordered three large salad bowls and decided to split it up. My mom paid, and we got back into the van. "Ugh! This is so annoying. I've never had to have salad before. I can't believe this day just keeps getting worse," Meg whispered.

"What was that? I heard something," Meg's mom said.

"Nothing, we're just talking. You don't have to know every single detail of my life," Meg said. Dang! I had never heard Meg speak in such a tone. I wondered why we decided to bother them with this road trip.

The next few hours were silent, with Meg and my mom asleep, Mackenzie watching a movie on her phone, and me just staring out the window. It was time for Mackenzie's mom to drive after a few hours, so she switched seats with Meg's mom.

We had been driving for about eight hours, and we still had nine more to go. The sun was setting, and it was getting dark. The sight was beautiful, with the sky's color a mixture of purple, pink, and orange. I should have been taking sky pictures, but I couldn't enjoy it. We needed to meet Sahil before it got too late. I knew the moms were doing a great job taking turns and driving, but I wished we could be quicker. Mackenzie and Meg were sitting in the third row watching *Glamour Girls.* They asked me if I wanted to join them, but I was very stressed and wasn't in the mood to indulge myself in other stories.

It was almost 9:00 p.m., and we hadn't eaten anything for dinner. We didn't have much of a choice after the salad chaos earlier today. Some of us hadn't finished our salads, so that was our dinner, and those who had finished their salads were allowed to have some of the junk food we bought. Mackenzie and I finished our salads, so we both dug into the snack bag and pulled out some chips and sodas. Meg didn't finish her salad, so she wasn't allowed any junk food, but she was being very stubborn. Her mom said, "Megan, come on. Finish your salad. That's all you're going to get tonight."

"I'm not hungry," she said, looking down at her phone.

Meg's mom even tried to make a compromise. "All right, let's make a deal. If you finish your salad, then you're allowed to have some cookies."

"Mom, I'm not a little kid. Stop babying me like that," Meg said angrily.

"Fine. If not cookies, then your choice of snack. You can even have two snacks if you want."

I didn't think Meg was going to buy it, but surprisingly she did. "Really? Two snacks?"

Meg's mom nodded. "Only after you finish your salad." Meg quickly put down her phone, picked up her salad bowl, and started eating.

As we were getting closer and closer to the destination, my mind was whirling with so many thoughts. So many questions about Sahil and even more questions about my biological father. My heart was starting to pound faster. *How did Sahil figure out who our biological father was and where he was? Why would Mom lie to us about our real father? I know it wasn't Mr. Troop, but maybe it was the guy Toby Rhodes used to do business with. Oh no!* I remembered the article I read online while I was at Toby's house. *The owner of the business did commit a crime and ended up in jail.*

Suddenly I remembered the glowing liquid Sahil told me to bring along. *What is that?* I looked back to the trunk and realized something. *Oh no! I need to make sure it doesn't spill.* I quickly made up an excuse. "Could we please pull over? I really need to use the restroom."

"I guess so. I've been driving for about four hours now. It's time to switch anyway," Mackenzie's mom said, and she pulled over to the nearest rest area. She leaned back in her seat and closed her eyes. All the moms seemed tired.

"You guys can still keep driving, right?" I asked.

"I can't for a while," Mackenzie's mom said.

"Don't worry. I'll take the next two hours," Meg's mom assured me.

My mom said, "Yeah, and I'll take another two hours. That leaves us with only one hour left. I'm sure you can do that." Mackenzie's mom nodded. "Thank you so much to all of you for helping us out here. It really means a lot," my mom told the other moms.

Meg's mom said, "No problem! We love to help."

I got out of the minivan and asked my mom to open the trunk. She asked, "Why do you need to open the trunk? The restroom is right in front of you."

"No, Mom. Try to understand. I need something to take with me to the restroom. You know it." Another lie.

"Oh, right. Sorry, sweetie. I'll open the trunk right away." Mom reached out for the trunk button and opened it.

I quickly went in there, opened my duffel bag, and took out the vial of liquid to check. *Thank God! It didn't spill.* I decided that it wouldn't be safe to leave the liquid in my bag, so I stuck it in my pocket and closed the trunk. I quickly headed for the restroom.

I got into one of the stalls and took the vial out from my pocket. The entire liquid glowed at first, and then something strange happened. The glowing went from the top of the vial to the bottom. I closely watched as the liquid swished around. It wasn't an ordinary chemical liquid. "Whoa! What are you?" I asked, holding up the vial.

The liquid made more moves, glowing throughout. Then suddenly it flew from my hands, but the vial didn't fall to the ground. It floated in the air. "Ahh!" I screamed.

"Is everything okay in there, sweetie?" Mom asked.

I didn't know when Mom came in, but I had to keep my mouth shut about whatever the vial held. "Uh, yeah, Mom. I'm fine," I replied.

I heard Mom sigh. "Sameera. Do you want me to come in?"

"No, don't. I mean I'm fine. I can take care of it."

"All right then," she said.

I tried to grab the vial from the air, but it moved around without letting me grab it. "Stay still. Let me put you in my pocket," I whispered to the vial. The vial didn't listen. Instead, it went to the stall near me and floated there for some time. "Stop it! You can't do this. You're supposed to be kept a secret." I felt stupid talking to liquid, but I didn't know what else to do. The vial floated back to my stall, so high that I couldn't reach it. "What do you want?" I asked. The vial just stayed in the same spot. "What can I do so that you stop all this and listen to me?" I asked. The liquid inside stopped glowing, but it still stayed high in the air, out of my reach. "This is so stupid! It doesn't even make sense. What has Sahil created?"

I took out my phone and called Sahil. Well, not really Sahil but his friend Carson. I had changed his contact on my phone to Carson. No one picked up the phone, so I called again. Still, no one answered. I texted.

Me: "Hello? I need to talk to Sahil for a minute. It's urgent."

Carson: *typing …*

Me: "Hurry!"

Carson: "Sorry, he can't talk right now. He's busy."

Me: "Freakin' busy! With what?"

Carson: "He told me not to say."

Me: "Fine, but when you get a chance to talk to him, please ask him to call me."

Carson: "He said he won't talk until you all reach here. So tell me what you want to tell him, and I'll pass the message."

Me: "It's not that simple to explain. I need to speak to him only."

Carson: "Well, you can try me, and if I don't understand, then just tell him when you get here. It's that simple."

Me: "Uh, how do I explain? Fine. There's a glowing liquid that Sahil had under his bed. He told me to bring it with me, and it's … well, it doesn't seem like an ordinary liquid. I want you to ask him what is inside it and why it's behaving strangely."

Carson: "Behaving strangely?"

Me: "Yeah, like the vial floats in the air, and the liquid inside moves around. The glowing goes from top to bottom. It's just very strange. I've never seen anything like it."

Carson: "Ha-ha! Is this some sort of prank?"

Me: "No. I'm serious!"

Carson: "Glowing liquid! Oh, it must be magical. Why don't you take a sip and see what happens?"

Me: "Look, if you don't want to help, then don't. Please don't mess around. Sahil would know what I'm talking about. And I can't drink it. He told me not to open it until I got there."

Carson: "Yeah, okay, baby. Sahil is not your older brother to tell you what to do in the first place. So why listen to him? Drink the liquid."

Me: "Stop! Why should I listen to you either? You're so annoying. You know what? It's no use talking to boys like you. You're all useless. Idiots."

"Sameera, sweetie? Is everything all right? You've been in there for a while."

What? My mom is still here? "Coming, Mom," I said. I stood on the toilet seat and grabbed the liquid vial from the air. *Yes, finally.* I got out of the stall.

"Oh, sweetie, I know it can be hard, but you'll get through it," Mom said.

I just rolled my eyes and walked to our van. When I got inside, Mackenzie asked, "Sameera, what took you so long?"

"Nothing. Just I'm, uh, getting used to, um, some things," I replied.

"Cool! Anyway, do you want to play a game?" she asked.

I frowned. "Why though?"

"Just to lighten up the mood. You know," Mackenzie said with her eyebrows wiggling up and down.

"Uh, can you stop that. It's a little creepy," I said.

Mackenzie chuckled. "Lighten up." She shook her head back and forth.

"No, actually, I'm fine," I said and looked away. *Wait … did she know about the glowing liquid?* I looked back at her, and she was staring at me with her eyes wide.

"Come on, Sameera! The game will be fun," Meg insisted.

I replied, "Uh, I don't really know."

"Aren't you just so frustrated about what your brother did? Thinking about him all the time? Don't you get bored?" Mackenzie asked.

"No, not really. It's for his safety."

"Right. Safety," Mackenzie said sarcastically.

"Why are you guys acting so weird?" I said.

Mackenzie smirked. "Acting weird, huh? Well, that's not what we were going for. We just wanted to help you relax and not stress out. Sorry if it seemed weird."

I laughed.

Meg's mom started the car. Finally, we were back on the road, and the van was quiet. My friends were so supportive. I felt like I should tell them the truth about meeting my biological father without our moms hearing. I moved into the third row and sat in between my friends. "All right. I have something I need to tell you guys, but only you two. Promise me you won't tell the moms." They both nodded. I whispered, "So we're going to Madison not only to see Sahil but my biological father as well."

"What! Are you serious?" Meg said. The others looked back.

"Keep it low," I whispered to Meg.

"After your mom already told you Mr. Troop was your father, you want to believe someone else is your real father? That's totally insane!" Mackenzie whispered.

"No, guys. You don't understand. Sahil said he was going to meet our real father," I explained.

Meg said, "Your brother jokes around a lot. You believe him?"

"I don't think he is joking this time. Even I felt like Mr. Troop wasn't my father. I believe Mom lied to me, and that's why I don't want to tell her what I'm telling you both right now. Let her go there and see for herself."

"I don't understand, Sameera. How could your mom lie to you? Especially about your own father?" Meg asked.

I thought for a second and said, "Well, I think she didn't want me to worry and spend all my time thinking about where he could be."

"Maybe. But I thought you were very smart. How did your brother beat you at this?" Meg asked.

I laughed. "I don't know for a fact if it's true. He could just be guessing. Only one way to know."

It was quiet for a few minutes, with my friends staring at the window and me staring straight ahead. It was completely dark, and all we could see was the road ahead with our headlights. I looked at my phone for the time. It was midnight.

"Hey, Sameera, do you mind if I ask you something?" Mackenzie asked.

"Sure."

"Did you actually have to use the restroom?"

I didn't know what to say. This was crossing the limits. I could only tell them so much without seeming like a lunatic. The magic liquid thing had to be kept between Sahil and me for now. If I told them everything I knew and had, they would go crazy. "Uh, well, yeah, I did have to go to the restroom," I lied.

"Are you sure?" Meg asked.

I replied, "Yeah. Why would I lie about using the restroom? It's something we all must do."

"Well, the way you were rushing in didn't seem—" Mackenzie started.

Then I interrupted. "Mackenzie! Why do you have to question me so much? I rushed in there because of … because of a girl's reason."

"Oh, got it. Sorry, Sameera."

"It's fine," I said. I got back into my seat in the second row next to Mackenzie's mom. I felt my phone vibrate, so I looked. It was a message from Carson.

Carson: "I'm sorry."

Carson: "I just want to help. No more jokes, promise."

Me: "I don't need your help."

Carson: "Please. I will tell Sahil what you told me about the glowing liquid."

Me: "Is he with you right now?"

Carson: "No, but when he is, I'll tell him."

Me: "Okay."

Carson: "Do you forgive me?"

I didn't respond. Instead, I just turned off my phone.

After a few minutes, I drifted into sleep, and I guess I was sleeping for a couple of hours. I woke up to the sound of car honks. *Beep! Beep! Beep! Beep!* "Oh, don't you hoot your horn at me! You're the one who tried to make a left turn on red!" Meg's mom was screaming at a car that passed by. We were on the local road now, no longer on the highway.

"All right. I think it's my turn to take over. I'll drive for the next two hours if I can," my mom said as we pulled over to the side. My mom and Meg's mom switched seats, and we were back on the road. Mom got us onto the highway.

"Do you think we should really be driving like this? I mean, it's been fourteen hours. There's a hotel in five minutes where we can rest for the night. We can get up at seven and start driving again. Do you want to take the exit?" Meg's mom asked.

I looked up, as that question caught my attention. *No, we can't rest for the night. We must keep going. It's my brother we're talking about.* I couldn't say that out loud because I knew that the moms were tired from driving, and I couldn't force them. Thankfully, my mom was determined. "It's all right. I've got it. If Mackenzie's mom doesn't want to drive anymore, then fine. I'll drive three hours, and we'll be there."

"Mom's right. We should keep going. We drove fourteen hours, and we only have three more. We can do it." I tried to give them some motivation. Mom smiled. Just then, my phone vibrated again.

Carson: "Hello?"

Carson: "Come on! I don't even know what we got ourselves into. My family was just going on vacation. Sahil wanted to come along for some other reason, so we took him. We didn't know it was going to be this bad. Right now, my family is at some museum, and Sahil made an excuse so that we could come to the Madison County Prison. He said his mom has no idea that his father is in prison. I could be having fun with my family right now, but I am here with Sahil."

Me: "Whoa! Go back a few steps."

Carson: "What do you mean?"

Me: "What's all this? I need a much more detailed explanation."

Carson: "Can you call?"

Me: "I can't. I'm in the minivan with my mom and friends. My friends already know, but I don't want my mom to hear me talking about any of this. We're almost there. Try your best to explain through text."

Carson: *typing ...*

Carson: "Fine. My parents don't know about this at all. They think that me and Sahil are just hanging out at a park. That's the lie. Sahil found out about his biological father, and he's here in Madison County Prison, so we're here to meet him. I didn't think he could go alone, so I agreed to go with him. Once again, I could be having fun with my family at the museum, but I'm not."

Me: "Hold up. How does Sahil know?"

Carson: "He didn't even tell me that yet. He wants to wait until you come."

Me: "Okay fine. Thank you."

Carson: "For what?"

Me: "Helping my brother."

Carson: "It's fine."

Me: "Don't worry. You'll get your vacation back."

Carson: "How? The week is almost over, and that means it's time to go home soon."

Me: "I appreciate you doing this for us. I want to apologize for what I said to you before."

Carson: "Calling me an idiot and useless?"

Me: "Yeah that."

Carson: "I'm used to it."

Carson: "By the way, you didn't tell me. How will I get my vacation back?"

Me: "I haven't thought about it yet, but I'm sure we'll find a way."

CHAPTER

19

A couple of hours later, Mom was starting to feel tired. She yawned and yawned and almost closed her eyes. "Mom! Watch out!" I screamed from the back.

Mom suddenly jerked, and her eyes opened wide. "Sorry. I'm just a little sleepy."

"Don't worry. I got the last hour," Mackenzie's mom said.

"Thank you so much!" my mom said as she took the nearest exit. Mackenzie's mom took over, and we were on the highway again with only an hour to go. I was getting excited to see Sahil but also nervous to see what else was in store for me. Mackenzie and Meg were fast asleep in the back, like nothing bothered them. I was getting a little sweaty.

"Phew. Is there any way you can turn up the air conditioner?" I asked Mackenzie's mom.

My mom looked at me strangely and said, "Sameera, are you okay? Do you have a fever?" She reached out to touch my forehead.

"No, Mom. I'm fine. Just a little stressed."

"About what?"

"Well … Sahil and … his condition right now. I'm worried about him."

"Relax. We're almost there. Whatever it is, we're all going to face it together."

"Yeah. You're right. I'm sure Sahil is fine," I said, trying to make myself feel better.

For the last hour, the minivan was silent. No one said anything or made any noise. It was kind of awkward for me because it seemed like the slowest hour of my life. I kept checking my phone for the time, but time stayed still. "A watched pot never boils," I heard Meg say.

I turned around. "Meg, I thought you were asleep."

"Well, I was … but the constant blinking light from your phone woke me up. Why do you keep checking your phone?"

I laughed, "Sorry … I'm just a little … you know, restless. I'm checking the time on my phone."

"Why? Is there a certain time you're supposed to be there?"

"No, it's just me. I'm a little nervous and excited at once."

"For what exactly?"

"Meg, you already know. To see my brother and …" I started to say, but then she interrupted.

"And your biological father?"

"Shh … keep it down. I don't want our moms to hear."

"My bad."

After what seemed like an eternity, I saw Mackenzie's mom pull into the parking lot that had a sign that read: *Madison County Prison*. "We're here, at last!" I looked around to see a glass building on my right and a brick building on my left.

"How do we know which is the right one?" I heard my mom ask.

I responded, "I can call Sahil … or, well, Carson."

"Do it then," my mom said.

I pulled out my phone and clicked on Carson. "It's ringing." No one picked up, so I tried again. Again, no one. "Come on! Pick up!" I said.

"Message him," said Mackenzie, who had just woken up from her sleep.

Me: "We are here. Where are you?"

There was no reply, so Mackenzie's mom said, "All right, I'm just gonna park, and then we can go in."

"If there's no response, then we'll split up. Three of you will go into the glass building, and the other three will go into the brick one," Meg's mom suggested.

"I call the glass building!" Mackenzie shouted. We all turned to look at her. She said, "What? I love glass buildings; they're cool. Brick buildings are so boring. They're, like ... everywhere."

"Mackenzie, focus! We're not here for a fun excursion," Meg said.

"Sorry. I guess I'll go to the brick one if I really must," Mackenzie said in a disappointed tone.

"There's no need for anyone to argue about who goes where," I said, "Carson just texted back, and they're actually in the back entrance of the brick building." Mackenzie's mom immediately reversed the minivan and headed toward the back of the building. There were many doors in the back as we passed by. I saw a short boy waiting outside one of the doors with his hands in his pockets. "I think that's Carson!" I yelled.

Mackenzie's mom parked the car in one of the lots, and we all got out. "Ahh, fresh air. That feels so good!" Meg said.

We all took our things from the van and headed toward the door, where a boy and a tall guard were standing. "Carson?" I asked.

"Yup! Sameera?"

I nodded.

"Hey, it's so good to see you all. This is my uncle. He works here, which made it easier for us to get in," he said, pointing at the tall guard.

The guard said, "I will take you all in, but first I need to check your bags and do a security scan."

My mom stopped him. "Wait ... where's my son? What in the world are you doing here? I need answers now! Start talking."

"You mean Sahil? Oh, he's inside. You'll get your confusion cleared soon. Let my uncle do his duty, and then he will take you all in," Carson said, and we all followed him. As soon as we entered, it smelled like rotten eggs. When I looked down at the floor, the carpet was brown and stained, and I cringed a little.

Mackenzie whispered, "Dang! Do they ever clean this place?"

"Girl, it's a freakin' prison, not your grandpa's lush mansion," Meg said.

Mackenzie nodded. "True, but they could better the condition of this place. I mean, look around."

"That's not for us to decide. Come on now. Let's get this over with," Meg said.

After Carson's uncle did a security check on us, he led us into another door. I looked around and saw many separated cells with red bars in front of them. I peeked into one of the cells and saw an old man drinking something from a steel glass and humming to himself. When he saw me, he froze. I kept walking.

"Where are we even going?" I asked.

"You'll see," Carson said, and we approached a plain white door that had a lock on it. Carson's uncle entered a code, and we all went in. We approached a wooden table where a man wearing what looked like a brown cowboy hat was sitting. He said, "Whoa, whoa, whoa, slow your roll! Where do you think you all are going? This is not some fancy wedding or party."

"Sir, I'm Carson, and this is my uncle who works here. We were here just a few minutes ago. Remember?"

"Okay, and these people?" the man asked, pointing at us.

Carson said, "These people are visitors. They need to meet someone, and then they'll be out."

"Hmm … no. Sorry. Guests aren't allowed. Now if you will please excuse me, I have better things to do than waste my time with a bunch of party people," the man said.

Carson said, "I told you, they're not party people."

"Look, I don't want any pranks. I need to see my brother now," I said.

The man laughed. "Sorry, kid. No can do."

"Why not?"

"You're a little too young to be a prison visitor," the man responded.

I frowned. "But we literally have three adults with us."

"Yeah, well … you can't all go in at the same time."

"Fine, then let's do three at a time. Meg, Mackenzie, and I will go in first, and then …" I started, but Mom cleared her throat. "Right, sorry. My mom, me, and …"

"We came to help you, Sameera, and if this is as far as we can go, then this is as far as we'll go. We don't have to go in. The rest is your family matter that we probably shouldn't get involved with. I suggest that Sameera, her mom, and Carson should be the only ones to go in. The rest of us will wait in the car," Meg said, looking at her mom.

Her mom said, "Yes, I agree with Meg. We don't want to be any trouble. You only asked us to help with driving, and I'm glad we were able to, but we should probably stay out of your personal business."

"Okay then. That works fine. Thank you both so much for helping me drive. I really appreciate it. You know what? I'll book you a hotel so that you can all get some rest and then book a flight back home. We'll manage from here," my mom said, looking at Mackenzie's and Meg's moms.

"Are you sure? We can wait in the car for you, and then we can all drive back together," Mackenzie's mom suggested.

My mom smiled. "That is so thoughtful of you, but since Sahil will also be coming, I don't think we'll have a lot of room in the minivan for all of us. I'll book a hotel and then text you the details."

"Oh, okay. Thanks. Well then, we won't bother you any further. We'll take our leave now. Come on, girls," Meg's mom said.

Mackenzie said, "Sameera, you'll keep us updated right?"

"Mackenzie, why do you need to know all this personal stuff about Sameera's family? No need to update her on anything," Mackenzie's mom said to me.

I smiled. "Don't worry. You guys are my friends, and I'll tell you everything when I get back."

"All right. Have a safe trip back home."

"You too. Bye!" Mackenzie, Meg, and their moms waved and left.

"Now what?" my mom asked.

"You can go on in," the man said and let us in. Carson's uncle led the way for my mom and me. Soon we approached a room with a bunch of filing cabinets.

"What are these files?" I asked.

Carson's uncle replied, "That's where all the information about the prisoners and their cases are kept."

Carson went through one of the drawers and mumbled something I couldn't quite catch. His uncle pulled out a key from his pocket and went over to open the drawers. Carson said, "Thanks! I don't know how to find the right one. I need Sahil's help. Let me go in and get him."

"Wait … what file are you talking about? Sahil doesn't have a case on him, does he?" Mom asked.

Carson looked at me. I said, "Mom, no. That's silly. He's too young."

"Then what is Carson talking about?"

Carson opened his mouth to speak, and then someone interrupted. "Oh, what a surprise! You guys came!"

"Sahil!" my mom screamed and ran up to him.

The guard who was standing in one corner of the room came over and said, "You guys are being a bit too loud. This is a prison. Please keep that in mind." He stepped back. Sahil looked like he belonged in the military. He was wearing a green heavy-duty jacket, khakis, and black boots.

"What's with this new look?" I asked.

Mom looked at Sahil. "Oh, honey, are you okay?"

"Yeah, Mom, I'm fine. The real question is are you fine?" Sahil asked.

Mom smiled. "Of course I am. What are you talking—well, I wasn't fine when I figured out that you weren't with your father. Why did you lie to me?"

"Enough! Father, father. It's not me who lied to you," Sahil said angrily.

My mom chuckled. "Honey, if it isn't you, then is it Sameera who lied? You ran away from home, so what do you have to say now?"

"I ran away for a good reason. A reason that you would never be able to believe. A reason that I'll never be able to forgive you for!" Sahil screamed.

Carson's uncle said, "Please keep it down. Otherwise, I'm afraid I'll have to ask you to leave."

"Sahil, where is he? Did you meet him?" I asked.

"Where is who?" Mom asked.

Sahil said, "Yes, I met him. You want to tell Mom now?"

"If not now, then when?" I asked.

My mom stood up. "Kids, who are you talking about?"

"Wait, Mom," I said and pulled Sahil to a corner.

Mom followed us and said, "What the freak is going on here?"

"Hey, Carson, can you take care of her?" Sahil asked.

Carson came over to my mom and said, "Hey, Mrs. Chacko, I need you to come with me for a second."

"I'm not going anywhere! These kids are hiding something from me, and I have a right to know because I'm their mother," my mom stated.

"Mom, just give us one second. We need to talk something out, and then we'll tell you. We promise," I said.

"Fine. Better make it quick," Mom said and stomped away.

"Hurry up and tell me what we're going to do," Sahil said.

I smirked. "Me? What do I know? You didn't tell me anything clearly!" I almost screamed.

Sahil nodded. "Okay. Chill, Sameera. I'll explain, but not everything right now. You already know the fact that I found our real father in this very jail. Now we must—"

"Hold up. Why and how?" I asked.

He replied, "I said I can't explain everything now. It's a long story. Right now, we don't have much time before Mom comes over here again. We must think of a way to get the truth out of her. It'll be the easy way or the hard way."

"It's you who got us into this mess, and I have no idea what to tell Mom now. You come up with something. You think you're such a genius."

Sahil thought for a second, and then I said, "I want to make sure we are both clear on this. Who exactly is our father?"

"Sorry to say it's not Mr. Troop," Sahil said and rolled his eyes.

I fixed him with a stare. "I know. I was able to make that out as well. Now … you'd better tell me who this guy is. I have a guess too, but I won't tell you unless you tell me first."

"Well, there's a file cabinet over there, and one of the files has all his information and his case in it. So if you want to start off with that …"

"Yeah, okay. Tell me his name," I said.

"Sabal Chacko."

"What?"

"Are you deaf? I said Sabal Chacko. S-a-b-a-l C-h-a-c-k-o," Sahil repeated.

My mouth fell open, and I dropped to the ground. *I'm sure I heard it right. I knew it! It is the same guy the old man Toby Rhodes was talking about. The successful businessman. Yes. It can't be anyone else but him.*

Mom saw me and came over quickly. "Sweetie, what happened? Carson, get Sameera a glass of water."

"From where? This isn't my house," he said.

"Oh, for crying out loud! Just forget it!"

I felt kind of dizzy but didn't tell her.

"Mom, please go. Our conversation isn't finished yet," Sahil said.

"No! I've given you two enough time. Now, whatever must be discussed, I'll be a part of it," Mom stated and helped me up.

I looked at Sahil and said, "I want to see it now. Sahil, find the file."

"See what now? File? What are you guys up to?" Mom asked.

"You'll see," Sahil said and went over to the file cabinet that Carson's uncle had already opened. Mom tried to follow him, but I reached out my hand to stop her.

I saw Carson standing in one corner of the room, looking at his phone and gasping. He sat on the bench and sighed. "Stay here, Mom," I said and went up to Carson. "Are you okay?" He showed me his phone, and I asked, "What is this?"

"Look at this picture. It'll answer your question," he said. I took his phone and looked. It was a picture of a happy family standing next to a beautifully painted concrete statue. There were many colorful glass paintings in the background. I looked down at Carson and asked, "Is this your family?"

"Obviously. Why would I be looking at someone else's family? My dad sent these pictures to me. They are having fun at the museum, and I'm here … at a prison. How fun! What picture will I send my family? Hanging out at prison with my uncle and best friend?"

I handed his phone back and sat down next to him on the bench. "I'm sorry this had to happen to you. I don't know why Sahil chose you to do this over me. I could've helped him with this mission if he had just talked to me. He knew you were going on vacation to Wisconsin, and he took advantage of it. But why did you agree? You know you could've said no, right?"

Carson looked up at me and said, "He's my friend. Of course, I would help him, and I don't regret it at all. I'm just a little upset and I guess a little jealous to see my family having fun without me. They think I'm having fun at an amusement park with Sahil, but little do they know I'm at a prison helping Sahil. You know what though? I feel good. I'm doing something good right now, so I'm okay. Thanks."

I looked straight ahead and took a deep breath. "It's my fault. The last time I saw Sahil was after I got into a fight with him. Then, a few minutes later, whoosh … he was gone. He ran away from home. I … really need to apologize. If I wasn't so immature, maybe I would've been here with him instead of you. I'm such a terrible sister. And you're … you're such a great friend. I can't thank you enough for being there for him," I said and put a hand on his shoulder.

"It's fine. No problem. Just don't call us boys stupid idiots or useless anymore. It hurt my feelings," Carson said.

I chuckled. "Don't worry. It won't happen again. I realize now you're not useless, and neither is Sahil."

"I don't know if you know, but Sahil was the one with brains. He was doubting Mr. Troop as his father. With all the research that he did online, I told him that there's no way that the man is his father. He is such a genius for discovering all that about his biological dad, and the way he investigated was interesting. No wonder I agreed to help him out. And now to see your mom's reaction when she finds out what a true genius her son is," Carson said proudly.

I was amazed. "Wow. Sahil did research and all that? He never used to do that before. Instead, he was a lazy person. He wouldn't even play those fun detective games with Mom and me. Huh. I really need to spend more time with him I guess."

"Yeah, I guess people do change. Now do you believe that your brother is smarter and is a true genius?" Carson asked.

I smiled. "Not quite there yet. I need to see the proof and everything before I can label him like that."

Carson laughed. "I'm glad we had this talk. It made me feel a lot better. And you're not a terrible sister. Despite all your differences, you still managed to come here all the way from New Hampshire in a day, so that's something to be proud of."

"Thanks, Carson. Now if you want, we can find a way to get you back to your vacation with your family. Maybe book you an Uber or something?" I suggested.

Carson thought for a second and then said, "You know what? I kind of want to see how this ends. Your mom's reaction and all that. My vacation can wait. Do you mind if I stay?"

"Of course not. It's up to you," I said.

"Hey, guys, come on! I found the file. Mom, I want you to wait a few minutes. We'll be back soon," Sahil announced.

Mom said, "You are not going anywhere. We found Sahil, and now let's go home. And, Sahil, I need to hear the entire truth on the way back."

I got up from where I was sitting and said, "Mom, please. This is important. We promise we'll tell you everything. Just give us a few minutes until we figure something out."

"I'll give you two five minutes, and after that, I don't want to hear any excuses. If you're not done by then, I'm leaving." Mom made her point very clear. She slowly walked over to the bench and sat there with Carson. I quickly went over to Sahil.

"Sahil, there's something I want to say to you first," I said.

Sahil responded, "No, wait. Me first. This is more important."

"Fine. Go ahead. Show me," I said. Sahil placed the file wide open on the table beside the filing cabinet. I took a step closer and said, "What in the world is this?"

"Look closely. This is Sabal," Sahil said, pointing at a printed picture.

I gasped. "No way. He looks exactly like the man I discovered back in Ohert City." I took out my phone to show him a picture of Toby and Sabal at the coffee shop.

"You've got to be kidding me! This is the same guy. What a coincidence! Why didn't you tell me before?" he asked.

I nodded my head. "Dude, you ran away from home before all this happened. I had no way to tell you."

"Right. Sorry about that again."

"No, I'm sorry for putting up a fight with you. If I hadn't argued with you then, we could've worked out this together," I said. Sahil smiled. I said, "But how do we know for sure that he's our real father? Just because he has the same last name …"

"Trust me, Sameera. I know. Let me tell you the story. You thought I was angry with you and ran away, but that's not the case at all. After you and I got into a fight about that dumb plan to bring Mr. Troop back, I researched further. After I fought with you, I wasn't creating a plan to bring Mr. Troop back but instead working on a project from a science kit Mom bought last year. I just decided that you were the older and wiser one and dropped my plan. For my project, I needed a glue stick, so I went to the storage room to get it. I opened one of the drawers and started digging through, but I found a picture of Mom and another guy. The back of the photo said, 'You are the one for me,' and it had a phone number on it. I didn't know what that meant. I was very confused because the man in the picture looked nothing like Mr. Troop. I knew something was fishy but kept it to myself. I put the picture back, took the glue stick and the phone number, and went back to my room. I immediately dialed the phone number, but nobody picked up the call. I searched that number on the internet and found that it belongs to someone in Wisconsin. I researched some other sources further and found out that the number belonged to a businessman named Sabal Chacko. I was like, *Hey, the guy has the same last name as me, but why does Mom have a picture of him and his number? Did she have another husband before Mr. Troop?* I tried to piece everything together, but I couldn't get the complete picture.

"I started to think Mom had another husband before Mr. Troop but didn't know how to ask her straight up. So I didn't. That picture. That phone number. The same last name. He had to be my father, but who the heck was Chris Troop then? He had a different last name. Why would Mom say he was our father? Then I read an article about Sabal Chacko and found that he's in this very jail. I really wanted to meet him, and I figured out that Carson and his family were headed toward this direction for vacation. I asked if I could tag along with them, and they were completely fine with that.

After a while, the doorbell rang at our house. That was Carson's family. They came to pick me up, so I took my stuff and went with them. I might've forgotten to close the door, but that's not the point. I discovered this prison was a mile away from the hotel Carson's family was staying at. I tried to contact this prison and get ahold of Sabal Chacko. They didn't let me speak to him, but they let me come visit. Carson didn't want me to go alone, so he agreed to come with me after lying to his parents. Brave boy! Anyway, I'm pretty sure you'll believe that he's the one."

I nodded. "Wow, Sahil. That's just … wow!"

He said, "We both went on our own little adventures to find out the same conclusion: there's a man in the world named Sabal Chacko. Forget the world. A man in this jail is named Sabal Chacko, and he is our biological father."

I didn't argue. "Yeah, yeah, what a use of our time."

He said, "Though we both found the same conclusion, I did better." I tilted my head and was confused. Sahil said, "I met him. I talked to him in person, and he said that he's our father. That's proof."

"They let you speak to him? Where is he? I want to speak to him too," I said.

Sahil replied, "But what about Mom?"

"We'll deal with her later. Carson seems to have her distracted for now," I said.

Sahil lifted the file and placed it in front of my face. "Wanna read the case first?" I took the file and looked at his case.

Name: Sabal Chacko
Age: 46 years old
Gender: Male
Marital Status: Divorced
Previous Jobs: Consider Chacker Business

> *Case:*
> On June 9, 2015, Sabal Chacko was reported for theft by one of his employees. He violated the rules of his own business by taking all the profit from his business and escaping. One of his employees stated that they didn't find a single penny in their drawer when they returned to work the next day. Another employee stated that they found a note from their boss, which said that he was giving up his business. On June 10, the police arrested Chacko in the middle of Madison, Wisconsin, after a day of tracking. Chacko stated that he was headed toward Vernon with the money for his parents, who were sick. He stated he was in debt and couldn't provide for his parents, so he had to take all the money from the business. After the authorities questioned him, they believed that he had committed a fraud. He was sent to jail early the next day.

There was a photo of him below his case, and he looked very depressed. "This is very sad. He was trying to do a good deed by helping his parents. The stealing part wasn't good, but he could've taken a loan or something. I can't believe Mom never told us about this," I said.

Sahil closed the file and placed it back in the cabinet. He said, "Yeah, but I'm not sure she knows the whole story. Anyway, he knows us. Probably not how you look now, but he knew our names. When I told him my name, he said that I am his son."

"I believe you. Can I meet him now … without Mom?"

"Yeah, I guess so. I'll ask the guard to take us in to meet him," Sahil said and asked the guard. He agreed immediately and led us toward another door.

Mom turned around and said, “Hey, you two! Come back here! Where do you think you’re going without me? Your five minutes are up. Tell me what’s going on, and let’s leave this place.”

Sahil looked at me and said, “Sameera, I already met him, so you go ahead. Go past those doors, down the hall, take a right, and it’s the cell all the way at the end. The guard will lead you. I’ll stay here with Mom.”

“Sameera is not going anywhere! We came here for Sahil, and we found him, so let’s head home now,” Mom yelled.

Sahil responded, “Sorry, Mom. We can’t just yet. Hurry up, Sameera, and go.”

“Mom, I’ll be back soon. I need to go meet someone,” I said quickly and followed the guard toward the door.

CHAPTER 20

The guard turned the key in the lock and opened the entryway, and I was embraced by a cover of chill air. Embracing myself against the chill, I strolled inside. I followed the guard to the right, and the last cell to the left was made of hefty, protected metal and had a sign that read No Admittance. I looked inside the cell to see racks supplied with frozen food lined against the dividers. Spiked icicles were pointed down at me from the roof. The guard pointed at the cell to show me where it was, and then he went and stood in a corner. I peeked inside the cell. It was a gloomy stone cage with a single tiny window that overlooked the town and the morning sun over the tall stone walls. There was a sense of coolness in the room, even if the walls were somewhat moist. Like a cabin, the bed was built of steel mesh. Steel, with bolts and locks, was used for the door. A sink and toilet were also present. "Hello?" I called. "Anyone here?" I heard footsteps, and I looked closer to see a man walking toward me. Apparently, he had been lying down on his mattress, but it was too dark for me to see him. He walked closer and put his face in between the bars. I studied him. His face was abnormally gorgeous and completely lined, his eyes indented and entering, and he had scraggly facial hair and a sweater vest that gave him a dubious proficient look. I had seen a photograph of him at the café, in which he'd been wearing precisely the same outfit.

He said, "Yes, can I help you?"

"Hi. I'm Sameera Chacko, and are you—"

Before I could finish, he said, "I am who you think I am. Your brother told me you would come."

I glared at him. "Sabal Chacko?"

He nodded. "I know it'll be hard for you to call me anything but that, so let's stick with my name for now."

I was confused and asked, "What are you talking about?"

"Oh, so you don't know who I am?"

"Of course, I do. You're Sabal Chacko, my biological fath—" I stopped midsentence because a weird feeling built up in my stomach.

"Yeah, right. I knew you didn't have it in you. Your brother though … he was just rocking it, calling me his dad and everything. I never felt so good in my life," he said. I looked down. He said, "I'm not expecting you to do the same, but at least you're here, and we're talking."

"I don't know why, but I just can't bring myself to call you that yet. I'm sorry," I said.

He responded, "That's no problem. It's just nice having people come by and visit—you know, especially my children. It gets a little lonely here sometimes. If you don't know already, I've been locked in here for about seven years now."

"Yeah, I know. I read your case, but I don't think it's very fair. I mean you *did* steal, so they have a right to punish you. Other than that, everything was good. You were trying to help your parents, and you gave the authorities an honest explanation. Seven years is just too much for that kind of thing."

"Well, seven years so far. I don't know how much longer." Sabal backed away from the bars, pulled up a wooden chair from behind him, and sat. "You know, it's normal to feel so many emotions at the same time. Especially when you're older and you figure out about your real father, it can be hard. But I don't want you to feel like you can't share your feelings with me. I'm probably like a stranger to you right now, but believe me, after seeing you and your brother, I just felt like my heart is slowly healing from all the emotional pain I've had in the last several years."

"I can understand. I'm curious. Can you tell me what it was like living with Mom and your life before you went to jail? I can't remember much of my childhood with you," I said.

He looked up at the ceiling and then back at me. "I can try, but that'll just make you feel worse. I've been a bad parent figure, and I don't know if I'll ever be able to see you and your brother again."

"It's okay. I want to know, and then maybe I'll feel a much closer connection toward you," I said.

He explained, "I'll try my best to explain. I had a love marriage with your mom because she was the most beautiful woman I'd ever met. I felt like I was the luckiest man in the world, and I had a great, happy life planned out for us. We would have two kids and then raise them to love life too. We got married in a village in Vernon, Wisconsin, and after about a year, you were born. We lived there for about a year, and then I found a much better place. We realized that it was going to be hard to raise our children in the village, so we moved to a much bigger city in New Hampshire. Plus, I had been working with business for so long that I felt like I could create my own business, so I built a company called Consider Chacker."

"Wait … tell me about the part where you met Toby Rhodes," I said.

He smiled. "I'm getting to that. I worked there for a year, hiring employees and trying to hit the money tree. While I was on one of my business trips, I met a homeless guy, and, as you said, his name was Toby Rhodes. I talked to him and got to know him a little better. I felt like he didn't deserve to be homeless. I bought him some food and gave him some new clothes to be fresh. One day, I invited him over to a nearby coffee shop, and little did he know that it was an interview. He thought I had invited him for a casual talk, but it was to talk about business. I asked him a few questions and told him about my business. After that, I strongly felt like he could represent my company because he had the skills and he was a natural. You don't find many people like that out in the world, so I hired him."

"Wow! I bet he didn't see that coming," I remarked.

Sabal continued, "He was a bit shocked at first, but I told him that it was no joke and that he could start making money too. We worked together for a couple of years, and then your brother, Sahil, was born. Your mom needed some help taking care of two kids at home, so I took off for a few weeks to be with my family. Then one day, Toby Rhodes called me back and told me how our business was growing rapidly. I needed to be there to watch my business grow, so I went back to work. Your mom was struggling a bit taking care of you both, but occasionally your grandparents would come over to help, meaning my parents. After going back and forth between my business and family life, I got to go on a few business trips. It was about a few days to a week, so I would still come home and have time for my family."

I eagerly listened.

"Things got bigger; my business started to sprout all over the country. We were making money like anything. That's when things started to take a turn. There was this one business trip I got invited to that was for a month. I was planning on going, but your mom didn't let me go at first. She thought I wouldn't get to see my children grow up. I told her that this was going to be the longest trip and I wouldn't go on trips longer than this. She was a little disappointed, but I promised to video call every day and see my children. I came back from the monthlong trip to figure out that there was another trip in store for me. That was also a month long, so I promised your mom the same things as the previous trip and left. After that, another and another. The trips started to get longer. One of them was over a year. I really couldn't afford to miss the trip because otherwise our business would face a huge loss. I had to go for all the trips."

"That's huge. Mom must've struggled to take care of us on her own," I said.

"Once, when I returned home from one of my monthlong trips, your mom wasn't happy. She told me to leave the house. I was a bit confused at first because I had just returned from a trip, and she wanted me to leave again. She explained that I didn't have enough time for the kids, and I only cared about money. Which I can't argue with because I did leave often, but I didn't only care about money. I cared about my family, which was why I was working. To make money for my family. For you kids to get an education and go to college. Your mom didn't care about those things at that point. She said that the kids were too young for us to be thinking about college. They really needed a father figure in their lives. I agreed but couldn't leave my business. Your mother told me to choose between my business or the family. I was so shocked because I loved them both and couldn't leave one for another. She said that if I want to live in this house, then I'd have to forget about my business."

"Oh man! That must've been a tough decision. What did you end up choosing?" I asked, fully into the story.

"I didn't know what to do at that point, so I went on another journey. I decided that since I was traveling alone all the time, it would be nice to take my family on a vacation. She thought that I had had enough of trips. I promised her that I would do a better job of maintaining my business life with my family life. That I would take my family on all my business trips so that I could be with my family and do business at the same time. Your mom thought I was crazy and didn't agree. She was concerned that if we kept traveling all the time, you kids couldn't go to a proper school and get an education. It was a hard decision to make, and since I couldn't make up my mind, she divorced me. I was so miserable, but I still had my business. My business wasn't of much use now that I didn't have a family to worry about, so I didn't work as much. I found a small apartment for myself and rented it out. I stayed up late nights, watching TV and getting drunk because I felt so miserable that I'd lost my family. I didn't have anything to look forward to every day after work. I went on fewer business trips, and soon, my business fell apart. I couldn't do a good job of keeping it together and leading my employees successfully. My employees were upset and wanted to quit the job. I felt like I had literally lost everything—my family, my business—and I didn't know how I was going to properly make money anymore. At that point, I felt like I should've just left my business in the first place and chosen my family. It was going to fall apart one way or another, and I regretted my decision so much."

"That's just … wow. I can't even imagine being in your situation. Did Mom ever know about any of this?" I asked.

Sabal shook his head. "She didn't have a single clue of where I was or what I was doing after she divorced me. I don't blame her for that. I minded my own business. She did too." I frowned, feeling bad for both.

He continued, "Once, my parents came to visit me in my apartment. They were a bit disappointed in me and what I had done. I felt so terrible, but they didn't leave my side. They were there to cook meals for me and talk to me. They asked me to move back to the village with them, but I refused. After they left, I felt a lot better. They really lightened my mood and the atmosphere of my apartment. I started going to work more regularly and trying to boost my business, but nobody seemed interested in working for me anymore. I didn't want them to quit, so I raised their allowance. Even then, they called me a lousy businessman. I didn't give up though. My parents had given me the strength to keep going, so I did.

"One day, my mom called and told me that Dad was not doing well. He was very sick and needed treatment. They asked me to help them financially, as they did not have enough money in the village. I gathered and counted every penny I had but figured out that I didn't have enough money to treat him. *How could this be?* That's when I knew that I had failed as a son. My parents were there for me and supported me all the time. They helped me take care of my kids and helped me in any way they could. I couldn't help it. If your mom hadn't divorced me, then I would have been able to go back to her and ask for help. I was all on my own now and had to think of a way to help my dad. So I gave them every penny I had, but my dad couldn't get the full treatment. In a couple of months, he died. My mom was begging me to come back to the village, as she was alone now. I didn't want to go, but I didn't have any other choice because I had no use for staying in New Hampshire. Nobody wanted to work for me. I decided to give the ownership of the company to Toby Rhodes. I wrote him a letter as proof, but I'm not sure if he accepted the position. I never heard from him after that. Whether he took over the company or not, I moved back to the village, taking a break from Consider Chacker."

"No way! Your business meant so much to you. I bet your employees must've missed you," I said.

Sabal laughed. "That's sweet to think, but they hated me for missing the business trips and letting them down."

"What happened next?" I asked.

"I didn't have a real job in the village. I did what all villagers do. Farming, working in the cattle farm, raising and milking cows, raising hens and chickens in the poultry farm, taking the eggs to market, and selling them. I grew some plants and harvested them as well. I didn't make a lot of money, but I was doing what I could to help the village. And if those duties were not enough, my mom also made me do some weaving. After I failed to help my dad with his treatment, at least I could help my mom. The village life lasted for about seven months, and then my mom fell ill. Once again, I didn't have enough money to treat her, but I couldn't make the same mistake as I did with my dad. I would do anything to save my mom. I was not the type of guy who would rob a bank, but I was willing to do anything for my mom to survive, even if it meant going to prison. I promised my mom that I would be back with the money and left for New Hampshire again. I turned to my business again for help. That was the only place where I had ever made enough money to thrive. I realized that since I helped Toby Rhodes during his time of need, he would help me in my time of need, but it turns out that he was no longer working there."

"Where the heck did he go? Who would want to leave such a big company, especially if they are the boss?" I asked.

Sabal replied, "I'll tell you. I talked to some of the other employees working there, and they said Toby was their boss for a while, but once he got a better job offer, he left the company just like that. I tried to borrow money from the other employees working there, but they weren't willing to help me after I had abandoned them the way I did. Instead, they were saving up to create a new business, taking down my name. So I had to do the impossible. Luckily, I still had a spare key with me to my company. One night, I went inside and took all the money from the business. I couldn't believe that I had to steal, but it was for my mom's good. I fled to Wisconsin with the money but couldn't reach Vernon in time to save my mom. While I was on my way, I got pulled over for inspection in Madison because the business employees filed a case against me. Then the authorities—"

I interrupted. "I know the rest of the story. It's written in your case. You've been here for seven years since then."

"Oh well, then I can stop talking," he said and looked down.

I said, "I'm sorry this had to happen to you. That's so terrible! Now Grandma must be …"

"Yeah, she's certainly no more," he said.

"And your business must be …"

"Yup, it's shut down," he said.

I asked, "Why didn't you call us? Or Mom? She could've done something to help you."

"Ha. You kids were too young to know about all this. And your mom. Why would she ever help me? I'd only ruined her life, so it was better if she didn't know all this," he said.

I replied, "Well, at least you were honest and told the truth. I really appreciate that quality of yours. Unlike Mom, who lied to us big-time about our real father."

"Really? What did she say?" Sabal asked.

I told him all about Mr. Troop and how Mom pretended that he was our real father. I didn't understand why Mom did that or how she knew him or even why he agreed to pretend he was our father. Sabal said, "That's a big lie, all right. She probably thought that I was a big disgrace to the family, so she never told you about me. And I can understand that."

"She shouldn't lie to her children like that. It isn't fair! We had a right to know about you," I said.

Sabal said, "Well, whatever had to happen already happened. It is what it is, and there's nothing we can do about it." It was silent for a few seconds, and then he asked, "How is your mom, by the way?"

"Mom is fine, and she is here actually."

"What? No way," he said.

"Yeah, she is waiting outside. You don't have to be stuck here anymore. We can tell Mom, and we can finally help you now. Get you out of this place."

Sabal just shook his head and said, "Right. And how do you plan on doing that? Sameera, this is my destiny now. I've caused a lot of trouble and can't face anyone again. This is my life now. Accept it."

"No. Stop! We've come all this way and can't leave without helping you. We will bail you out or something," I said.

"It's not as easy as you think it is. I've been here for so long that even bailing me out is too expensive."

"We'll do something. Gather all the money we have. And I have friends who can help! How much will it come to? A thousand dollars? Maybe two thousand?"

He shook his head and said, "Fourteen thousand dollars. It was two thousand for the first year, but then each year, the bailing money doubled."

"Oh, wow. That's a lot! But you can't just stay here forever. It's better to bail you out now instead of later. Come on. You don't deserve this, Father." I stopped. I didn't have a weird feeling in my stomach anymore. Instead, I felt my heart was complete. I had never felt this satisfied calling Mr. Troop my father, but this feeling was real. I was satisfied. "Father."

Just then, Sahil rushed in. "Sameera, I can't keep Mom out anymore. She really wants to know what we're up to."

"She can come in if she wants to," I said.

Sahil raised his brows and said, "Really? Are you sure? She'll go mad if she sees her ex-husband again. I think it's best that you just come outside instead of her coming in."

"I don't want to leave him here," I said.

Sahil smiled. "Who? Dad?" I nodded. "I guess it's only fair if he decides. What do you want us to do, Dad?"

Sabal looked up and said, "It doesn't matter anymore. Take me with you or leave me. I'm just happy I got to see you both. I know I've been such a horrible father. Not having time to spend with you kids. I really messed up, and I don't think your mom will ever forgive me."

"If she hears your story about what happened after she divorced you, then maybe—" I started, and then he interrupted.

"No, no. She'll never believe it. I've never been there for her. I always put my business before my family and made fake promises to her all my life."

"Come on, Dad. Just give it a try. You never know. Maybe we could be a complete family again. You could finally spend time with your children and live the happy life you've been dreaming of," Sahil suggested.

Sabal replied, "It's going to be very hard to face your mom. I don't even know what to say."

"Don't worry. We just need your approval to bring Mom in. We'll handle the rest," I said.

He slowly nodded.

Then Sahil screamed, "Mom, you can come in now!"

My mom rushed in and pinched Sahil. "Ouch!"

"What the heck do you both think you're doing? Holding me captive like a prisoner. Seriously, Sameera, what's going on?" I slowly raised my hand and pointed in the direction of Sabal's cell. Apparently, he wasn't visible. Mom said, "Where are you pointing at? There's nothing there."

I turned around to see that Sabal wasn't in sight. I walked over to the cell and peeked inside. He was sitting down on his mattress. "Come on! Why are you hiding? There's nothing to be ashamed of. Please do it for us. Your children."

Sabal slowly walked over to the bars, where he was visible to Mom. He said in a nervous tone, "Hey, Jeena."

Mom frowned. "What the … who even … I'm sorry … but is that?"

"Mom, just calm down. That is who you think it is, but you must hear the whole story," I said.

Mom shook her head back and forth and said, "I … how … did … kids … this isn't really happening. I'm just dreaming. No, that's not who I think it is."

Sahil said, "That is Dad. Our real dad. Just give him another chance to make it right."

"I'm sorry, but I can't. Let's go home now," Mom said angrily and started to head out.

Sahil ran up to our father's cell and held onto the bars. "I won't leave Dad here. Do what you want, but I'm not coming home without Dad. Either you go home with Dad and me or you go without us."

"Sahil! Get out of there! You're coming home with us! It's not a request; it's a demand!" Mom yelled.

I went up to Sahil and said, "Sorry, but I don't think he can come home with us. We tried our best, but Mom is not even willing to hear his story."

"Geesh, Sameera, you're giving up so easily? You choose Mom over Dad after how much Mom has lied to us?" Sahil said.

I thought for a minute and then realized that Mom was sort of a villain for keeping our real dad a secret from us for so long. I said,

"Oh my gosh, you're right, Sahil. Hey, Mom, I'm not coming with you either." I walked over to Sabal's cell and held onto the bars.

Mom screamed, "Sameera! Stop being childish! You're supposed to be leading by example for your brother; instead, you're following your younger brother. You should be ashamed of yourself!"

"No, Mom, you should be ashamed of yourself!" I screamed back. Mom gasped. "Yeah, Mom. After you lied to us so much about our real father, I can't come with you. You brought another man to live with us and pretended that he was our father. How could you!" I started to feel the rage build up inside me.

Sahil said, "I agree. Dad is more honest than you. He told us his whole story of how he got here, and you don't seem to care! You're such a big liar!"

I noticed tears come out of Mom's eyes. She tried to hide them, but we could still see. She didn't say another word and ran back the way she came from.

"Children, you shouldn't have yelled at your mom. It must've really hurt her feelings," Sabal said.

I smirked. "I don't feel bad at all. She deserves it! She could've just told us the truth in the first place, and then we would've respected her."

"You must go and apologize. She might've made some mistakes in her life and lied to you, but it must've been for a good reason. I mean, she's your mom after all. Maybe she was just trying to look out for you both. She didn't want you to get hurt."

"There's nothing wrong with telling us who our biological father is. If she really was over you and loved Mr. Troop, then she could've just told us that clearly! She didn't have to pretend that he was our father to marry him. That's just crossing the line," I said.

Sabal nodded and said, "Yes, I see your point, but you must realize that you asked your mom to give me another chance. Do you see how hard it was for her to accept that? Similarly, I'm asking you to give your mom another chance, and I see it's hard for you too."

It was quiet for a few seconds. "Wow, you make a good point, Dad! But I just really wish you could come with us. You could teach us a lot of things," Sahil said.

Sabal replied, "That's a wild dream for me too, but I can't help it. It'll be a long and expensive process to get me out of prison. Anyway, I want you to go now and apologize to your mom."

"Okay, fine. We'll do it. Come on, Sahil," I said and got up.

Before I went out the door, Sabal stopped me. "Sameera, wait." I turned around. "Come here."

I walked back over to his cell and stood. "Yes?"

"I'm sorry. I didn't mean to hurt you," he said, his voice low.

I scrunched my face and said, "You hurt Mom. I don't think you hurt me. What are you even talking about?"

"You know. You're the one who wrote the letter, right?" he asked.

I looked up like that question was still not ringing a bell. "What letter?"

Sabal rolled his eyes. "You don't have to pretend anymore. Everything in that letter is true. I was never a part of your life. I have hurt you, but that has made you stronger. I have been a bad parent figure, Sameera, but I just want you to know that I'm proud of you. I'm proud of how far you've come."

My eyes shot up at him as I realized exactly what he was talking about. "Father … no. How did you even—that letter was not meant for you."

He let out a chuckle. "Then who was it for? Do you have another father? It fell out of your pocket right as you approached my cell."

I didn't even know what to tell him anymore. That letter was for Mr. Troop before he left and before I figured out that he wasn't my father. How did I forget about it? It was also a coincidence that I put on the same pants as I did the day Mr. Troop left our house. But I wasn't going to tell Sabal all that. Instead, I said, "It was sort of a misunderstanding. I, uh …" I scratched my head, hoping for ideas to get past this. "It, um … I wrote that letter a while back. Before I knew anything about you," I lied.

He nodded his head and said, "Oh, I see. What do you think of me now that you know my story?"

I didn't know what I thought of him. I didn't know how I felt about him. "I … uh … I don't know really … but the letter doesn't mean anything. That I can say." He was silent. "I'm gonna go check on Mom really quick," I said and rushed out the door.

I saw Mom sitting on the wooden bench in the room with filing cabinets. Sahil whispered to me, "I don't even know where to start."

"Let's just start with an apology first, and then we'll somehow convince her to hear Father's story," I suggested. We slowly walked up to Mom and sat on either side of her on the bench. She still had tears coming down from her eyes. "Mom, I'm sorry for yelling at you," I said.

Sahil said, "Me too."

"Are you okay?" I asked. Mom nodded. "Come on. Talk to us."

"I'm fine. I just needed a minute. Hearing my own children yell at me and say everything you said … I am not used to that," Mom explained.

I responded, "Yeah, I just got a little too angry after you lied to us, and you know …"

"I'm sorry kids. I shouldn't have told such a big lie. I was just trying to do the best for this family. I didn't want to dwell on the past and bring back old memories and bad experiences to you both," Mom said.

I replied, "But it isn't bad. And Father isn't bad. He told us the whole story. He struggled a lot after you divorced him, and eventually it sent him to prison."

Mom looked down and sighed. "I really don't want to know anything about him right now. Let's just stay at a hotel for the night. We'll drive home tomorrow, and I'll tell you guys everything. I'll be completely honest."

"But, Mom, how can we just leave Dad here?" Sahil asked.

Mom laughed. "What are you talking about? There's nothing we can do about it. This is his home now. You shouldn't get too attached to him. He wasn't a good person."

"We won't go anywhere until you at least listen to Father's story," I said.

Mom rolled her eyes. "How did you even find this place?" Sahil explained his side of the story, what he discovered and how he acted on it.

Mom said, "Fine. You seem like you've put a lot of effort into this whole mystery solving, so I'll do it. I'll listen to his story, but you must promise me that we'll leave this place right after."

"Yup, yeah, for sure," Sahil and I said at the same time.

Mom slowly got up and said, "I'm not doing this because I care about him or anything. I'm doing it for you both. You are my children, so I'd do anything for you. Come on. Let's get this over with," She started to walk back inside.

I said, "Wait. Where did Carson go?"

"I sent him back home with one of the officers," Mom replied.

I was quite surprised and asked, "You sent him all the way back to New Hampshire?"

"No, silly. He told me his family was vacationing here in Wisconsin, so I sent him back to his family. I didn't want him to be influenced poorly by all these family matters," Mom explained.

I said, "Oh, okay. I see. Sahil, you need to apologize to him whenever you see him again. You shouldn't have dragged him here with you."

"I didn't though. I wanted to come here alone, but he asked to tag along. I told him that it was going to be no fun, but he didn't care. He just wanted to be a good friend," Sahil responded. "Let's just go in now please."

Mom walked in, and Sahil and I followed behind her. Mom slowly approached Sabal's cell, not seeming interested at all. Sabal looked up in confusion and then looked back down. "Mom, you have to talk," I whispered.

Mom looked at me and clenched her fist. After a couple of minutes, Mom finally said, "I … uh, need to, um, hear the full story." Mom didn't even look at Sabal.

Sabal looked up. "Why?"

Mom still didn't look at him as she said, "Because my kids asked me to."

"Oh, okay. Well, thank you, children," Sabal said.

Mom finally jerked her head up at him and said, "They're my children."

"Oh, well then. Here goes my story." Sabal told mom the same story that he told us. We were bored, but we waited patiently.

After Sabal explained everything to Mom, she had more tears coming. I went up to Mom and said, "Mom, stop crying. It's okay."

"I can't believe the entire story," she said. I looked at Sahil and shook my head in disappointment. Our plan didn't work. Mom didn't believe it. I guessed we were going to just leave Dad there and go home—go back to how things were before, with Sahil, Mom, and I living together.

"Hey, Jeena. Now, if you don't mind, may I ask you a question?" Mom nodded. "Tell me about you. What happened after I left? Another man came and pretended to be the father of my children?"

"Ugh! The kids told you everything, didn't they? Fine. I guess you have a right to hear my story too," Mom said. I didn't know Mom's side of the story either and was eagerly listening.

Mom turned to face us. "I lied to you both about Mr. Troop. He isn't your dad, but he was a caretaker for you both for a couple of years after your dad and I got divorced. And … uh well, his first name is Chris, and his last name is Troop; he doesn't have a middle name."

"What! Why did you lie to us, Mom?" Sahil asked.

Mom replied, "Let me finish. Sameera and Sahil, your father left you a long time ago, because of financial reasons. I didn't want my kids to grow up without a father. I was thinking of marrying another man to make us a complete family. No one was willing to marry a woman who already had kids. I was upset for some time until I came stumbling upon a job where I met a man named Chris Troop. He seemed lonely, so I went and talked to him one day. He told me he wanted a family but didn't have one. He told me his story of how his family abandoned him, just as your dad abandoned us. As he was telling me his story, I felt a connection with him. I told him my story, and after that, I guess we knew we were meant to be friends ... at first. He told me that he worked as a caretaker part-time and would love to take care of my children if needed. I had to stabilize financially and had to work two part-time jobs, sometimes even throughout the night. He looked after you kids for a couple of years, and it really helped me. You probably couldn't recognize him because you both were very young. Then after you both got a little older, you didn't need a caretaker to look after you anymore. I had a well-paying job and had time to look after you both. Chris had also moved on with his life, and I didn't see him again until I enrolled you both in summer camp. I couldn't tell you how happy I was to see him. After all these years, I still felt grateful for how he'd helped me during a time of need. He was looking to get married, and so was I. I wanted to start a fresh life. And I ... I'm sorry, Sameera, but I lied to your friends, Mackenzie and Meg, saying that Chris was your father and I wanted to surprise you. And Chris liked the idea too, so he played along and acted like he was your father. Then just a few months ago, he told me he got a job offer in California and that he was going to go for it. I realized at that point that he, too, was just like Sabal—chasing after jobs and not having time for a family. I thought I could marry him, but it would've been no use because he would never be around. I thought I understood him, and he understood me, but I realized that he got divorced for the same reason I divorced your father. I didn't want to make the same mistake again. So I let him go, but since I had already made you believe he was your father, I didn't want to confuse you."

"Wow, Mom! You know you could've just told us if you wanted to marry another man. You didn't have to make up lies that he was our father. That made it even worse," I said.

Mom responded, "I know, sweetie, but I wanted you both to feel connected with him the way I did in the beginning. After all, he used to take care of you for a while, and the only way I thought was to make him feel like he was your father. But apparently, you guys were smart enough to figure that out. I'm sorry, kids. I shouldn't have lied to you. I was just trying to make a complete family. You don't understand how hard it was for me after your father left."

It was quiet for a few seconds, and then Sahil said, "I understand, Mom. It would've been tough raising two kids on your own, and we're sorry for all the trouble we caused you."

"I'm sorry too, Jeena. I owe you an apology big-time, but I don't think an apology will make up for everything I've put you and the kids through. I want to make it up to you, Jeena. After I get out of this jail, I'll do anything for you," Sabal said.

Mom smirked and said, "No need. There's no point in doing anything anymore. The kids have grown up, and they are responsible enough to take care of themselves. I don't need you anymore. I only need them."

Just then, I heard my phone vibrate in my pocket. I picked it up. "Hello?"

"Hey, Sameera, it's Mackenzie. Don't worry, I'm not calling to ask how things are going there. I know you want to keep it private."

"Oh, it's okay, Mackenzie. We're all good," I said.

Mackenzie said, "Anyway, that man from Ohert City called. Toby Rhodes. He said he wants to talk to you."

"Wait—what? Why? How did he get your number?" I asked.

Mackenzie replied, "Well, we exchanged numbers while we were at his house. Remember? He said he wanted to keep in touch with us."

"Okay, but I'm busy now. Tell him I can't talk now," I said, looking in the direction of my mom.

Mackenzie said, “He said it’s very important, and he wouldn’t even tell me about it. He only wants to speak with you.”

“Okay, fine. Send me his number. I’ll talk to him quick,” I said and hung up. A couple of minutes later, I received his number. “Hey, guys, I’ll be right back. I need to take an important call,” I said and walked to another corner of the prison.

CHAPTER 21

I called Toby Rhodes. "Hey there! Is this Sameera?"

"Yes, this is her. What do you need to talk to me about?"

"Great! I was going to ask, how much money do you need?"

That question was so shocking to me. *Why would I need money?* "Sorry, but I don't know what you're talking about. Are you sure you have the right person?" I asked.

Toby laughed. "Ha-ha. Yes, I do. And I also know where you are right now. Trying to bail my old friend out of jail, huh?"

"What? No. I mean I am here with my father right now, but how did you know?" I asked.

He replied, "I called your friends for a casual conversation, and they told me about the fact that you went to meet your father in jail. Am I right?"

"Yeah, that's right."

"So, tell me, how much money do you need to bail him out?" he asked.

"Mr. Rhodes, please don't take the trouble. It's too much money. We'll figure something out."

"Who do you think I am? Homeless? Let me tell you, I used to be. I remember telling you my story, but I recently started up a new business," he said.

I responded, "Whoa. You did? You're kidding!"

"Not at all. Your father taught me a lot of things at Consider Chacker. That inspired me and gave me the courage to start my own business. It's only been a week, but it's going well," he said.

"I know they say that you're always young at heart, but is this the age to do business? I thought you retired."

"I want to spend the last several years of my life feeling proud and doing something courageous. So here I am," he said.

I asked, "What's the name of your business?"

"It's called Ask Rhodes. It's like Consider Chacker in some ways but not the same."

"That's amazing! Congratulations! I'm so happy for you," I said.

He chuckled and then said, "I know you are happy for me, but you aren't happy for your father. You want him to live a better life, and so do I. That's why I'm offering to help. He really helped me when I needed it, and now he needs help. I'm willing to pay back."

"Really? That's so nice of you! I don't know how to thank you."

"Just tell me how much money," he said.

"Fourteen thousand dollars."

There was a long period of silence. "Hello? Mr. Rhodes? Are you still there?"

He cleared his throat and said, "Ah-hum. Yes, I am."

"Do you think you can help us?" I asked.

He said, "I uh … um, fourteen thousand? Well, that—"

I interrupted. "I know it's expensive. That's why I warned you earlier."

"It's not that I don't want to help. Look, I really love Sabal. He was a great guy and treated me so well. I want to help. I really do. But even all my business money combined will not get you to fourteen thousand," Toby explained.

I frowned and said, "That's okay. I didn't expect to bail him out or anything."

"Hey, wait. I didn't say that I was done. Fourteen thousand is not something I can come up with right now. Let's see. So, if I stretch myself, I can spare about seven thousand now," Toby said.

I replied, "That's half of the money we need."

"Yeah. Sorry, kid. That's all I've got now. But don't you worry. The way my business is going, seems like we'll get you to fourteen thousand in about two months. You can get your father bailed out in about two months," he said.

"That … I guess it will be amazing, but, Mr. Rhodes, you don't have to take the trouble and work to make money for us. Seven thousand is good enough. We can think of a way to get the other half."

"I want to help. That's how I'll pay him back for what he did for me," Toby said.

"All right, but can I talk to my father about this?"

"Don't say anything to him about me right now. Once I get the full money, then we can tell. Anyway, I need you to send me your mom's bank account information so I can transfer the money," Toby said.

I replied, "Will do. Thank you so much! I really appreciate it."

As soon as Toby hung up, I ran to my father and exclaimed, "We'll bail you out in two months!"

My mom, who was still standing near the cell, said, "Sameera, you're not going to do anything illegal to get money like your father did."

"It's not illegal! Someone is going to help us," I said.

Mom asked, "Who?"

"Well, the person told me not to say his name, but it's an old friend of my father," I said, looking at Sabal.

The way Sabal grinned made me think he knew who I was talking about. Then his expression changed. Sabal said, "No one can help me. I told you, it's too expensive."

"It's expensive, not impossible," I said.

Sahil asked, "Who is helping Dad, Sameera?"

"I told you, I can't tell right now. Plus, you don't know him. You've never met the dude." I turned to Mom. "Mom, I need your bank account information," I said.

Mom replied, "What the heck? No way. I'm not giving you my bank account information."

"Please! I need it! Otherwise, we can't help Father," I said.

Mom responded, "I'm not giving him a single penny."

"Mom, you don't understand. You don't have to pay a single penny. I told you, someone is going to help him. They will transfer the money to your account, and then we can bail him out," I explained.

Mom smirked and then said, "Do you even know how much it costs to bail someone out? Especially being here for several years? No, Sameera, we can't do this, and we won't." Mom was very firm with her decision.

Sahil said, "Please trust Sameera. She thinks she can help Dad. Please, please, please. I want Dad to be free from this jail. I want him to come home with us."

"Sahil, stop pleading! I said no!" Mom screamed.

Sabal said, "Forget it! I knew it was too good to be true. There's no one who can help me out of this jail."

Mom looked up at Sabal and maturely said, "I'm sorry you had to go through everything you did. When I divorced you, I had no idea what was going to happen next. I got a good job and was able to make a living and thought you would be doing the same. I never imagined that you would end up like this. I mean, your business was going so well, and you were very successful at the time. I just want you to know that I never intended to hurt you in any way. I was overly frustrated when you didn't have time for the kids and might've overreacted. So I'm … sorry."

Sabal wasn't even looking at Mom. Instead, he was staring at the floor. A few seconds later, he finally said, "So are you saying that you forgive me?" Mom slowly nodded. Father said, "I don't deserve this. I realize that I've been a terrible parent figure and husband. I'm willing to do anything to make it up to you all."

"No, Dad, it's okay. You weren't a bad person, and you didn't mean to do bad things. We already forgive you, and we want to bail you out of this jail. Right?" Sahil asked, looking at me and Mom.

I said, "Yeah, I do." I looked at Mom, who seemed doubtful. "Mom?"

She looked at me and said, "We can bail him out of jail, but he can't come home with us."

"Why can't he live with us, Mom? He's our father. You just should remarry him, and then we'll be a complete family again," I suggested.

Mom smiled weakly. "I'm sorry, but I can't."

"Why? Do you have plans to marry Mr. Troop or something?" Sahil asked.

Mom said, "No, honey. I just want to be by myself for some time. Being a single parent is hard, but I raised you both on my own. And I think I did a pretty good job."

"Jeena, I understand that you want to keep the kids to yourself just because you raised them yourself, but I'm their parent too. I think it is important that I'm a part of their life," Sabal said.

Mom raised her eyebrows and said, "Wow. Well, look who's talking now! You made me feel the same way when you always left us to go on your business trips. I thought you were very selfish and didn't care about us. See, you got a taste of your own medicine. I'm extremely sorry, but the kids will live with me." Sabal opened his mouth to speak, and then Mom said, "Now, do you still want to be bailed out? Do you think you can manage a living space for yourself? If not, we'd be more than happy to leave you here."

"Yes," he said.

"All right, Sameera, whatever your plan is to get the money, here's my bank account info," Mom said, pulling out a sheet of paper from her purse. "Don't lose it and don't give it to anyone else." I agreed.

I went to the corner of the room and messaged Toby Rhodes the bank account information. I received a reply immediately.

Toby Rhodes: "Thank you. The money will be in there shortly. Check back in about ten minutes."

I went and told Mom, "The money will be in there in ten minutes. Well, not all the money, but half of it for now. The other half will be there in two months."

"We'll get seven thousand now?" Sabal asked.

I nodded. "Mmhmm."

"Wait. Dad has to be stuck here for another two months?" Sahil asked.

Sabal replied, "Don't worry, buddy. Time will fly. These seven years have gone by. What's the harm in waiting for two more months? I'll be waking up each day knowing that I'm one day closer to leaving this prison."

"I can't wait for you to leave this prison. Wherever you live, I'll come and visit you often. Wait … you'll still be living in New Hampshire, right?" Sahil asked.

Sabal's smile started to fade, and he said, "I'm not sure. Wherever I can get a job. At least I'll be happy knowing that you kids still have a place for me in your hearts."

I suddenly remembered something and pulled out my phone. I messaged Toby.

Me: "Will you hire my father to work with you after he's out of prison? He said he will live wherever he gets a job, and I really want him to live near us."

I didn't get a response immediately, but I got one after a few minutes.

Toby Rhodes: "Depends on what kind of job he wants."

I was kind of confused because I thought my father loved doing business with Toby.

Me: "My father loved doing business with you. Of course, he would want to work with you again!"

Toby Rhodes: "That doesn't always have to be true. His interests may be different now, and besides it's been so long since he worked at Consider Chacker. He might've lost touch."

Me: "Wait a minute. Are you saying you don't want him to work for you? Be honest. You don't have to try to be considerate. I won't feel bad."

Toby Rhodes: "It's not like that at all! Of course, I would be willing to offer him a job at my place, but I want him to take the decision, not you. Once he's bailed out of jail, I can talk to him. If he wants to work at my place, then we can decide. It's that simple."

Me: "Oh, okay. Sounds good. Thank you again for the money!"

I joined Mom and Sahil back near Sabal's cell. I said, "Hey, Father! Did you know that Mr. Rhodes started his own business?"

Sabal looked up at me. "No, I didn't. That's very cool!"

"Yeah. It's called Ask Rhodes, and he said he set up the business similar to your old one," I said.

Father nodded and then said, "Proud of him."

I paused and moved my feet closer together. "So, if he were to offer you a job at his company, would you take it?" I eagerly asked.

Sabal looked down and then looked straight ahead. I couldn't read his expression. He just made a sound, "Hmm."

"What is there to think about? It's a simple question. Yes or no?" I asked.

Sabal met my eyes and replied, "I don't think I'm ready to work in a business again yet. After I leave prison, I'm planning on going back to the village for some time."

I was shocked and gasped. "What? Why? There's no one left in that village to go back to."

Sabal fiddled with his fingers and then explained, "Yes, I know, but I think it'll be best to pay a visit to my parents' house. I wasn't there for either of their funerals, so it kind of occurred to me that I should go soon. Meet some of the other villagers and ask them about what exactly happened to my parents. I really think I need to go there for some time,"

Sahil went over to Sabal's cell and held onto one of the bars. He asked, "So when will you be back after visiting the village?"

Sabal shrugged. "I don't know. It could take some time."

Mom stepped forward and put a hand on Sahil's shoulder. "Kids, please don't bother him so much. Let him do what he wants. I think we should leave now. There's nothing else to do here. Once the full money is here, I'll come back to bail him out," Mom said.

Not letting go of the cell, Sahil said, "We'll come too."

Mom sighed. "No, Sahil. You both don't need to come here again. It'll be no use for you. Plus, school will start soon." I rolled my eyes.

Pretending he hadn't heard Mom, Sahil said, "I'll go to the village with you, Dad." I was surprised to hear those words come from Sahil's mouth.

Mom said, "No way. You're not going."

"Yes, I am. He's my dad, and I want to spend some time with him before it gets too late. I'm just learning from the experiences," Sahil argued.

I cocked my eyebrows and asked, "What experiences?"

"The ones we had when we were younger when Dad kept leaving us. And the fact that Dad didn't get to spend much time with his parents when he had the chance to," Sahil explained. "So please don't stop me. I know this is not some fun vacation or whatever, but I want to go. Go with Dad to the village and see Grandma and Grandpa's house."

The room was silent before Father said, "Oh, wow, kid. You really want to do this, don't you?"

Mom took her other hand and put it on Sahil's other shoulder. She made him let go of the cell bar and turned him around to face her. "Sahil, please try to understand. You can't go. You'll miss school. And you will not enjoy the village. It won't be as luxurious as the city you're used to living in."

I took Mom's side. "Yeah, Sahil, you can't just go wherever you want, whenever you want."

"What do you know, Sameera? I know I made a mistake last time when I left without telling, but at least this time I'm with my real dad," Sahil said.

Mom let go of Sahil and sighed. "The kids are really growing up. We'll see, Sahil. We'll see."

Sahil stomped his feet and screamed, "No, Mom! I'm old enough, and I can make my own decisions. I want to go with Dad to the village, and I will go!"

Mom's eyes widened. "Fine, go, but don't blame me if anything goes wrong." Sahil nodded. "Let's go to a hotel now," Mom said.

"We'll see you later, Father!" I called as Sahil, Mom, and I left Madison County Prison.

We stayed at the Hilton hotel for the night and started driving home the next day. On the way home, I heard my phone buzz and pulled it out. It was a notification from Instagram that Meg had posted something. I quickly clicked on it and saw a photo of Mackenzie and Meg in their swimsuits, hanging out by some pool and drinking sodas. They had wide smiles on their faces and looked very happy. The caption read "Girls' Day out!" with two heart emojis. I felt a bit left out and jealous that they were having so much fun despite knowing my situation. I didn't even like or comment on her post. Instead, I just turned off my phone and put it away. I tried not to think about that and changed the subject because there were other important things I needed to figure out.

I turned to Sahil. "Hey, that vial of liquid you told me to bring. What exactly did you intend to do with it?" He didn't respond to me. He was just starting out the window. "Sahil, I asked you a question."

"Sorry, I can't answer," he said.

I was confused and said, "Why not? You can tell me anything. You know that, right?" He nodded. "Then tell me. I won't get mad. Promise," I said.

Sahil turned around to face me and said, "It's science. I, uh … made the liquid so that whoever drinks it would fall fast asleep. And um … they would stay asleep for a couple of hours."

"And why would you need that?" I asked.

Sahil's face turned a little pale. He replied, "I thought I would need to use it in the prison in case someone tried to stop me from seeing Dad."

"Makes sense, but you forgot it at home. What was the use for me to bring it with me all the way there after you had already gone to the prison and met Father?" I asked.

Sahil swallowed hard and said, "I thought I would need to use it on Mom."

"What!" I screamed so loud that Mom turned around to look at us. I quickly made up an excuse. "We were just playing a game, Mom. No worries." I looked back at Sahil and whispered, "Why the heck would you need Mom to fall asleep?"

"You said you wouldn't get mad. Sorry, it's just … I was so worried about if you were going to make it, and I thought Mom would create a huge scene after seeing Dad," Sahil responded, looking down.

I yelled, "Oh my gosh! That's so insane! How could you do that to her? She's our mom!"

"I know. I realized that I shouldn't use it on her after you arrived. Mom looked so worn out, and I couldn't make her life more miserable."

"Do what to me?" Mom asked, still staring at the road.

I frowned and said, "Nothing. It's just a game."

"Huh? What game is this?" Mom asked.

Sahil said, "It's a game where we pretend to be different characters and try to figure out each other's secrets and crimes."

"Whoa! That's just heated. Play something else … quieter," Mom requested.

I nodded and whispered, "Keep it down, but keep talking."

"I don't have anything else to say! I've told you everything already," Sahil whispered.

I replied, "Fine, but why was the vial of liquid acting strangely? It literally moved around and floated in my stall when I was in one of the rest areas. I couldn't believe my eyes. How did it do that?"

"Oh, did that work? Awesome! Lemme tell you. I'm a legend. My creations are a success!" Sahil exclaimed.

I said, "Yeah, whatever, but how did you do it?"

"It's remote controlled. I had the remote control in my pocket the whole time but forgot the vial of liquid, so I might've pressed a few buttons by accident. Didn't know that it would work," Sahil explained. I didn't say anything for a few minutes and then looked at Sahil. He said, "What?"

"You know, I've been wanting to tell you something. The fact that you solved this mystery about our biological father and invented all this cool stuff. Whether it worked or not, you put your mind to it and tried at least. You're a true genius, Sahil. A true genius."

"Thanks! That means a lot coming from my own sister, but I thought you would be jealous of me—the fact that you're the science nerd, but I'm doing all the cool experiments and stuff," he said.

I smiled. "Not at all. I'm happy for you."

CHAPTER 22

Two Months Later

It was finally time to bail my father out of prison. Unfortunately, since the fall season had arrived, it was time to go back to school. Toby Rhodes had transferred the rest of the money into Mom's account. Mom was in a rush and said on her way out, "Come on, kids. I'll drop you two at school and then head to the airport."

"Mom, are you sure we can't come with you to see Dad?" Sahil asked.

Mom went up to Sahil, patted him on the back, and said, "I know you want to come, but, honey, we can't afford two more flight tickets. I'll just go, bail him out, and come back home."

"With Father, right?" I asked.

Mom shook her head. "We've already discussed this. He won't be living with us. If he wants to come back to New Hampshire, he can, but he's on his own."

"Yeah, I'm sure he'll come back after visiting the village," I commented.

Sahil said, "But, Mom, I was supposed to go to the village with him. I need to go with you."

"Sahil, he's coming to Ohert City to stay with Mr. Rhodes for a few days. Then he'll go to the village back in Wisconsin. You can go and visit him in Ohert City," I explained.

"Come on now. You're going to be late for school," Mom said.

Sahil and I took our backpacks and got into the car. "Shotgun!" called Sahil.

I pushed him aside and said, "You are too young to sit in the front. It's me who'll take shotgun." I got into the front seat, forcing Sahil to get into the back. Mom got into the driver's seat and started driving us to school.

After we arrived at school, Mom said, "Good luck at school, and be good kids. You'll get a ride home with Meg. Both of you."

"I don't wanna. I'll go home on the bus or with Carson," Sahil said.

I said, "No you won't."

Mom said, "Sameera, please take care of yourself and your brother. I'll be back tomorrow."

"I'm not a baby! Wait. We're just staying by ourselves after school? Uh, I don't think we can handle it," Sahil said.

Mom smiled. "Honey, there's no other way. Besides, you two will be going to Mackenzie's house for dinner, so all is taken care of."

"What! Why can't we go to Carson's house? We always go to Sameera's friend's house," Sahil complained.

I said, "We've troubled him enough. You'll come with me to my friend's house, okay? Now don't make Mom angry."

Sahil frowned.

"Okay. Bye! Love you!" Mom said as we got out of the car.

I saw Mackenzie go into the building. I told Sahil, "Meet me right here after school. Got it?" He nodded. I walked up to Mackenzie.

"Hi, Sameera. It's so great to see you again. Time to rock this school year!"

"Yeah, good to see you too. Hopefully it's a good school year." I smiled.

Just then, Meg approached us and said, "Hey, besties! How are you all doing?"

"Great! We were just talking about how excited we are for this school year," Mackenzie said.

Meg grinned widely. "I know, right! High school's gonna be so much fun." Mackenzie and Meg started chitchatting about something I couldn't quite keep up with. Then they started walking together inside the school, laughing. I felt kind of left out but followed them in without saying a word. I hadn't really hung out much with Mackenzie and Meg ever since they helped me and my mom get to Wisconsin. However, after we got back, I did share all the details. I told them what it was like seeing my biological father after so many years, both sides of my parents' story, and what our plan was to bail him out. They showed a bit of happiness for me and then moved on. Ever since then, Mackenzie and Meg had been busy with their baking show preparations. I realized that since I was so caught up in my own family drama, I never got a chance to ask them how their show went.

After school, I met Sahil outside. "Hey! Meg should be here soon. How was the first day?" I asked.

He replied, "Great! I saw a lot of friends from last year. Plus, one of my classrooms has a huge fish tank."

"That's cool! I had a pretty good time today too. Not much homework, so that's always nice," I said.

Just then, I heard someone say, "Sameera, over here!" I turned to my right to see Meg peeking out of a red Honda Civic. Sahil and I ran up to the car and got into the back seat.

Meg's mom started driving, and it was quiet for a few minutes. Then Meg's mom, who seemed to love starting conversations said, "Hey! How was school?"

"Good," Meg replied, not actually meaning it.

"And, Sameera?" she asked.

I replied, "It was pretty good. I have less homework, so I have more free time."

"Yeah, that's nice!" she commented.

"Hey, Meg. I never asked. How was the baking show you and Mackenzie participated in?"

Meg seemed thrilled at the question I had just asked. “Great! Mackenzie and I placed second overall. I wish you could’ve come to watch us.”

“Wow, second place is amazing! I’m sorry I couldn’t make it. Maybe next time,” I suggested.

Meg nodded. “For sure!”

I noticed Sahil was silent for the entire ride back home. After we got home, I asked Sahil, “So what do you want to do?”

“I dunno,” He mumbled under his breath. Sahil sighed and went to sit on the couch.

I followed him and asked, “What’s going on?”

“Nothing. I just want to be by myself for a bit,” Sahil said, without looking at me.

I sat down next to him and said, “You never say that. Tell me what’s really going on.”

After a few seconds, he finally said, “I am excited to meet Dad again, but thinking about it brings me back to how I even got there. By ruining Carson’s vacation. Sameera, I still feel bad about that.”

“Come on. You can get over it. I’m sure Carson already got over it by now.”

“No, I don’t think he has. He hasn’t been talking to me like usual. We haven’t hung out ever since that incident. I feel like we’re drifting apart, and it’s all my fault. By the time he went back to his family, the vacation was over. He didn’t even get to enjoy it. I wish he could get his vacation back,” Sahil said and slapped his forehead.

I said, “If you feel bad, then apologize. Will you?”

“I already did, and he said he was fine, but I don’t feel content,” he replied.

I thought for a second and said, “Then why don’t you try doing something nice for him?”

“Like what?” he asked.

I raised my eyebrows and said, “I don’t have to tell you everything. You know him better than I do. Think of something he would like. I’m sure you’ll feel better after doing something nice for him.”

Sahil exhaled and said, "I really hope so."

"Hey, look. I felt bad for dragging my friends with me to Wisconsin, but we were helpless. We couldn't book a flight at the last minute, and Mom couldn't drive all by herself to Wisconsin in one day, so we used a little help from my friends. That's what friends are for and ... siblings."

Sahil smiled and said, "Thanks, Sameera! I'm going to find something nice to do for Carson now."

He got up from the couch, and before he could proceed any further, I said, "If you don't want to go to my friends' house for dinner, we don't have to. We could make something together at home."

"But we don't know how to cook, and I'm not planning on rebuilding the chemical kitchen," he said.

I laughed. "No chemical kitchen. We'll make real food, and so what if we don't know how to cook? We'll figure it out. There's the two of us."

"Yeah, I'd really like that," he said and went upstairs.

I stayed seated on the couch and thought about all the things that had happened to us in the past few months and the past few years. How quickly everything happened. Just then, I got a call. I picked up the phone.

"Hello, Sameera. It's Mackenzie. I just wanted to make sure you are coming over for dinner."

"Oh, yeah, well we've just decided to eat at home," I said.

She replied, "Wait, but why? Your mom is out of town, and she wanted you to come to my house."

"I know, but Sahil and I decided to cook something at home," I explained.

Mackenzie said, "I feel like you're trying to avoid me, Sameera. Did I do something? I'm sorry if I did."

"No way, Mackenzie. You didn't do anything. It's not that I'm avoiding you. I want to spend some time with my brother. He's been through a lot to find our father, and I don't think he wants to go anywhere right now," I explained.

Mackenzie responded, "I understand. Well then, let us know if you need anything from the store. My mom is going to go soon."

"Thanks, but I think we have everything we need," I said.

Mackenzie said, "Okay. Well then, I'll see you later." She hung up.

A couple of hours later, Sahil came to the kitchen and asked, "What are we making today?"

"I dunno. What do you want to make?" I asked as I took out some plates and utensils. Sahil took a deep breath and said, "Can we make some pasta?"

"Sure! Search for the recipe. I think we have the ingredients," I said.

After we figured out how to make pasta, we easily made it and ate it. "This is really good!" Sahil said as he took a fork full.

"Yeah, I'm glad we decided to do this," I replied.

After a few minutes of silently eating, Sahil said, "I had a good time. I like it when we don't fight."

"Same. It's nice to get along," I said.

After we finished eating, Sahil went upstairs to get something. He came back down with a CD case and said, "I'm going to watch a movie. Wanna join me?"

"What movie?"

"It's called *The Maze Runner*."

"What's it about?"

"You haven't read the book? Well, you'll have to watch the movie to find out."

"I think I'm good. You go ahead and watch."

"Okay then," Sahil said and turned the movie on.

While he was watching the movie, Meg texted me.

Meg: "Hey, Sameera, wanna come over? I got some new clothes. They're fashionable. We could wear them and put on a mini fashion show. OMG! It'll be so much fun!"

Me: "That sounds fun, but I don't know if I should leave my brother alone. My mom told me to keep an eye on him."

Meg: "No problem! Can I come over with the clothes then?"

Me: "If you really want to."

Meg: "Sorry, am I bothering you? If I am, don't worry about it. We can hang out some other time."

Me: "No, it's okay. Come over. My brother is watching a movie anyway, and I have nothing to do. Let's hang out!"

Meg: "Cool! I'll be over in a few."

I went to Sahil and said, "Meg is coming over to hang out soon. We'll go upstairs. Are you good here?"

Sahil paused the TV and said, "Um, yeah, I'm fine. Why do you ask?"

"Just wanna make sure."

"I'm not a baby—okay? I can take care of myself. You don't need to keep checking on me."

"I won't. Call me if you need anything," I said.

Sahil nodded, turned around, and turned the TV back on.

CHAPTER 23

The doorbell rang, and I went to go get it. "Hey, Meg! Come on in." Meg came in with a handful of shopping bags. "Wow, did you go to the mall today?" I asked.

Meg laughed. "No, I went last week with Mackenzie, but we didn't get to try any of these on, so I thought you and I could try these."

"Wait … you both hung out again? Without me?" I asked with concern in my voice.

Meg replied, "Well, yeah, we tried calling you, but you weren't answering, so we assumed you were busy with your family." I sighed and looked down. She said, "I'm sorry, Sameera. We didn't think you would be in the mood to go shopping at that time. Anyway, I'm here now, and we can hang out."

I frowned and said, "Oh, well you could've at least texted me and asked, but I guess you were just being the so-called considerate friend."

"Yeah, but we didn't do much. We just went shopping, ate some food, and watched a movie. That's all," She explained.

I said, "That's like more than half a day. You say that's not much?"

"Are you jealous, Sameera?" Meg asked, grinning at me.

I thought for a second and then realized that maybe I was. I was jealous that Mackenzie and Meg hung out without me but didn't tell her. "No … um, I'm not. It's just, uh, I didn't know you guys hung out."

"Well, that's the past. Now I'm with you in the present. Come on. Let's go upstairs to your room and try on these cute outfits," Meg said, taking my hands in hers. We went upstairs to my room and put on a fashion show.

"OMG! These are so cute!" I said, holding up a purple top with puffed sleeves.

Meg, who was fixing the sequence on her white crop top, said, "I know, right! I wish Mackenzie were here. I think these clothes would look even cuter on her!" I slowly nodded. She said, "Hey, should we call her over? It could be double the fun!" I dropped my top on the floor and gasped. Meg kept bringing up Mackenzie even when she was not here. Meg and I were together, and Meg was talking like Mackenzie was the center of attention. I didn't want Mackenzie to come over because Meg and Mackenzie had already hung out without me the week before, so it was time for Meg and I to hang out for once without Mackenzie. Meg pleaded, "Come on, Sameera! It'll be so fun!"

I made up a lie. "Well, my mom told me not to have anyone over in the first place, but I thought that having one friend over wouldn't hurt, so I let you come. And now you want to have more people over? I don't think so."

"It's just one other person. Besides, we don't have to tell your mom. You don't even have to mention I came over," Meg suggested.

I exhaled and decided to tell her the truth. "Fine. I am jealous. Okay? I'm jealous because you both hung out without me, and I'm jealous because even though the three of us are best friends, you both had a secret without me."

"What are you even talking about? Why would you think we have secrets?" Meg put the clothes to the side and sat on my bed.

"Um, well, that's not the point. You and Mackenzie—" I started, but Meg interrupted. "What's the secret that we have?"

"I don't know. You both hung out twice without me, so you must have secrets."

Meg laughed. "Seriously? We don't gossip. We're not those kinds of girls. But why does it seem like you're trying to avoid Mackenzie?"

I thought for a second and then realized how much I had tried to avoid being around Mackenzie in the past few days. I didn't mean to, but she got to hang out with Meg a lot, so now it was my turn.

Meg said, "Do you not remember that she and her mom came with us to help you get to Wisconsin? You can't just forget that favor and pretend that she doesn't exist," Meg said.

I couldn't take it anymore. Now I felt like I couldn't talk to Meg about anything. I just wanted to leave, but the funny thing was it was my house, so Meg should leave. *Yeah, Meg, why don't you just get out of my house? If you don't respect my feelings and my privacy, then just go! Go hang out with Mackenzie since you seem to love her so much more than me.* But I didn't say all that. I felt rage build up in me because Meg didn't understand me, but I didn't say any more. Instead, tears welled up in my eyes. "I'm … uh, actually sorry, but …" I said, sniffling between my words.

Meg's expression straightened, and she said, "You want me to leave? Okay then. I'll go." She gathered all the clothes that she had brought with her. I was wearing her purple top with puffy sleeves, but she didn't even bother to ask for it back. She just took what was in her reach, put them in her bag, and left my room. I kind of felt bad for just kicking her out like that, but I thought it would be better not to talk to anyone for a while.

I took off the purple top and put my clothes back on. I sat on my bed, sighed heavily, and let my head drop. Tears were streaming down my face. I heard Sahil come up the stairs, yelling, "Sameera! Sameera!" I quickly wiped away my tears. Sahil opened the door and came in. "Geesh, were you crying?"

I hid my face and said, "It's none of your business. You should've knocked before coming in."

"Sorry, but I couldn't hold my excitement. But why are you upset?" he asked, trying to be sympathetic.

I said, "I said it's none of your business. Why are you so excited?"

"I asked first," he said. I kept quiet. Sahil came and sat next to me on my bed. He looked up and said, "Something is bothering you, and you think that I'm not old enough for you to talk to me about it."

I kept staring at the floor and said, "Well ... yeah, I guess so. I don't really want to talk to anyone right now."

"Why did Meg leave so early?" he asked. I thought about why Meg left. I also thought about Mackenzie and how I had not been talking to her like usual. I could apologize to her, or I could apologize to both for my behavior, but for some reason, I couldn't gather up the courage to. I felt like everything that had happened to me in the last few months wasn't my fault. For the first time ever, I felt alone. Meg and Mackenzie were the only people I talked to about literally everything. And now I couldn't.

Sahil said, "You are not alone, Sameera." I immediately looked up. It was like he had read my mind. "I know that I'm younger than you, and you think this is none of my business, but it is. It is my business to know how you are doing. You are my sister, and I care about you." I was so shocked. He had never talked like that. It was like he had suddenly become sensible. He was not normally like that. He was normally careless and unsympathetic. I didn't know why he was doing it, but I wanted him to stop. He said, "If you don't want to talk right now, that's fine. But I want you to be okay."

"I am okay," I said.

He stood up and said, "This whole situation about our biological father has been hectic, even for me, Sameera, but we'll get through it. I promise."

I remembered Sabal Chacko and realized that if it weren't for our adventure to Wisconsin, Mackenzie and Meg would've never hung out without me, and we would still be close. I said, "I wish that never happened. We were completely fine without knowing about our real father. Now everything is messed up."

"What? You're not happy we found our real father?" Sahil asked.

I replied, "Not we, just you."

"Whatever. You're not happy to know your real father?"

"I am, but that ruined my friendship with Mackenzie and Meg," I explained.

He gasped. "Like how?" I ended up telling him how my friends hung out without me while we were in Wisconsin and then continued hanging out together even after we got back.

Sahil said, "That's just … sad. You were jealous that they hung out without you?"

I said, "I, uh … you know how you felt when you and Carson were drifting apart after our journey to Wisconsin. That's how I feel right now with my friends."

"That's understandable. All I had to do was apologize to Carson for ruining his vacation and offer to hang out at the arcade—his favorite place. He's happy about that, and I feel like we're on track to becoming close friends again," Sahil explained.

I nodded. "Yeah, that's a good idea. I really should apologize to my friends, especially after everything I've put them through—from finding you to helping me and Mom get to Wisconsin."

"That's mature of you," Sahil pointed out.

I smiled. "Thank you."

"For what?" he asked.

I said, "For sitting here and talking to me like an adult. That's mature of you."

"No problem. All right. I'm gonna go finish my movie now," he said and got up.

I stopped him. "Hey, wait … what's the exciting news you had?"

"Well, Mom just called on our home phone. She said she successfully bailed Dad out of jail. He'll be in town soon. I'm so excited!" Sahil exclaimed.

"That's great!" I said. He skipped down the stairs. I pulled out my phone and texted Mackenzie.

Me: "I'm sorry."

A few minutes later, she wrote back.

Mackenzie: "For what?"

Me: "For avoiding you for the past few days."

She didn't respond. I guessed she wanted an explanation for why I did that.

Me: "It's just that I was jealous you and Meg hung out without me. I felt kind of left out."

Mackenzie: *typing ...*

Mackenzie: *typing ...*

Mackenzie: "I'm sorry you feel that way. That was not our intention at all. We were just trying to have fun and make the most of our last few days of summer break. We tried calling you, but you were unresponsive, so we went along with our plans. I'm sorry. We should've waited for you."

Me: "No worries. I'm glad you guys had fun. I just don't want us to drift apart. High school is going to be a lot on us, but I want us to stay best friends throughout."

Mackenzie: "Of course, Sameera. Nothing can break our friendship. You, me, and Meg. BFFs forever. Xoxo"

Me: "Thanks, Mackenzie! Hey, how about we all hang out at the mall this weekend?"

Mackenzie: "That would be fun! I'll check with Meg."

Me: "I'll check with her. I was about to text her now anyway."

Mackenzie: "All righty, sounds good. See you later!"

I swiped out of Mackenzie's messages and tapped on Meg's name. I typed: "Sorry about the other night. I overreacted. Could we please pretend that never happened? I'm grateful to have such amazing friends like you and Mackenzie, and I don't want to lose you guys. Mackenzie and I were planning to hang out at the mall this weekend. Wanna join us?"

CHAPTER 24

Mom was finally back the next day after bailing Sabal out of jail. I was sure he wasn't going to come live with us, and I felt like we had done all that for nothing. At least we got to meet our biological father, but he wasn't going to live with us, so what was the point? I had missed having a father most of my life, but it didn't really affect my personal growth. I always wondered what it would be like if Mom hadn't divorced Sabal. How close would we be to him? I was sitting at the kitchen table, sipping on orange juice and gulping down oatmeal. Mom was wiping down the kitchen. I remembered something. "Hey, I never asked. So where is Father going to live after visiting the village?"

"Oh, right. I told Sahil yesterday that your dad is going to live close by after visiting the village. He got a job nearby, not the same one as before, but I think you both can go visit him anytime. He will just be two neighborhoods away," Mom said.

I said, "Wow, that is exciting! But I just don't think it will be the same. I mean, we've never had a close relationship with our real father."

"I know. You both don't know him that well, but that's why he's here. You can develop that relationship with him. It's not too late for that. I've been a little selfish lately, the whole time trying to make a complete family thing, but I want you to know that I was doing it for you both. I wish you had a father during your childhood," Mom said.

I smiled. "That's okay. You did a great job raising us on your own, with a little help of course. Thanks, Mom! And I guess thanks to Mr. Troop, too, for everything he did. I know it's hard for you to adjust, Mom. You don't like Father anymore, but you're doing it for us."

"Well, I never said that I don't like him. I just ... It's been a long time, and I ... it'll take some time to get used to," she said.

There was a pause for a few seconds, and then Mom said, "Anyway, do you have any plans this weekend?"

"Yeah, I'm planning to hang out with Meg and Mackenzie at the mall," I replied. I still hadn't received a reply from Meg about the other night. I was hoping she wasn't upset with me. I would see her at school today. Hopefully I could talk to her in person. My friends always looked out for me and cared about me. Mom cared about me too. She didn't lie and pretend for her benefit. She did it for us—her children. And I truly respected that.

Mom smiled. "Great! Enjoy yourself." Mom handed me my lunch bag and said, "Sweetie, here's your lunch. I'm getting late for work. Is Sahil still in bed? Please do me a favor and wake him up, will you? I don't want you guys to miss the bus."

"Sure, I'll wake him up."

"Thank you, sweetie." Mom kissed me on my forehead, took her bag, and left through the garage door. I woke up Sahil, and he got ready for school.

I didn't see Meg at school that day. I sat with Mackenzie during lunch. "Hey, have you seen Meg today?" I asked as I set my lunch bag down on the table.

Mackenzie took a bite out of her PB&J sandwich and said, "I don't think she came to school today. She is sick."

"Oh no! What happened?" I asked as I opened my lunch bag.

Mackenzie shrugged, still focusing on her sandwich. "It could be anything. The flu ... a stomachache. Maybe she got hurt physically or ... emotionally," she said in between bites.

Emotionally? Because of me? How could that be? I already apologized to her. Did she not get my message? "Oh well. I thought she would've told you," I said.

Mackenzie put down her sandwich and opened her bottle of apple juice. She took a sip and said, "She didn't tell me anything. I texted her today, but she still hasn't responded. I heard from our history teacher that she called in sick. That's all I know." I looked down. Mackenzie stopped sipping and chewing and asked, "Is something wrong, Sameera?"

I looked back up at her. "No. Nothing's wrong. I just ... I don't know if Meg is upset with me."

Mackenzie cocked her eyebrows at me. "Why would she be upset with you?" I decided to tell her about the night Meg came over to my house. "Ah, I see. I don't think you should make it such a big deal if you already apologized. I'm sure she didn't skip school to avoid you. She might really be sick," Mackenzie said.

I smiled. "You're right. It's probably just that. I'm not going to overthink it. Let's just enjoy lunch," I said, and we continued eating in silence.

After school, I went up to my room and pulled out my phone from my backpack. I saw a missed call from Meg and a text from her as well.

Meg: "It's totally fine, Sameera. I forgive you. And sure, we can pretend that night never happened. You're an amazing friend, and I don't want to lose you either. Sorry for getting back to you so late, but I've been really sick the past couple of days. I have a stomach flu. It was worse this morning, so I've mostly been in bed all day. If I feel better, I might be able to come with you guys to the mall this weekend."

A flood of relief washed over my body. She really was sick. Not that I was happy about that. I was just glad that she wasn't upset with me.

Me: "Thanks, Meg! And I hope you feel better soon!

Meg: "How's it going with you? Anything interesting happening lately?"

Me: "Not really. Still awestruck after meeting my biological father two months ago."

Meg: "Oh yeah. What an adventure that was!"

Me: "It sure was! If it weren't for Sahil, I would've never experienced that adventure. He's the true genius."

Meg: "Definitely."

Meg: "Anyway, after I do feel better, I was thinking. I never spend that much time with my dad, but the story of your family made me realize the importance of a father in my life. I realize I'm very grateful to have a father, and I want to spend some time with him before it gets too late. You know? Is it okay if we hang out at the mall some other time?"

Me: "Of course! Mackenzie and I will wait until you're ready."

EPILOGUE

And so … there you have it. How Sahil became a true genius. I doubted him at the beginning. I really did, but now I realize that a true genius doesn't always start out as a true genius. He may have seemed dumb in general situations, but when it came to a tough situation, he proved himself as smart and determined. If it weren't for his curiosity and the clues he found, I would've never met my real father. I would've been lied to all my life. I would still be believing that some other man who looked nothing like me was my father. Ugh! I wonder if Mom would've ever told us. Based on what I've experienced, I don't think so. I'm so glad to have my real father back in my life. Even though he doesn't live with us, I'm glad that he lives just two neighborhoods away and I can go see him and talk to him anytime I want. He came back from visiting the village, and turns out that his mom is still alive. Someone was able to fund Grandma's treatment, and now she's doing well in the village. I think I know who that someone is. Isn't it great how my father helped another man when he was in need, and the same man was able to help my father when he was in need? I guess that's just the cycle of life, and I learned a lot. My father says that once he's working and making money again, he's going to repay Toby Rhodes for all the money he spent on Grandma's treatment and getting my father out of jail. I'm so grateful for this old guy who I tried to shun away from when I first met him. I'm so grateful for my best friends, who never left my side, and most of all for my brother, Sahil. I may fight with him or yell at him, but that doesn't mean I don't love him. He's my brother, after all, and I couldn't have asked for a better one.

AUTHOR'S NOTE

Why I wrote this book ...

First off, I write books mainly because I have many ideas in my head that I think would be neat to transform into stories. At first, I didn't know where to start or what kind of story I was going to write, but I knew what I wanted my title to be. Eventually, I decided that I wanted to write some sort of an adventure story. I came up with two characters that I could work with. One was a sensible teenager, and the other was her clumsy younger brother. I gave them simple characteristics, such as Sameera being a science nerd and Sahil being a sports fan. I first thought of revolving the story around a summer camp and how their interests toward science and sports led them on an adventure to discover more about themselves.

At the time I was writing this book, I was watching many TV shows/movies and reading many books that revolved around a family with a single parent, usually a mother. Whether it was since the parents were divorced or one parent passed away, I didn't completely understand their situation. I used to wonder why many stories portrayed the father figure as unimportant and how it was like not having a parent. Fortunately, I have a good family with both of my parents, but at the same time, it makes it harder for me to relate to the people who have only one parent. There were a few times at my school where I came across people who had only one parent. Oftentimes I didn't know what to say to them or how to feel about their situation because I grew up with both parents and didn't understand what it was like for people who didn't.

I wrote this story mainly to explore this concept of single-parent families and to bring in the importance of family. I wanted to understand single-parent families better and feel more sympathetic toward them. I decided to write how it is like living with an absent parent through the eyes of a thirteen-year-old. Obviously, everyone has different views and feelings about this topic. In my story, I didn't want to portray the father as an unimportant figure because I know that fathers are very important in the lives of their children. They work so hard to support their families, especially their children. The children may not realize the hard work and effort their fathers put in for them to have a good life, like my characters did, but the journey they went through helped them learn a lot about why their father wasn't involved in their lives. That's why, in this story, I tried to portray the hard work and struggles of the father as the reason he couldn't be fully involved in his children's lives. Through these characters, I got to share my understanding of this topic much better, and I added my own twist to make it a unique and unforgettable experience. Hope you enjoyed reading this book as much as I enjoyed writing it!

Printed in the United States
by Baker & Taylor Publisher Services